THE SHOOTING IN THE SHOP

A FETHERING MYSTERY

THE SHOOTING
IN THE SHOP

SIMON BRETT

FIVE STAR

A part of Gale, Cengage Learning

Detroit • New York • San Francisco • New Haven, Conn • Waterville, Maine • London

GALE
CENGAGE Learning˝

Copyright © Simon Brett 2010.
Five Star Publishing, a part of Gale, Cengage Learning.

Set in 11 pt. Plantin.

LIBRARY OF CONGRESS CATALOGING-IN-PUBLICATION DATA

Brett, Simon.
    The shooting in the shop : a Fethering mystery / by Simon Brett. — 1st ed.
        p. cm.
    ISBN-13: 978-1-59414-924-5 (alk. paper)
    ISBN-10: 1-59414-924-0 (alk. paper)
    1. Seddon, Carole (Fictitious character)—Fiction. 2. Jude (Fictitious character : Brett)—Fiction. 3. Women detectives—England—Fiction. 4. City and town life—England—Fiction. 5. Large type books. I. Title.
PR6052.R4296S515 2010
823'.914—dc22   2010028832

First Edition. First Printing: November 2010.
Published in 2010 in conjunction with Tekno Books and Ed Gorman.

Printed in the United States of America
1 2 3 4 5 6 7 14 13 12 11 10

To Isla,
who hasn't had a book dedicated to her yet
and
to Saira Sherjan,
whose partner Deborah Sherry won,
in a fund-raising auction for St John's Ambulance,
the right for Saira's name to appear in this book

CHAPTER ONE

In a sense, the murder let Carole Seddon off the hook. All the social niceties she had been worrying about throughout December seemed much less important after someone had been killed.

For many years Carole had tried to ignore Christmas. As a child, she had observed it with the tense middle-class rigour that her parents had brought to everything they did. In the early years of her marriage to David the festival had been slightly less fraught and when their son Stephen was small they had gone through the required rituals with an attitude which at times approached the relaxed.

But Carole's painful divorce from David had put an end to the idea of Christmas as a season of goodwill. The adolescent Stephen had reacted—as he did to most pressures—by burying himself in work, and as soon as his age made it decent for him to do so, had contrived to spend Christmas away from both of his parents.

But Stephen's life had changed. He was now married to Gaby. They had an adorable daughter Lily. And for some months Stephen had been talking in terms of 'a proper family Christmas'. It was a prospect that filled Carole Seddon with a sense of deep foreboding.

She wasn't sure whether knowing that Jude would also be around over this particular Christmas made things better or worse. In previous years her neighbour had been away for the duration 'with friends' (into details of whose identity Carole didn't probe). That was really all that was said about Christmas. Carole would be staying in Fethering, Jude would be away with friends. And by the time the New Year started, the last thing anyone wanted to hear about was the details of someone else's Christmas. Which suited Carole very well.

Jude was the closest the tightly buttoned Carole had to a friend, and the knowledge that she would be next door at Woodside Cottage throughout the holiday should have been cheering. But Carole had never been good at seeing the positive side of anything, and Jude's presence in Fethering over Christmas did present her with a lot of challenging questions.

For a start, how did Jude celebrate Christmas, if at all? Carole was properly wary of her neighbour's New Age tendencies. Would there be crystals and joss sticks involved? And then again, how much of Carole would Jude want to see over the Christmas period? She was notoriously casual about social arrangements. Already Carole had had a card through the door of High Tor, inviting her to Woodside Cottage on the Sunday before Christmas for an 'Open House, from twelve noon until the booze runs out'. This did not accord with any of Carole Seddon's rules for entertaining. When was she meant to arrive (assuming, that is, that she actually went)? And, even more unsettling, when was the right time to leave? She liked party hosts to be very specific about such details. 'Drinks 6.30 to 8.30'—you knew where you were with an invitation like that. Even better, 'Drinks and Canapés 6.30 to 8.30'—then you knew you wouldn't be getting a full meal and could have a little cottage cheese salad waiting in the fridge for when you got home.

But open house . . . that could mean anything. Was there food involved? Was there an actual sit-down meal and, if so, at what point during the time between twelve noon and the moment the booze ran out would the guests be sitting down to it?

The whole thing made Carole Seddon very nervous. She couldn't imagine a less appealing concept than that of an open house. Houses like High Tor should, in her opinion, be permanently closed, with invited guests arriving by prearrangement only. If people started coming to your house any time they felt like it, the potential for embarrassment was unimaginable.

Amidst all her agonizing about the invitation, Carole wouldn't admit to herself what was really worrying her. It was meeting Jude's other friends. Her neighbour was currently working as a healer (a word from whose pronunciation Carole could never exclude an edge of scepticism), but it was clear that, before she moved to the middle-class gentility of Fethering, Jude had had an extremely varied and colourful life.

Carole had never quite got all the details of this life, just hints from things mentioned in passing. This was not because Jude was secretive—she was the most open of women—but because Carole always felt reticent about probing too overtly. This did not mean that she was not intrigued by her friend's past, and she had pieced together quite a few gobbets of information about it. At various stages of her life Jude had been a model, an actress and a restaurateur. She had been married at least twice, cohabited with other men, and had a stream of lovers (more numerous in Carole's imagination than they ever could have been in reality). But whenever Carole got to the point of asking for more flesh to be put on this skeletal history, the conversation seemed invariably to glide on to other subjects. Jude was not being deliberately evasive; she was just such an empathetic listener that people—even self-contained people like Carole—soon found themselves talking about their own lives and problems rather than hers.

But the thought of Jude's friends was worrying. The thought of the other guests who might attend the Christmas open house. It wasn't that Carole had never met any of Jude's friends. The people who used her healing services often became more than clients and Carole had been introduced to some of them. She had even met one of Jude's lovers, Laurence Hawker, who had lived out the last months of his life at Woodside Cottage.

But Carole was worried about the ones she hadn't met. Worried about the kind of people they might be—positive, relaxed people like Jude herself. People for whom being alive seemed part of a natural process rather than, as it often felt to Carole, a challenging imposition. People who would think that Jude's neighbour was irredeemably dowdy, with her antiseptically tidy house, her pension from the Home Office, her Marks and Spencer's clothes, her sensible shoes, her straight-cut grey hair and rimless glasses over pale blue eyes. Carole Seddon knew that she could never compete with the faint aura of glamour which always hung about Jude.

With that perverse vanity of the shy, she was much more worried about what people might think of her than she was inclined to show any interest in them.

The other thing that worried her was that one of Jude's friends at the open house might ask how she usually spent Christmas. Or worse, might find out how she actually had spent the past few Christmases.

In her bleakest moments Carole thought her ideal would be never to prompt any emotion from anyone. But now her granddaughter Lily was in her life, this was becoming a difficult stance to maintain. There was one emotion, however, which Carole Seddon never wanted to prompt in anyone, and that was pity.

When she had moved permanently to Fethering, raw from her divorce and smarting from her not-completely-voluntary early retirement from the Home Office, she had known the risks of appearing pitiable. A woman the wrong side of the menopause, on her own in a seaside village . . . she was morbidly afraid of slipping into the stereotype of the solitary swaddled figure reading a magazine in a shelter by the beach.

It was to counter this danger that she had bought a dog. Gulliver was a Labrador and his original purpose had been to stop Carole from looking as if she was alone when she went for walks on Fethering Beach. She couldn't be seen to be walking because she had nothing else to do; she was walking to exercise Gulliver. No one could pity her for that.

They could pity her, though, if they knew that she had spent the last few Christmases completely on her own.

Not that it had been too bad, from her point of view. Each year she had stocked up with nice food. Not turkey and all the trimmings, but slightly more lavish fare than what she usually ate. A bit of wine, too—the amount she drank increased each year, a direct result of her developing friendship with Jude. That, together with a good book from the library and the Christmas Eve *Times* Jumbo Crossword, was all she really needed. She didn't watch much television, though seeing the Queen's Speech was an essential ritual engrained from her childhood. Otherwise she might track down an obscure documentary on some minor channel, but would watch nothing that made any acknowledgement of the season. Or she would listen to the radio. She found radio mercifully less Santa-obsessed than television.

The only moment when she made any reference to Christmas was when she rang her son Stephen at eleven o'clock sharp to wish him the compliments of the season. Neither asked the other how they were celebrating, both perhaps afraid of truthful answers, but the required politesse—and even a degree of cheeriness—was maintained.

Then Boxing Day dawned; the major stress was over for another year. And on the few occasions when she was asked about her Christmas, Carole could say with complete veracity what so many people said: 'Oh, you know, quiet.'

This year, however, things would be different. Not only was there Jude's open house to negotiate, but also Stephen, Gaby and Lily were going to come to High Tor for Christmas Day. Carole Seddon faced the prospect with apprehension, leavened by occasional flashes of excitement.

Stephen had rung on Thursday the eighteenth of December, exactly a week before Christmas Day, to confirm arrangements. Sometimes Carole found his mannerisms distressingly like those of his father. David, despite being a control freak in many ways, had never been good at making arrangements. With him each detail of a plan had to be tested from every angle before he would commit himself to it. And in that morning's phone call Stephen behaved in exactly the same way.

'Mother, I thought I'd better just run through the timetable for Christmas Day,' he said, his voice echoing David's nervous pomposity. His calling her 'Mother' was a bad sign. When he was relaxed—which he had been, increasingly, since marriage and fatherhood—he called her 'Mum'.

'I thought we'd got it agreed,' Carole responded. 'I talked to Gaby about everything. Have any of the arrangements changed?'

'No, not really, but obviously the whole schedule is kind of predicated on when Lily sleeps.' There were office noises in the background. Phoning his mother from work showed how much importance Stephen attached to the call.

'Yes, Gaby told me. She said Lily's usual pattern these days is having her morning sleep around half past ten, so if you leave Fulham then she can sleep in the car . . . Fulham to Fethering an hour and a half, maybe two . . . you'll be with me between twelve and twelve-thirty, which will be perfect.'

'Yes.' Her son's silence reminded Carole uncomfortably of her ex-husband assessing a plan for flaws. 'Did Gaby talk to you about food for Lily?'

'Yes, she gave me a list. I've got lots of milk and yoghurts, Ready Brek, Weetabix, sweetcorn, frozen peas. I can assure you, Stephen, your daughter will not starve during her stay at High Tor.'

'No, no, I didn't think she would.' But Stephen still sounded troubled. 'Did you talk to Gaby about the turkey?'

'What about the turkey?'

'Well . . . erm . . .'

Oh no, the 'erm' was one of David's favourite mannerisms. Carole was not being allowed to forget her ex-husband.

'Stephen, if you mean whether or not Lily is given any turkey to eat, yes, Gaby and I have discussed it. I will purée some and put a little on a plate for her. If she likes it, she can eat it. If she doesn't, fine. I won't be insulted by Lily turning her nose up at my turkey.'

'Oh, good.' Still he sounded hesitant. There was something he wanted to say to her, something awkward, something he knew she wouldn't like.

Just before Stephen put it into words, Carole realized, with a sickening sense of recognition, what it would be.

'Mother . . . I . . . erm . . . spoke to Dad last night . . .'

'Oh yes?' Now she knew what was coming, Carole's defences were quickly in place.

'He hasn't, in fact, finalized his own plans for Christmas.'

'That's no surprise to me. Your father was never great at committing himself to arrangements about anything.'

'No. He has had an invitation to have Christmas lunch with some friends locally . . . you know, in Swiss Cottage.'

'Good.'

'But they're not people he knows very well. He's not sure whether he'll be an imposition on them.'

'Well, that's for him to decide, isn't it?'

'Yes.' There was another long silence from Stephen's end.

Knowing exactly what he was about to say, Carole had to restrain herself from hissing out, 'Oh, get on with it.'

'The fact is, Mum . . .' He was trying to soft-soap her now. '. . . I was just wondering . . . erm . . . whether, since we're all going to be together on Christmas Day—'

'No, Stephen.'

'I mean, it's not as if you and Dad are at each other's throats these days, like you used to be. You were fine at our wedding and—'

'No, Stephen.'

'Why not?'

She wasn't about to quantify the reasons why having David in High Tor on Christmas Day would be such undiluted agony, so she restricted herself to a third 'No, Stephen.'

'I was thinking from Lily's point of view, Mum. I mean, she wasn't born when you and Dad divorced, so why should she get involved in all that grief?'

'She will not be aware of any grief,' said Carole firmly. 'Christmas Day at High Tor with just you, Gaby and me will be a very pleasant experience for her. Whereas spending Christmas Day with her grandfather also present would be an unmitigated disaster.'

'Lily wouldn't be aware of that.'

'But I would!'

'Then she'd have memories of a nice, happy Christmas Day with all the family together.'

'Stephen—A, she is far too young to remember anything from this Christmas, and B, where do you get all this stuff about "a nice, happy Christmas with all the family together"? Is that how you recollect your childhood Christmases?'

He was embarrassed into silence, but Carole had by now got the bit between her teeth. 'And from what Gaby's told me of her family background, I can't imagine that her family

Christmases were much cheerier either.'

'But we don't want Lily to grow up in an atmosphere that might cause her problems in later life.'

'Lily will survive. She will not notice her grandfather's absence on Christmas Day. And she's much more likely to develop problems in later life if she's brought up in an atmosphere of lies. Yes, a happy nuclear family is a lovely idea, and some people are fortunate enough to grow up in one. But you didn't and I didn't, so let's drop the pretence, shall we, Stephen?'

Carole had said more than she wanted to. Actually to admit to having had an unhappy childhood, and to suggest that Stephen had had the same, went against all her middle-class principles of reticence. What was worse, she had almost ended up shouting at her son. But she was so furious about the way he had tried to use Lily to blackmail her into doing something which she knew would be disastrous.

The conversation had unsettled her, though. David, even by his absence, could still sour the atmosphere between her and Stephen. The phone call had not been an auspicious harbinger for the week ahead.

CHAPTER TWO

'So how many people are coming to your open house?'

'I've no idea. That's why it's called an open house.'

Carole couldn't be done with this. 'You must have some idea . . . roughly . . .'

'Well, I can guarantee it'll be more than ten and less than a thousand.'

Jude was being far too skittish for her neighbour's taste. 'But surely you have to think in terms of catering?'

'There'll be plenty of nibbles and things.'

'And hot food?' asked Carole, hoping for an answer to the sit-down meal question.

'Oh yes, some hot food,' replied Jude, with infuriating lack of precision.

'And drink?'

'Certainly drink. Plenty of wine.'

'But the invitation says "until the booze runs out".'

'Yes.'

'Well, the time at which the booze runs out is going to depend on how many people are there, isn't it?'

Jude nodded and immediately went into a parody of an old-fashioned math teacher. 'If it takes three men twenty-five minutes to empty a seventy-five-centilitre wine bottle, how long will it take twenty-five men to empty the same bottle and, working at that rate, how many bottles would be required to keep a party of sixty-three people going for three hours and seventeen minutes?'

'I do wish you'd treat this seriously, Jude. And, incidentally, you clearly have done a numbers check. You said you were expecting sixty-three people.'

'No, I didn't. That was just a random example for my pretend mental arithmetic challenge.'

'Oh. Well, you should have thought about it. Your open house is the day after tomorrow, you know.'

'Yes, I do know. But come on, it's only a party, nothing to get hung up about.'

Though Carole Seddon would never be heard to use the expression, for her a party was exactly the sort of thing to get 'hung up about'. She sniffed. 'Well, I would want a bit more information about numbers for any social event I was catering for.'

Someone of less benign character might have made some sharp riposte to that, but all Jude said was, 'It'll be fine, I promise you.'

'And you're confident you'll have enough to drink?'

Jude grinned mischievously. 'I'll have enough till it runs out.'

'But you don't know when that's going to be. Suppose someone arrives at the party after it's all run out?'

'I promise you, there'll be plenty.' Jude ran a chubby hand through the blond hair piled up on her head. She was dressed, as ever, in an array of draped garments which embellished rather than disguised the contours of her ample body. 'I've got plenty in,' she went on, 'and a lot of people will bring bottles, anyway.'

'Oh, is it a "bring a bottle party"?'

'No.'

'It didn't say it was on the invitation.'

'It didn't say it was because it isn't. It's just that when you invite people to a party, a lot of them do instinctively bring along a bottle.'

Another thing of which Carole would have to make a note. And another moral dilemma. What kind of bottle should she take along to the open house? Jude, she knew, had a preference for Chilean Chardonnay, but would her other guests like that? And then again, what sort of price level should one aim for? Carole rarely spent more than five pounds on a bottle of wine, but when her contribution joined the others on the Woodside Cottage sideboard, she didn't want to be shown up as a cheap-skate.

'Anyway,' said Jude, slurping down the remains of her coffee and picking up her tatty straw shopping bag from the ultraclean floor of the High Tor kitchen, 'I must get on. Bit more shopping to do.'

'For the open house?' asked Carole, still intrigued by the stage management details of the forthcoming event.

'No, I've got most of that. A few presents outstanding, though.'

'Oh, I've done all mine,' said Carole, instinctively righteous. 'Well, I've done Stephen, Gaby and Lily. Those are the most important ones.' The last sentence was a bit of a cover-up. They were not only the most important ones, they were the only ones. Carole didn't buy presents for anyone other than Stephen, Gaby and Lily. For many years the only name on the list had been Stephen. But she didn't want to admit that, even to Jude. Once again there loomed the awful fear of being pitied.

'What have you got for Lily?'

'Oh, she's easy. There are so many things out there for little girls. I got her some lovely baby outfits from Marks and Spencer. Their children's clothes are very good, you know. And not too expensive. I checked the sizes with Gaby, but of course, being Marks, she can exchange them if she doesn't like them.'

'Oh,' To give something on the assumption that it might well be changed seemed to Jude to be a negation of the principle of present-giving. She spent so much time matching the gift to the personality of its recipient that no one ever contemplated returning one of hers.

'That's what I do with Stephen too,' Carole went on briskly. 'I always give him two Marks and Spencer shirts. And I put the receipts in the parcel.'

'So that he can change them?'

'Yes.'

'And does he often change them?'

'How would I know?'

'Well, if you see him wearing a shirt you recognize as one you gave him, then you'll know he hasn't changed it.'

'I'd never thought of that.' But now she did think of it, Carole realized she *had* recognized some of the shirts her son had worn over the years. Maybe he did appreciate his mother's taste, after all. She didn't allow herself the thought that he might have worn them simply because they were her gifts.

'And what about Gaby? What have you bought her?'

'Oh, toilet water. Lily of the Valley. You can never go wrong with toilet water.'

Jude's plump face screwed up in disbelief. 'Toilet water? You're giving your daughter-in-law toilet water?'

'Yes,' Carole replied defensively. 'Toilet water's always a safe present.'

'A safe present for a maiden aunt fifty years ago, perhaps. But Gaby's in her early thirties. If she opens her present on Christmas morning and finds she's got toilet water, she'll be depressed for the rest of the holiday.'

'We don't open presents till after lunch on Christmas Day,' said Carole primly.

'Well, whenever she opens it, a bottle of toilet water is going to have the same effect.'

'Are you suggesting I should give Gaby something else?'

'Of course I'm suggesting you should give her something else. And you should give Stephen something else, too.'

'But what's wrong with his shirts?'

'They are totally impersonal. They could have come from anyone. Come on.'

Carole's pale blue eyes blinked behind her rimless glasses. She didn't think receiving a present that could have come from anyone was necessarily such a bad thing.

But she felt her thin hands grasped in Jude's plump ones as she was pulled up from her chair. Her dog Gulliver looked up hopefully from his permanent position in front of the Aga. People getting up could sometimes presage being taken out for a walk.

'Where are we going?' asked Carole plaintively.

'Shopping.'

'Where?'

'Gallimaufry,' Jude replied.

Her neighbour's entire body registered disapproval at the choice of destination.

CHAPTER THREE

The architecture of Fethering was a living history of its development from an assemblage of fishermen's huts to something more like a small town than the 'village' which description stubbornly remained in all official documentation. The returning economic confidence of the late fifties and early sixties was expressed in the High Street's shopping parade. This terrace of buildings had resolutely resisted being rebranded as a 'shopping centre' or, even worse, a 'shopping mall'. It still remained essentially as it had been built, a row of matching shop fronts, pillared by red brick and with a residential flat over each one.

When originally completed, the shops had had their names fitted into a strip above their windows, all co-ordinated in identical lettering that looked like—but probably wasn't—brass. Continuous shifts of ownership and corporate branding meant that most of the original signs had gone. Only the Post Office retained its brass lettering, though beneath it the part that dealt with postal services was now just a tiny corner of a large convenience store.

Over other frontages were displayed the logos of the chain that ran the local bookies and of Allinstore (probably the most inefficient supermarket since records began), signs for Polly's Cake Shop, Urquhart & Pease and another estate agent (both apparently riding out the slump in house prices), the hairdresser's Marnie, three charity shops and a couple of other premises which seemed to change hands every six months.

Simon Brett

Amongst these last was Gallimaufry, which had opened early in September with champagne, balloons and a lot of local press coverage. It was a shop whose contents intrigued Jude, but were dismissed by Carole (who'd never been inside the place) as 'overpriced rubbish'.

The word 'gallimaufry' had culinary origins, describing a dish made of odds and ends of leftovers, but soon came to be applied to any kind of hotchpotch or mix of unlikely elements. And the word was certainly apt for the stock in the store on Fethering Parade. What appealed to Jude about the place was that she never knew what she might find there. It wasn't a dress shop, though there might well be some Indian print shifts on display. It wasn't a furniture shop, though it sometimes sold intricately carved stools and tables from Africa. Gallimaufry didn't specialize in any particular lines, and yet it was the kind of Aladdin's Cave where anything might be discovered.

The Aladdin's Cave parallel was emphasized as they entered the shop that December morning. Stock items were draped from hooks and hangers, intertwined with strings of fairy lights. Large candles in sconces higher up the walls made the scene even more exotic (and prompted in Carole sour thoughts about health and safety risks). The effect was studiedly casual, that apparently random set-dressing which could only be achieved by meticulous preparation.

If the pot luck element in shopping at Gallimaufry, the fact that she never knew what she would find there, was what appealed to Jude, the very same quality was what had kept Carole away from the place until that Friday morning. She reckoned there was quite enough imprecision in life without going out of one's way to discover it. Carole Seddon liked to have things cut and dried.

Of course, the success of a shop like Gallimaufry would always depend on the mind behind it. An eclectic buying policy

22

was not necessarily good news, and the retail trade was littered with businesses that had gone belly-up because their premises were filled with stuff that nobody wanted to buy.

But the mind behind Gallimaufry appeared to be a shrewd one. A careful analysis of the requirements of Fethering consumers had been conducted and, rather than filling a single large niche, the new store had aimed for many small niches.

Though the village had its less salubrious area—rather appositely called 'Downside', some ill-maintained roads of former council housing to the north—Fethering was, generally speaking, quite well-heeled. The bungaloid straggle of interlocking villages between Worthing and Littlehampton, nicknamed locally the 'Costa Geriatrica', contained many people who had retired on good pensions (in the days when there were still good pensions to retire on). Even with a recession looming, there was plenty of spare cash in the Fethering area. The skill for a retailer was to get its owners to part with it.

And that was a skill that, gathering from the crowd when Carole and Jude entered the shop that Friday morning, the owner of Gallimaufry possessed. It was also clear, from the lavish embraces they exchanged, that Jude knew the owner of Gallimaufry very well.

Introductions were made. Carole silently disapproved of the woman's name almost as much as she did of her shop. Lola Le Bonnier. Surely nobody was actually christened that? No amount of vindictiveness of parents could land someone with the name of Lola Le Bonnier. Maybe it was a misfortune of marriage.

And the woman was wearing a wedding ring. She was tall, slender, in her thirties with hazel eyes and chestnut hair skilfully shaped short around the nape of her neck. She was dressed rather too stylishly for Carole's taste, but there was no denying the look was effective: an Arran cardigan with impossibly large wooden buttons over a pink silk T-shirt fringed with so much lace that it looked like lingerie, and skintight jeans disappearing into the tops of knee-high brown leather boots with implausibly high heels. Carole supposed rather sniffily that if you owned a shop which sold overpriced knick-knacks, then you had a duty to dress like an overpriced knick-knack.

'Hello,' said Lola Le Bonnier, giving a firm shake to Carole's hand. 'I don't think I've seen you in here before, have I?'

'No,' came the reply that its speaker knew was too brusque.

'Well, browse at will.' Lola made an elaborate gesture at her stock. There was something theatrical about her voice too; it had a husky, breathy, *actressy* quality. 'Plenty of stuff still here, if you're looking for that final present for "the person who has everything". All heavily discounted too. Everything must go. Welcome to credit-crunch shopping.'

There was a wryness in her tone as she said this, an implication of understatement. Maybe the confidence of Gallimaufry's champagne opening in September had been diluted by the harsh realities of the economic downturn. Perhaps, even though the shop was crowded, people were more cautious than they had been about parting with their money.

Certainly the stock was covered with labels bearing come-ons like 'Final Reduction' and '50% Off'. Carole's interest was stirred. 'Overpriced knick-knacks' held more appeal for her when they ceased to be overpriced. They'd still be 'knick-knacks', obviously, but it might be worth her casting her eye over them.

'Oh, by the way, Lola,' said Jude suddenly, 'if you and Ricky have got any time on Sunday, I'm having an open house. Starting twelve o'clock, going on till God knows when. You'd be very welcome.'

Really, Jude, thought Carole, if you go around randomly scattering invitations to every shopkeeper you happen to meet, no wonder you haven't got a very clear estimate of how many people are going to come to your party. And I see the timing of the event has changed. 'God knows when' might be very different from 'when the booze runs out'.

'Thanks,' said Lola Le Bonnier, her response as casual as the invitation itself had been. 'I'll check with Ricky. Sunday's Varya's day off—she's the au pair, but Ricky's mother will be with us by then . . .'

'Oh, she's the actress, isn't she?'

'That's right, Jude. Flora Le Bonnier.'

'You've heard of her, haven't you, Carole?'

'I don't believe so,' came the sniffy response.

'She is—or at least was—quite a *grande dame* of the English theatre.'

'Very *grande*,' Lola confirmed. She gestured to a pile of books by the till—glossy hardbacks with a monochrome glamour photograph of an aristocratic-looking woman on the front and the title *One Classy Lady*. 'Her autobiography. No way I'd get away with not stocking that in here. But fortunately she's devoted to her grandchildren, so we might be able to leave them with her and come to your party for a while.'

'Well, be great to see you if you can make it.'

'We'll definitely try.' Lola looked at her watch. 'Actually, I'll ask Ricky straight away. We're just about to go up to London for a lunch thing. Christmas "do" for one of the record companies he's worked for.' She looked across at a woman busy dealing with purchasers behind the counter. 'Got to be on my way, Anna.'

There was a slight tug of resentment at the corner of the woman's mouth as she took in this information, suggesting to Carole that maybe Lola made rather too frequent demands on her to hold the fort. The assistant was probably early fifties, with thick make-up, cupid-bow lips, sculpted eyebrows and ash-blond hair. Marilyn Monroe gone to seed, or perhaps Marilyn Monroe at the age fate never allowed her to reach.

Carole realized with a slight shock that she did actually recognize the woman, though she was used to seeing her with her hair covered by a hat or scarf. Anna was one of Fethering Beach's regular dog-walkers. She had a small West Highland terrier with a little Black Watch tartan coat. If Carole took Gulliver out a bit later than usual in the morning, around half past seven, she would quite often pass the woman. Being Carole, of course, she had never spoken to her, just given the abrupt 'Fethering nod' of acknowledgement which was customary at that time in the morning.

'All right,' the woman called Anna replied to Lola, contriving to keep the irritation out of her voice. 'Will you make it back before closing time?'

Lola Le Bonnier's lower lips jutted forward doubtfully. 'Try to. But when Ricky gets chatting to his music industry mates, it's sometimes hard to drag him away.'

'We are open till eight tonight.' Again the woman put her argument into the words rather than intonation.

Lola was busy reaching behind the counter for a violent-pink fake fur coat and a bag shaped like an upmarket leather coalscuttle. 'I'll try and get back before you close. But you and Bex will be OK. You're a star. Bless you, Anna. See you, Jude love—hopefully on Sunday.'

And, without allowing time for any responses, the owner of Gallimaufry swept out of her shop. Anna exchanged a look with a teenager whose fringe was purple-streaked, and who Carole reckoned must be Bex. The expression of sullen boredom on the girl's face suggested that not much help would be coming from that quarter. Anna would effectively be managing the shop on her own until eight o'clock.

CHAPTER FOUR

Jude was already away cooing at the array of discounted goods that Gallimaufry had to offer, so Carole thought she'd better join in. She was still slightly upset by her neighbour's reaction to her proposed presents for Gaby and Stephen, but at least she'd show willing by looking for alternatives.

'Perfect!' squealed Jude as her friend approached. She had perched a tinsel crown on her head, and she was holding up a box whose contents were a sudoku jigsaw puzzle. Carole thought it was a pointless present. Her mental workouts were with words rather than numbers. Now, if they made a jigsaw of *The Times* crossword, that might have engaged her attention. Except, of course, you could only answer the clues once, and when you'd done that, all you'd be stuck with was a jigsaw.

'It's the perfect present!' Jude continued.

'For whom?'

'Georgie.'

Carole had a rule with herself, that she would never ask for information about her neighbour's friends. If such information was volunteered, fine, but she didn't want to appear curious. It was a rule she broke frequently, as she did now, asking instinctively, 'Who's Georgie?'

'Former client of mine. Came with a terrible pain in the neck.'

'And you cured her of it. You *healed* her?' asked Carole, failing to keep her distaste out of the word.

'Well, she got better. I think getting divorced probably was more effective than anything I did for her. Her husband was the real pain in the neck. Anyway . . .' Jude rattled the box— 'Georgie's hooked on numbers. She'll love this.'

Carole couldn't stop herself from saying, 'Well, I wouldn't like it.'

'Nor would I. But that's the point about presents. They aren't meant to appeal to you. They're meant to appeal to the recipient. And this particular jigsaw will suit Georgie down to the ground.'

'Good,' said Carole flatly. Then a new thought came to her. 'Is Georgie going to be at your open house?'

'Possibly. I think I invited her.' Yet more inappropriate vagueness about the serious matter of giving a party. 'But I'm spending Christmas Day with her. First one she's had without the husband around. Which in one way makes her quite ecstatic, and in another way worried about being lonely. So I said I'd join her.'

This was new information. Jude had said she was Christmassing in Fethering, without being more specific about exactly where in Fethering. But Carole didn't comment, instead focusing her attention on the potential presents on display. She couldn't see anything that came within a mile of suitability for either her son or daughter-in-law. Who could possibly want a wind-up skeleton? Or an apron in the pattern of a Friesian cow? Or a Russian Father Christmas doll, inside which was a smaller Russian Father Christmas doll, inside which was an even smaller Russian Father Christmas doll, inside which . . . ? Yes, Gallimaufry really was a place for people with more money than sense.

On the other hand, the discounted prices were not bad. Assuming, of course, that there was an appropriate price for something you wouldn't give houseroom to.

'Oh, look, these are great!' Jude enthused.

'What on earth are they?'

'They're finger puppets of famous philosophers. Look!' And in no time one of Jude's hands was playing host to Socrates, Spinoza, Descartes, Nietzsche and Wittgenstein.

'But what *use* are they? Who could possibly need anything like that?'

' "Oh, reason not the need!" ' Jude quoted. 'King Lear got it right, you know. If we stuck only to what we needed, life would be a very dull business. It's the things we *don't* need that make it bearable.'

'I thought you were supposed to have green principles.'

'What on earth gave you that idea?'

'Well, come on, Jude, you're into healing and wind-chimes and essential oils and joss sticks and crystals and—'

'And all other kinds of New Age mumbo-jumbo?'

'Now I didn't say that.'

'No, because I saved you the trouble.' There was the shadow of a grin on Jude's rounded face. She enjoyed these sparring sessions with her neighbour. For her they contained a strong element of teasing, and even Carole didn't take them quite as seriously as she used to. 'Anyway,' Jude went on, 'just because I believe in some things you don't believe in, it doesn't mean I believe in everything you don't believe in.'

'So you're not worried about saving the planet?'

'Yes, I am, but not to the exclusion of everything else. I don't want to save a planet that ends up dull because nobody allows themselves any kind of indulgence. It's the little embellishments of life that make it worth living. And those embellishments needn't be expensive. There's an old Chinese proverb—'

'Is there?' said Carole, with a sniff that summed up completely her view of old Chinese proverbs.

'Yes. It says, "If I had one penny left in the world, I would spend half of it on bread, and the other half on flowers." '

Carole sniffed again. 'The penny isn't legal tender in China. It never has been.'

'I think the proverb may have been translated for English audiences.'

'Oh.'

'Anyway . . .' Jude's brown eyes twinkled as she waved her hand, wiggling Socrates, Spinoza, Descartes, Nietzsche and Wittgenstein in front of her neighbour's face. 'Do you think these'd be suitable?'

'Suitable for what?'

'As presents.'

'For whom?'

'For Stephen or Gaby?' Jude replied innocently, precisely aware of the response her words would attract.

She was not disappointed. 'Don't be ridiculous!'

'Well,' said Jude, full of mock-penitence, 'you know them so much better than I do. I was just thinking something like this'— another wiggle of philosophers—'might appeal to their sense of humour.'

Carole wondered momentarily whether her son had a sense of humour. Gaby did, she felt sure, and Stephen had relaxed so much since their marriage that maybe by now he had developed one too. Maybe a sense of humour was contagious, like chicken pox.

'I think', she said, 'I'm going to do better sticking to the M and S shirts for Stephen.'

'Well, all right, but you still can't give Gaby toilet water.'

Carole grudgingly conceded that there might be some truth in that. She looked around at the display of discounted knick-knacks with something approaching despair. 'But I still haven't a clue what would be right for her.'

'It's always struck me,' Jude began tentatively, not wishing to be too pushy with her suggestions, 'that Gaby's full of fun. She's got a very bubbly personality.' Carole agreed that this was the case. 'She's also very girly in some ways.'

'Ye-es.'

'So I think you should give her something to put on.'

'Clothes, you mean? But I don't know her size.' Carole anxiously surveyed the hanging garments in Eastern silks, crumpled linen and PVC. 'I wouldn't begin to know what Gaby would like to wear.'

'Oh, come on, you've seen her enough times. You know the kind of stuff she likes.'

Carole tried to focus on what her daughter-in-law did actually wear. Jeans and sweatshirts mostly these days, as she spent most of her time at home looking after the baby. While she was still working as a theatrical agent, Gaby had had a couple of dauntingly businesslike trouser suits, but those hadn't seen the light of day since Lily's birth.

'She likes sparkly things,' Jude prompted.

Yes, now Carole came to think of it, a lot of Gaby's tops did have glittery designs on them. And she wore quite a bit of costume jewellery in what her mother-in-law would have described as diamanté. 'So you're saying I should get her a brooch or something?'

'No, I'm saying you should give her something frivolous. Something like this perhaps?' Jude's hand, by now denuded of Socrates, Spinoza, Descartes, Nietzsche and Wittgenstein, reached up to pull something down from its hook. It was a six-foot-long stole formed by sprays of feathers alternately white and silver.

Carole scrutinized the object. 'Well, it wouldn't be very warm, you know, as scarves go.'

'It's not a scarf, it's a boa.'

'Maybe, but what for?'

'For fun!' Jude replied with something approaching exasperation. 'For when Gaby wants to glam herself up a bit. For when she wants to forget that she's a wife and mother and remind herself she's a girl.'

Carole continued to look dubiously at the boa. 'Do you think she'll like it, though?'

'I'm sure she will. And I can guarantee that Lily will like it too. In a few years' time she'll be using it for dressing up.'

The granddaughter argument swayed Carole, and when she looked at the cost of the boa, she was won over completely. Originally, it had been twenty-five pounds, which would definitely have come under her definition of overpriced. But that had been slashed to ten pounds, and then a further reduction had been made to four pounds fifty. Carole decided she had found Gaby's present.

Emboldened by this success, she started wavering about the Marks and Spencer shirts for Stephen.

'You could still give them to him,' Jude suggested, 'so that he doesn't die of shock at not getting them after all these years. But then you could give him something else as well.'

'What kind of "something else"?' asked Carole suspiciously.

'Something frivolous.'

'Stephen's never going to wear a feather boa.'

'No, I know he's not,' Jude replied, though she couldn't deny that the image was quite amusing. 'But there are other frivolous things in here.'

Carole looked around the shop. In her view, a Santa Claus Willy Warmer was simply in bad taste. And she wouldn't have dared to be present when Stephen opened such a thing. Nor was she attracted by a key ring with a small Rubik's cube attached. The combined digital stopwatch and bottle opener didn't do much for her either. And as for the thought of giving anyone a sumptuously boxed, gold-plated Belly Button Fluff

Extractor . . .

'Maybe I should just stick to the shirts . . .' she announced uncertainly.

'No, Carole, don't give up so easily. Put yourself in Stephen's shoes for a moment. What would he like? What are his interests?'

'Work, mostly.'

'And his work involves . . . ?'

'Money and computers, in some combination which I have never quite worked out.'

'Well, I'm sure Lola stocks something for computer buffs.'

'I doubt it. This isn't a technology shop.'

'Ah, look, the very thing!' Jude swooped on a basket full of wind-up toys. 'A Glow-in-the-dark Computer Angel!'

'What?' asked Carole weakly, as the package was thrust towards her. Under a plastic bubble there was a translucent green plastic figure of an angel. Printed above it were the words: 'Your Computer Angel deals with all your computer problems, glitches and viruses. Just wind her up and her flapping wings will spread her protection over your desktop or laptop. And when you turn the lights off, your Computer Angel will glow in the dark.'

'How does it work?' asked Carole.

'Blind faith.'

'No, I mean how does it work as anti-virus protection?' After long resistance to the idea of computers, Carole had recently become something of an expert on the subject. 'There isn't a software CD with it, as far as I can see. And it doesn't have a USB plug.'

'Carole,' said Jude patiently, 'it's a joke. It's just a fun thing. To bring a smile on Christmas Day to the face of a computer obsessive like Stephen.'

Her neighbour still didn't look convinced. But then she saw

the price tag: £7.50 reduced to £4.00, then reduced again to £1.50.

As she paid for her purchases, Carole and Anna at the till exchanged half-smiles, as if to say, 'Yes, we have seen each other before.' But neither took the opportunity to embark on conversation.

And so Carole completed her Christmas shopping. Which meant that, as well as the Marks and Spencer shirts, Stephen Seddon would shortly be the proud owner of a Glow-in-the-dark Computer Angel.

CHAPTER FIVE

Carole at first demurred at Jude's suggestion they should lunch at the Crown and Anchor. Some atavistic instinct told her it was self-indulgence to go out for a meal so near to Christmas. But, as it often did, Jude's more sybaritic counsel prevailed, and so they made their way from Gallimaufry to Fethering's only pub and the lugubrious welcome of its landlord, Ted Crisp.

A large man with matted hair and beard, he nodded acknowledgement of their arrival and started pouring two large glasses of Chilean Chardonnay before they gave an order. The interior of the pub was decorated for Christmas, but there weren't that many Christmas customers. Therein lay the cause of his lugubriousness, as he wasted no time in telling them.

'Look at the place. Empty as a barn. This should be the time of year I'm coining it, doing all the local office Christmas lunches. Should be packed out for the whole of December, and what have I had? Bugger all.'

They looked around and saw his point. A few frail Fethering pensioners had braved the cold weather to take advantage of the Crown and Anchor's Midweek Special deals. A small, thin woman sat in an alcove nursing a pint of Guinness. Low winter sun through the pub's windows turned the long hair, cascading down over a flowered smock, a golden colour, giving her the image of a hippy chick from the Sixties. But neither she nor any of the other customers looked as if they were big spenders.

'Is it still because of what happened in the summer?' Jude

35

asked Ted tactfully. She was referring to the time when the Crown and Anchor had been invaded by Hell's Angels and a murder had taken place on the premises. The pub had nearly been closed down and, although it subsequently emerged that Ted Crisp had been the victim of criminal harassment, memories in Fethering were long and adverse publicity slow to dissipate.

The landlord nodded assent. 'Yeah, that's it. Going to take years to build up the business again. And now with all this financial chaos going on, people are even less inclined to come out and spend their money down the pub. They'd rather sit at home with a pile of half-price cans of supermarket lager.'

'It'll get better,' said Jude.

Carole picked up the baton of reassurance. 'Of course it will. You've still got Ed Pollack as your chef, haven't you?'

'Yes, he seems happy to stay . . .'

'That's good news.'

'. . . as long as I can afford to keep him on,' Ted continued gloomily. 'I sometimes worry about how long I'll be able to keep Zosia on, too.' He was referring to his Polish bar manager, who had been introduced to the Crown and Anchor by Jude.

'Don't be silly,' Carole said. Then, looking around, asked, 'Where is Zosia, by the way?'

'Got some Christmas drinks thing at the university.' The girl was managing to fit a degree in journalism around her work at the pub. 'So I'm on my own here today.' He looked mournfully around the bar. 'Not that I'm exactly rushed off my feet.'

'Ted, it'll all be all right,' said Jude soothingly. 'This is a great pub. Ed's a great chef. Word'll soon spread again about how good the food is at the Crown and Anchor. By the summer you'll have a waiting list for tables.'

'If I'm still here then.'

When he was in this kind of mood Ted was not to be

comforted, so Carole and Jude thought their best course of action was to order their lunch. He handed menus across and stood with ballpoint pen and pad poised. 'Can't tempt you to the full Christmas menu, can I? It's very good.'

'I'm sure it is,' said Carole, 'but I'll be doing all that on Christmas Day.' And she felt a little flurry of excitement at the thought.

'I might go for it,' said Jude.

'What, the full Christmas menu?' asked her astonished neighbour.

'Why not? I like turkey and stuff—not to mention turkey and stuff*ing.*'

'But you can't have all that before Christmas.'

' 'Ere, are you trying to restrict my trade?' asked an aggrieved Ted Crisp. 'If the lady wants to order a full Christmas menu, don't go putting her off.'

'I'm sorry, Ted,' said Carole contritely. The teasing element with which he usually made such remarks seemed to be absent that day. The lack of business really was getting to him.

To compensate, Carole ordered a fillet steak, the most expensive thing on the menu and, while Ted took their orders through to Ed Pollack in the kitchen, the two women moved to one of the pub's alcove tables. The thin woman with the Guinness seemed to be giving them the once over. Closer to, she no longer looked like a hippy chick. Out of the sunlight, her flowing hair was grey and the contours of her face were scored with wrinkles, like an apple that had been stored for too long. Carole and Jude were aware of the curious stare from her faded brown eyes, but quickly forgot about her when they sat down. Their conversation soon homed in on Lola Le Bonnier. Carole was intrigued as to how Jude had met the owner of Gallimaufry.

'Just going in and out of the shop, really. Then one of her kids, her baby Henry, had a problem with asthma, so she brought him along to me for a session.' Professional discretion prevented Jude from mentioning the condition which had brought Lola herself to Woodside Cottage for a consultation.

'Can you actually *heal* asthma?'

'I can sometimes ease it a bit.'

At another time Carole might have asked more about that, but on this occasion she was more interested in Lola Le Bonnier, who, she observed, didn't conform to the usual image of a shopkeeper.

'No, I think Gallimaufry for her is really just a rich girl's hobby.'

'And she's rich through her husband, is she? The Ricky she mentioned?'

Jude shrugged. 'Lola may also have money of her own, I don't know. But certainly Ricky never seems to lack for a few bob.'

'Have you met him too?'

'Only a couple of times recently. But I saw a bit of him in London in the early seventies.'

'When you say you "saw a bit of him" . . . ?'

Jude grinned. 'I do not mean we were lovers, no. He did try it on with me a couple of times, but I was a rather conventional teenager and—'

'You mean you were a virgin?' asked Carole, intrigued by this potential new insight.

'God, no. But I was sleeping with someone else and at that stage was very much a one-man woman.'

Intriguing. Was the implication that she was no longer a 'one-man woman'? Carole hadn't heard much about her neighbour's teenage years, but before she could ask a supplementary question, Jude had moved on. 'Anyway, Ricky was involved on the periphery of a lot of pop groups back then. Did some producing, promotion, that kind of stuff. Very trendy.'

'And successful?'

'He behaved as if he had a lot of money.'

'But you don't think he did?'

'I'm not saying that. The music business has always been full of bullshit, and Ricky Le Bonnier could splash it about with the best of them. I never did know with him—and I still don't—how much of what he says to believe. He sounds like a name-dropper, but when you get down to the details, he does actually know the names he drops quite well. So if he says he's been in Mustique with Mick Jagger, he probably has. If he says he's toured with Led Zeppelin, then that's probably true too.'

Carole was tempted to ask, 'Who are Led Zeppelin?' but she stopped herself. She knew full well who Led Zeppelin were and, had she asked the question, would have sounded like an elderly judge from a *Punch* cartoon. She knew she played up too much to her fogeyish image at times.

'You know,' Jude went on, 'Ricky's one of those people who's clearly had a varied and busy life, but rarely tells you all the details of it.' Takes one to know one, thought Carole tartly. 'Anyway, needless to say, Lola isn't his first wife. Always rather prided himself as a ladies' man. He's had at least two other wives that I know of. I vaguely remember hearing about one of them dying tragically . . . a drug overdose or something. And I think he had at least one kid, a daughter who'd be grown-up by now, though I don't know which wife was her mother. Or maybe she's a stepdaughter, I'm not sure. I mean, Ricky's about my age, so there's probably a good twenty years between him and Lola. I seem to remember he hitched up with her about six years ago. Like so many men of his age and with his kind of past, he's rebranded himself with a new family. Then he and Lola moved down here, and live in a great big manor house just outside Fedborough. Fedingham Court House, it's called. Apparently Ricky's a local lad, was brought up somewhere around here, so he's kind of come back to his roots.

'Anyway, they settled into the country life by buying a pair of Dalmatians, then Lola presented Ricky with a couple of babies in quick succession and, so far as I can gather, the marriage works very well. He's an amusing guy, good company, Lola appears to be devoted to him. And she's a bright girl, I can't see her putting up with any nonsense.'

'When you say "bright" . . . ?'

'Got a degree from Cambridge. Did a lot of theatre and revue while she was there, I gather—Footlights and what-have-you— even started working as a professional actress. Then moved into PR, a lot of music business stuff . . . which is presumably how she came to meet Ricky.'

'But is she—?'

Carole's question didn't get asked, however, because at that moment Ted Crisp delivered their lunch order. Carole tucked into her steak, while Jude began to make inroads into a huge pile of turkey, stuffing, chipolatas, crispy bacon, roast potatoes, brussels sprouts, bread sauce and cranberry sauce. For the first time that year Christmas seemed very close.

They were so involved in eating that they didn't notice the thin, long-haired woman in the smock finish her Guinness and make her way out of the pub. Nor did they notice the curious look she gave them as she left.

CHAPTER SIX

In the event, in spite of all her misgivings, Carole rather enjoyed Jude's open house. Not that she hadn't been desperately nervous before it. In fact, for the first time in her life, she had even contemplated having a bracing drink at High Tor before she braved the rarefied atmosphere of Woodside Cottage. She had an unusual amount of alcohol in the house in anticipation of Christmas lunch with Stephen and family, and her supplies included a half-bottle of brandy to light the Christmas pudding. The temptation to have a quick nip from it before she went next door was surprisingly strong. But Carole curbed the urge. Drinking when on one's own—secret drinking, as her parents would have called it—was, Carole knew, 'a slippery slope'. And she'd spent much of her life rigidly steering clear of slippery slopes.

After considerable internal debate, she had decided that one-fifteen was probably the proper time to arrive for a party that was scheduled 'from twelve noon until the booze runs out'. And although she'd never have admitted to having done it, her location in High Tor enabled her to check from her bedroom window that enough guests had arrived for her to make her own entrance comparatively unnoticed.

With regard to a bottle, she decided finally to go down the Chilean Chardonnay route. She had bought six for the Christmas lunch (as well as a bottle of champagne), but recognized that that was over-catering for a party of four, one of

41

whom was a baby and one of whom would be having to drive back to Fulham afterwards. So she could spare one to ensure that it took a little longer for the booze at Woodside Cottage to run out.

Carole didn't put on a coat. It would have been daft to do so when she was only going next door, but that wasn't the reason why she left it at High Tor. If she found the open house too much of a strain, then she wouldn't have to delay her unobtrusive exit by searching for her coat.

At one-fifteen sharp Carole Seddon made the stressful journey of a few yards to Woodside Cottage, gloomily anticipating that the house's owner was the only person she would recognize. Also, she felt sure that Jude would be surrounded by other guests and not notice her arrival. Then Carole would stand around like a lemon, and the full scale of her own social ineptitude would be revealed for all to see.

She needn't have worried. Jude answered the door to her tentative knock and immediately enveloped her in a huge hug. She swept up the proffered bottle of Chilean Chardonnay. 'Lovely; our favourite, isn't it? Look, there are some poured glasses on the tray over there. Help yourself. And I'm sure there are lots of people you recognize.'

Carole was about to say she doubted that, but as she looked into the room she was surprised by how many faces she did know. It was almost like a parade of the Fethering people who had been involved in Carole and Jude's previous investigations. There was Sonya Dalrymple, who had got them involved in solving the murder at the Long Bamber Stables. Now divorced from her odious husband Nicky, she looked more blondly beautiful than ever. There was Connie from the hairdresser's on the parade, which used to be called Connie's Cuts, but had been renamed Marnie. She stood glowing with happiness beside Martin, the husband she had remarried after his second wife had been found guilty of murder. Sonny Frank from the betting shop was there, along with another of its regulars, Gerald Hume, who was an intellectual soulmate of Carole's.

'Hello,' he said in his precise, mandarin way. 'What an inestimable pleasure it is to see you. I had been hoping that you might be attending this gathering, given your geographical proximity to our hostess. Now what can I pass you to drink? "A beaker full of the warm South, Full of the true, the blushful Hippocrene"?'

'Yes, I'd rather it was less blushful than Keats recommended, though. A glass of white, please.'

Gerald handed the drink across. When Carole thanked him, he riposted with a quotation she could not immediately identify: ' "The labour we delight in physics pain." ' Replying to her quizzical look, he said, '*Macbeth.*'

She raised her glass to his. 'Are you still a regular at the betting shop?'

'Oh yes,' he replied. 'And about to experience two days of deprivation.' Seeing her puzzled expression, he elucidated. 'No racing on Christmas Eve or Christmas Day.'

In its perverse way, the first sip of her cold Chardonnay spread a pleasing warmth through her body. She looked around the sitting room of Woodside Cottage, transformed for Christmas. It was more cluttered than ever with boughs of holly, fir and other evergreens stuck to the walls and standing in jugs and vases. All natural decorations, she noted. No paper chains, no tinsel, no lametta, certainly no fairy lights. Simply variations of green interrupted only by the red of holly berries. Whatever she did, Jude had style.

And she also, however casual her approach to it might have seemed, knew how to run a party. Hardly surprising, when Carole came to think about it, because one of Jude's previous incarnations had been as a restaurateur. Somehow spaces had been found on the crowded surfaces for trays of drinks and bowls of intriguing-looking nibbles. There was no room for a table where the guests could sit down, but enticing smells from the kitchen suggested more substantial hot food would soon be on its way.

And yet Jude didn't seem to be distracted by her culinary responsibilities. She was flitting amongst the throng, as ever surprisingly light on her feet for a woman of her bulk. She was dressed in layers of wafting garments, predominantly purple, mauve and pale, pale violet. On top of her intricately plaited bundle of hair was the room's only concession to tinsel, the crown she'd picked up in Gallimaufry. As she had done so many times before, Carole wondered how it was that Jude could get away with the way she dressed. If she herself had gone around with a tinsel crown on, she would look ridiculous, like an ageing woman in an anonymous Marks and Spencer's black dress who'd had a drop too much at the staff Christmas lunch and forgotten to remove the hat she'd got in her cracker.

But then Carole was Carole and Jude was Jude.

At that moment Jude's lack of concern about the kitchen was explained as issuing forth from it came Zosia, the bar manager from the Crown and Anchor. Her blond hair was in its usual stubby pigtails and her customary broad grin was in place, as she balanced trays of chicken satay sticks, prawn tempura, stuffed mushrooms and other delights.

Carole couldn't help reflecting that Zosia was another person who had come into their lives through murder. It was the death of her brother Tadeusz that had brought the girl to England and, though she never let the surface of her cheerful public persona crack, there must have been times when she still felt the loss.

If Zosia was helping Jude, then Ted Crisp must be holding the fort at the Crown and Anchor. But even as Carole had the thought, she saw the landlord across the room, standing on his own, large and forlorn. With a murmured apology to Gerald Hume, she crossed towards him.

Seeing Ted in public always gave Carole a bit of a charge. The sheer unlikeliness of her having had a brief affair with the man gave her more sense of herself as a woman than she usually felt. And her confidence was increased by how uncomfortable he was looking. She'd been worried about her own social ineptitude, her not recognizing anyone at the open house, and yet here she was grinning away at familiar faces as she crossed the room, whereas it was Ted who appeared to know no one. Not surprising, really. He hardly ever stirred from the premises of the Crown and Anchor. So Fethering residents who weren't regulars at the pub . . . well, he probably hadn't met them.

He did look rewardingly pleased to see her, and uncharacteristically kissed her on both cheeks. She had forgotten how surprisingly soft his beard was against her skin.

'So if you and Zosia are both here, who's looking after the Crown and Anchor?'

'She's trained up the young staff very well. They can manage for one lunchtime . . . not that there'll probably be much business.' But he didn't sound as down about the situation as he had when they last met. In response to Carole's enquiring eyebrow, he went on, 'Suddenly got a bit of a break yesterday. Lunch booking for thirty-five tomorrow. Firm's Christmas do.'

'That was very short notice.'

He grinned with satisfaction. 'That was because they were let down by the place they had booked. Someone there screwed up the reservation.'

'Where was that?'

His satisfaction grew. 'Home Hostelries' latest flagship venue. The Cat and Fiddle up near Fedborough.' Ted Crisp had many

45

reasons for welcoming incompetence from that particular chain of pubs.

They were joined by a bustling, bubbling Jude. 'Now I do want you two to meet my friend Saira.' The name was pronounced like the grape variety 'Syrah'.

The woman indicated was in her early thirties. The shape of her face and the line of her hair suggested Indian or Pakistani ancestry, but her skin was surprisingly pale. Her brown eyes were flecked with hazel and she had a broad, toothy smile.

'Actually, we know each other,' said Carole, glad to see another familiar face.

'Oh, I should have thought of that. Through Gulliver?' asked Jude.

'Yes. I'm sorry, I've always known you as Miss Sherjan. I didn't know your first name.' Rather formally Carole shook the woman's thin hand and explained to Ted, 'Saira Sherjan's one of the local vets. Part of the practice at Fedborough. She's patched up various injuries for Gulliver.'

'Pleased to meet you,' said the publican.

'And how is Gulliver?'

'Fine at the moment, Miss Sh—Saira. Still constantly reproaching me for not taking him on enough walks. But, touch wood, he hasn't managed to cut himself on anything on Fethering Beach recently.'

'Good. He's a lovely dog.' The woman's affection for animals glowed within her. For her, being a vet was a vocation rather than just a job.

'Not very bright, I'm afraid.'

'What Labrador is?'

'Can I get you a drink, Saira?' asked Jude, waving the bottles of red and white she had in each hand.

'No, I'm just on the water.' She grinned at Carole. 'That is partly because I'm on duty as Emergency Cover this evening.

And also because I'm in training for the London Marathon.'

'So are you going to lay off alcohol right through Christmas?'

'You bet.' Saira Sherjan was evidently strong-willed. 'Excuse me, I'll just go and get some water.'

As she watched the finely toned figure move away, Carole asked Jude how she'd met the vet. 'You don't have any animals.'

'Oh, through friends,' said Jude, with her characteristic airiness, and darted off to fill more glasses. At this point Gerald Hume rejoined Carole to say he must be going. 'I have an investment programme arranged for the afternoon.'

'The betting shop?'

'How well you know me.'

'I didn't know you did Sundays there as well as weekdays.'

'The habit of losing money is a deeply entrenched one,' said Gerald Hume. 'If we do not chance to meet again before the outbreak of festivities, I trust that you will have an enjoyable Christmas.'

The response, 'Oh, I'm sure I will,' was instinctive. It was how she had covered up the loneliness of her recent Christmases. But, with a sudden surge of good cheer, for a moment Carole entertained the hope that her answer could be accurate for once. With Stephen, Gaby and Lily, she actually might have an enjoyable Christmas.

CHAPTER SEVEN

Carole was suddenly aware of a loud, cultured voice saying, 'Ah, well, that's something Elton John would have thrown a real tantrum about. Though fortunately, when I was working with him, he was in one of his calmer phases.'

She didn't need telling that the speaker was Ricky Le Bonnier, but serendipitously Jude was passing and effected the introduction. Smiling, he took her hand in both of his and said, 'Carole, such a pleasure to meet you.'

He certainly had charm—or even what someone less hidebound than Carole might have called 'charisma'. Ricky Le Bonnier was tall, quite bulky above the waist, with grey, thinning hair hanging long to about jaw level. His glasses had narrow rectangular lenses set in frames whose designer appeared to have been influenced by the technology of the Eiffel Tower. He wore cherry-coloured corduroy trousers and a fuzzy cardigan with an abstract pattern of blues and greys.

Although he was in the centre of a small audience, Ricky Le Bonnier appeared to have brought two women with him, but neither was his wife Lola. The first was elderly, ensconced so deeply in one of Jude's heavily draped armchairs that Carole had to bend double to talk to her. She was introduced as Flora, Ricky's mother, and the expression of adoration that she fixed on her son might well have explained his robust self-esteem.

Although she had claimed to have no knowledge of the name, Carole recognized the woman instantly. Every period television drama of the previous decade seemed to have featured Flora Le Bonnier, usually as the proud head of some patrician family. And before that she had had a long career in British films. But it looked as though her acting days might now be over. She was thin, probably quite tall if she stood up, with a beaky nose and white hair expertly fluffed out by an expensive stylist. Her hands were curved rigidly inwards, the finger joints knobbly with arthritis. Propped against the armchair were the two sticks that, presumably, she needed for walking.

The other woman, perhaps in her late twenties, was introduced to Carole as Polly, Ricky's daughter—though clearly not from his current marriage. Nor did she actually look very like him. Polly was thin, dark and wiry, attractive in a daunting, don't-mess-with-me manner. She wore tight black jeans and a sweater which emphasized her trim figure. Her hands were fiddling restlessly with a mobile in a fluorescent pink phone sock. Polly's dark eyes darted around the room, looking for someone else she knew, someone who might give her the excuse to move away from her current conversational group.

Carole told Ricky that she'd met Lola in the shop.

'Ah yes,' he said. 'Gallimaufry, the great Le Bonnier indulgence.'

'Lost cause more likely,' snapped Flora. If Carole hadn't recognized the face, she could not have failed to recognize the voice. Husky, finely modulated, marinated in centuries of aristocratic history.

'That remains to be seen,' said her son easily. 'As we know from all the doom merchants in the media, England's high streets are suffering in the current economic climate, and there will inevitably be some casualties.'

'I wouldn't know. I never read newspapers,' was his mother's rather grand response. 'They are full of inaccuracies and libel. Which is why I have made it a rule throughout my professional life never to speak to the press.'

'All right, Mother, we all know you don't read the papers. But you watch television and listen to the radio. You can't pretend that you don't know things are tough on the high street.'

'Very well. And I also know that first to the wall will be mimsy-pimsy shops which sell over-priced rubbish for people with more money than sense.'

Carole was glad to meet someone whose opinions of Gallimaufry coincided so exactly with her own (even though she had ended up buying a glittery boa and a Glow-in-the-dark Computer Angel there), but she was more interested in the subtext of the old woman's words. The impression came across that not only did Flora Le Bonnier disapprove of the shop, but she hadn't much time for its owner either. Ricky's mother was not a fan of his most recent marriage.

Carole's mind went back to the moment in Gallimaufry when Jude had issued the invitation to her open house. Lola had suggested that Ricky's mum might look after the children while she and Ricky came to Woodside Cottage. In the event, it appeared that Lola herself had been left holding the babies. And somehow Carole couldn't imagine her using the expression 'Ricky's mum' in Flora Le Bonnier's rather daunting presence.

'Oh, come on, Grandma,' said Polly, 'give the place a chance. It's hardly been open three months. Lola's worked bloody hard on it and we should all give her as much support as we can.'

Carole was surprised to hear this expression of solidarity. According to hallowed fairytale stereotypes, Polly should resent her stepmother, but that appeared not to be the case. Maybe the two young women were near enough in age to bond as girlfriends.

Ricky Le Bonnier evidently considered that he had been silent too long. 'I think, next to putting your own money into a musical or opening a restaurant, going into the retail business must be one of the riskiest investments out there. But as you say, Polly, if anyone can make a go of it, Lola can.'

This prompted a barely disguised snort from Flora, as her son continued, 'Mind you, it can work for the lucky few. I knew Gordon and Anita Roddick when they started up Body Shop—not far away from here, the first store was in Brighton—and, God, I wish I'd got in on the ground floor of that. Some of their franchisees have just minted it over the years.'

'I wouldn't worry about that, Ricky, because you've done very well yourself. You've made your money through the music business,' said his mother, as though this was an article of faith.

'Oh yes, I'm not complaining. Mind you, the people who really clean up there—apart from the artistes, of course—always end up being the middlemen, the lawyers, the accountants. At the more creative end of the spectrum, the producers and so on are usually the ones who miss out. Very few creatives are also good businessmen.'

He favoured Carole with a big, confidential smile. He had that ability, shared by many professional charmers, of being able to make the person they're looking at feel for that moment that there's no one else in the room. 'My background's as a record producer. Worked with a lot of big names in the past . . . Led Zeppelin, Procol Harum, Jethro Tull. My name was never in the foreground, but, to give them their due, a lot of the artistes always make a point of recognizing my contribution . . . you know, when they're interviewed, that kind of stuff.'

Still rather sensitive about her own retired status, Carole asked, 'And are you still working?'

He chuckled and made a broad gesture to his womenfolk, whose message seemed to be, 'Isn't it amazing that people still have to ask questions like that about Ricky Le Bonnier?' 'Carole,' he said gently, 'I'm the kind of guy who's never not working. I'm always switched on. I don't do downtime. So, yes, in answer to your question, I am still working.'

'Still in the music business?'

'You betcha. They say it's all changed, and certainly it isn't the same world I grew up in. God, we knew how to enjoy our work in those days. We knew how to lunch. We knew how to have a proper all-nighter in the studio with a few bottles and, er, other stimulants, to aid the creative process. Today's Perrier-sipping wimps in the music industry couldn't keep up with the pace we used to live at. But, hell, it worked! The stuff that came out of those studio sessions was pure gold. Now the accountants have moved in—as they have in most of the creative industries—but they still have to turn to me for help when they get stuck. Oh, yes, the skills of Ricky Le Bonnier remain very much in demand.'

'So when did you last actually produce a record?' asked Polly coolly.

For the first time Ricky looked slightly thrown by the question. His daughter, it seemed, had the ability to get under his skin. For the first time Carole was aware of considerable tension between them.

'It's not actually to produce the record, Polly love, that they look to me for these days. I work more in an advisory capacity. I allow them to pick my brains when they need a bit of expertise—not to mention experience.'

'And do they *pay* you for your "expertise—not to mention experience"?' There was no doubt now that Polly Le Bonnier was deliberately needling her father.

He looked down at his mother with the same expression he'd used when Carole had asked whether he was still working. He sighed and addressed his daughter. 'Look, love, you should know by now that your daddy just attracts money. He doesn't have to go out of his way to find it. He works hard for it, certainly, but your daddy is a money magnet.'

'And a babe magnet?' There wasn't much affection in Polly's tone.

Her father looked down to Flora in her armchair and shrugged helplessly. She smiled up at him lovingly as he said, 'Guilty as charged.'

Polly's snort was very similar to the one recently emitted by her grandmother. Then the girl looked at her watch. 'Can we get back soon? You know I've got to catch the seven-thirty-two train back to London this evening and I haven't seen much of the little ones.'

Ricky's hands rose in a placatory gesture. 'Just a few more people I want to see. I haven't spoken to the lovely Jude properly yet.' And he drifted off. Flora was also lifting herself out of her armchair with the help of her sticks, saying she needed 'the little girls' room'. Carole noticed how little movement she had in her clawlike hands; she couldn't grip the sticks, only push them into the right position to support herself.

Left alone with Polly, she asked, 'When you mentioned "the little ones" . . . ?'

'Lola's two. Mabel and Henry.'

'Your stepsister and stepbrother?'

'Yes, though it's more like I'm their aunt, really, given the age difference.' Polly seemed noticeably to have relaxed now her father was not beside her. 'But I don't get a chance to see much of them . . .' she looked again with irritation at her watch '. . . and, quite honestly, I'd rather be with Mabel and Henry at this moment than at a drinks party full of people I don't know.' Realizing how ungracious this must have sounded, she was quick to apologize.

'Oh, don't worry,' said Carole. 'I'm not much of a one for parties myself. It's just that I live next door, so I know Jude and . . .' She shrugged.

'Bit of a life force, isn't she?'

Carole had never put it into words before, but of course, yes, that was exactly what Jude was; a 'bit of a life force'. With inevitable and dispiriting logic, Carole wondered what, by comparison, that made her. She didn't pursue the thought.

'So you're not spending Christmas down here, Polly?'

'No, I'll be at my boyfriend's parents'. They live in Gloucestershire.'

'Oh. Very beautiful county,' said Carole with all the fatuity of small talk. 'Or, at least, bits of it are.'

'The bit where they live certainly is. Near the Slad Valley. Laurie Lee country. No, we'll have a few days down there, living in the lap of luxury, miles away from the real world, and then we'll have to come back to the harsh reality of making a living.'

'And how do you do that? I mean, what do you do?'

Polly Le Bonnier wrinkled up her prominent nose. 'I'm an actor.'

'Like your grandmother.'

'Yes. Or rather, not like my grandmother. Anyway, she isn't really my grandmother.'

'What do you mean?'

'I'm not Ricky's real daughter. I'm his stepdaughter. He married my mother.'

'Ah, and is she still—?'

But Polly clearly didn't want to talk about her mother. She moved brusquely on. 'No, I'm not like my grandmother. She was successful. I may have a famous name—which arguably isn't mine by right, anyway—but I'm only an actor when somebody will employ me. The rest of the time I'm an occasional barmaid or waitress.' She sounded rueful rather than dispirited about her situation.

'Ah. Well, maybe things'll pick up for you next year.'

'Maybe.' Polly didn't sound like she'd put a very large bet on the possibility.

'And your boyfriend . . . Is he also . . . ?' Rather proudly Carole remembered a phrase Gaby had used when speaking of the clients at the theatrical agency where she used to work. 'Is he also "in the business"?'

'Yes. To some extent. But Piers is a comedy writer too, so he's not so dependent on the acting as I am. Mind you, that may change.'

'What do you mean?'

Polly opened her hands in a gesture of self-deprecation. 'Just that I'm having a go at writing something.'

'A comedy script?'

'No, no, it's more . . .' She seemed embarrassed to be talking about her writing. 'It's a book, I suppose. Well, it is a book, yes.'

'Have you finished it?'

'A couple of times.' Carole looked at her curiously, so the girl explained, 'I mean I've got to the end a couple of times. I've finished two drafts.'

'Have you shown it to anyone?'

'To Piers. He says he thinks it's terrific. But then he would say that, wouldn't he? Mind you, unwilling as ever to give me unqualified praise, he says he doesn't think it'd have much chance of getting published. But I've also shown the manuscript to a friend who works in a literary agency. She was quite flatter-ing about it, though I'm not sure . . . Oh, I'll finish another draft—which I nearly have done—then see what happens. And in the meantime keep looking for acting work.'

'Well, I wish you a lot of luck with the book.'

'Thank you.'

'Is it fact or fiction?'

Polly responded with a wry smile. 'Bit of each, perhaps.'

'Ah. Contemporary setting?'

'No, I suppose I'd have to say it's historical. About the past, anyway, and about how people reinvent their pasts. Most of us do that to some extent.'

'Do we?' Carole thought about whether she'd ever done it, and decided that yes, she had. 'I suppose you're right.'

'I don't have to look far for people who've reinvented their past,' said Polly.

'Are you talking about your father?'

'Him, and others.' She gave a sardonic grin. 'Anyway, I'm getting quite intrigued by history, you know. Digging back into the mix of truth and fantasy, finding out where things went wrong.'

'Went wrong for you, do you mean?'

'Good heavens no.' The girl laughed at the idea, then wryness returned to her voice as she went on, 'I know where things went wrong for me.'

She didn't let the thought linger or leave time for a supplementary question. 'So maybe the book will make my fortune, change my life around. Huh, I should be so lucky. Anyway, for the time being, Piers is the only writer in our household. He's starting to do quite well,' the girl said wistfully. 'He's had a few credits on television sketch shows. You may have seen the name Piers Duncton scrolling down at the end. And now a television sitcom of his looks like it might get commissioned. You know, he's got very good contacts. He was in the Footlights at Cambridge, and that kind of network counts for a lot in show business.'

Carole made a possible connection. 'So when he was at Cambridge, did he know Lola?'

Polly nodded. 'Yes, they were in revues and things together. Did the Edinburgh Fringe, all that stuff.'

'Did you meet Piers through her?'

The girl shook her head. 'Other way round. I'd met Piers before he went to Cambridge. In the National Youth Theatre.

And somehow our relationship survived the three years he was up there.' She made it sound as if the process hadn't all been plain sailing. 'So I met all his Footlights mates, including Lola.'

'And was it through you that your father—or, rather, your stepfather—met Lola? You introduced them?'

Polly twisted her lips into an expression of mock ruefulness as she echoed her father's words of a few moments before. 'Guilty as charged.'

CHAPTER EIGHT

Carole was surprised how long she stayed at Jude's open house. She was so busy nibbling Zosia's exquisite nibbles, drinking more white wine and, to her amazement, chatting away easily to people (some of whom she hadn't even met before), that she didn't notice the passage of time. Only at the end of a long conversation with a retired geophysicist about the semantic history of the word 'serendipity' did she finally take a look at her watch. She was astonished to see that it was nearly five o'clock. The booze showed no signs of running out, and the crowd of guests hadn't dwindled by much, but Carole thought it was probably time she left.

Her circuit of goodbyes took a gratifyingly long time and it was nearly six by the time she was sitting by the Aga in the High Tor kitchen. Gulliver looked up at her pathetically, hoping for an after-dark walk, but Carole was feeling selfish. She'd do the *Sunday Times* crossword first, and then take him out just on the rough ground behind the house to do his business. The dog couldn't really complain; he'd had an hour's thorough workout that morning on Fethering Beach.

Though *The Times* crossword was an essential part of Carole Seddon's daily routine, she very rarely did the *Sunday Times* version, and its quirks were unfamiliar to her. She found her mind kept sliding away from the clues and her vision kept wandering abstractedly into the middle distance. It took quite a while for her to conclude that she was a little drunk.

But this realization did not generate the guilt which would usually accompany it. Instead, Carole felt rather mellow. In spite of her misgivings, she had really enjoyed the open house. She hadn't had to explain herself, she hadn't had to apologize, she had just chatted away to people. Not like Carole Seddon at all. Just like a normal person, in fact.

The mellow feeling stayed with her for the rest of the evening. She took Gulliver out for his necessary visit, and ignored the reproachful plea in his dark Labrador eyes for a longer walk. She had eaten so many nibbles that she only required a single slice of cheese on toast for supper. Then she watched some mindless medical drama on television (not feeling her customary guilt for watching something mindless) and caught up with the news headlines. She was in bed by half past ten.

Waking at about three with a raging thirst, Carole Seddon felt rather less mellow and started worrying again about Stephen and his family's forthcoming Christmas visit. She was awake for over an hour.

As she lay there, willing sleep to return, she became aware of a light visible through her curtains. A strange, almost pinkish glow. Carole wondered if it presaged snow, and went back to sleep, dreaming of a White Christmas.

But the strange glow she had seen had another cause. The next morning Carole Seddon heard that there had been a fire on Fethering High Street Parade. Gallimaufry had burnt down.

CHAPTER NINE

Jude had heard the news in a phone call from one of her clients, and straightaway rushed round to High Tor. Carole was miffed at not having been first with the information. Her head still a little fuzzy from the day before, she had taken Gulliver out for his walk before seven that Monday morning, and it was only by bad luck that she had chosen the route to the beach down by the Fethering Yacht Club and the Fether estuary. Nine times out of ten her walk would have taken her past the shops on the High Street, so she would have been able to see the destruction for herself. And also to spread the news.

As they sat down to coffee at the High Tor kitchen table, it turned out that Jude had little detail, except for the fact that the fire had taken place. 'There'll probably be something on the local news at lunchtime,' she concluded.

'I could check the BBC Southern Counties website,' said Carole, and scurried off to do so. Jude was amused by the way her neighbour, for so long a technophobe, had suddenly become hooked on computer technology. It was also characteristic of Carole that she kept her laptop permanently on a table in a spare bedroom upstairs, as if she were unable to acknowledge its portability.

Jude didn't bother following, she just sat and enjoyed her coffee. She wasn't expecting there to be any new information on the BBC website yet, and so it proved. 'We'll have to wait for the next bulletin,' said Carole disconsolately. 'No other way of finding anything out.'

'We could visit the scene of the incident,' suggested Jude.

'What, you mean actually go down to the parade and have a look?'

'Yes.'

'Oh, we couldn't do that.'

'Why not?'

'Well, there'll be lots of other prurient ghouls down there, you know, like people who slow down to look at car crashes.'

'They're probably not prurient ghouls. They're just curious.'

'Huh.'

'Are you saying you're not curious, Carole?'

'Well, I . . . Well, I . . . I suppose it's only natural to want to know what's happened locally, particularly when it involves people one knows, or rather people one has met . . .'

'Yes.'

'And there could possibly be something one could do to help.'

'Yes, there could. Come on, Carole, get your coat on.'

'I'll take my basket, so that it'll look as if I've gone out shopping.'

'If you want to.'

'And if I have Gulliver with me, it'll look as if I'm taking him for a walk too, rather than just being . . .'

'A prurient ghoul?'

'Exactly.'

They could smell the fire long before they could see anything. In fact, Carole was amazed she hadn't smelt it during her earlier excursion with Gulliver. Though no smoke was visible, their nostrils were filled with the stench soon after they stepped out of High Tor. Acrid, redolent of the harsh tang of burning plastic.

As predicted, there was a substantial crowd gathered in front of the High Street Parade. The antennae of Fethering residents had always been finely tuned to catastrophe. But none of the prurient ghouls could get very close to what had once been Gallimaufry. The whole parade had been cordoned off by police tape. There were still two fire engines at the front, and maybe more at the back, the side that faced towards the sea, but the main fury of the flames appeared to have been subdued. A few sparks could be seen in the interior, and some exposed beams still steamed from their recent immersion by the firemen's hoses.

Basically the building had been gutted, the roof had collapsed, and it stood like a blackened empty box between the adjacent shops which, to the uninformed observer, did not seem to have suffered much damage.

Carole and Jude recognized quite a few of the locals. They also registered the presence of the small, thin, long-haired woman they'd seen in the Crown and Anchor last Friday. She was dressed in a faded green velvet coat over scruffy jeans, and was looking at the wreckage of Gallimaufry with something approaching satisfaction.

They might have commented on the woman's reaction, had Gerald Hume not come bustling towards them out of the watching crowd. He opined, with all the certainty which he had brought to his career in accountancy, that the fire had been started by an electrical fault. 'That's what it usually is,' he said.

'Do you have any proof that that's what caused it?' asked Jude.

'That's what it usually is,' he reasserted.

Nobody else seemed to have any more reliably authenticated information, but that had never stopped the residents of Fethering from expressing their opinions. There was an atmosphere almost of bonhomie about the gathering. Christmas was only days away, and the burning down of a shop served as a pleasant diversion. It would have been different had it been one of the long-established businesses on the parade. But Lola Le Bonnier was a recent incomer, she lived near Fedborough rather than actually in Fethering, and she had been a bit too flashy for the taste of most locals. The same went for her shop. There was something hubristic in the whole enterprise of Gallimaufry. Even the name was a bit fancy and clever-clever. Did Fethering really need somewhere selling overpriced knick-knacks? Nobody actually used the expression 'Serve her right', but that was the dominant feeling amongst many of the crowd.

Jude, who knew and cared for Lola, didn't share this view. But Carole wouldn't have taken much convincing to side with the sceptics. 'The trouble is,' she said, 'when you're running something like a shop, it's all very fine to make the place look exotic and trendy, but you can't ignore basic Health and Safety procedures.'

'What do you mean by that?' asked Jude, uncharacteristically combative.

'I mean, having all those candles and fairy lights with stuff draped all over them . . . well, it was just asking for trouble, wasn't it?'

'We don't know that's what caused the fire,' said Jude doggedly.

'No, but we can make a pretty well-informed guess that—'

Carole didn't get to finish her sentence. A policeman with a loudhailer started asking the crowd to move along, telling them there was nothing to see, that there was a danger they might get in the way of the firemen's work, and that they would be informed when it would be safe for the other shops on the parade to reopen.

Many of the spectators were unwilling to leave, but Carole and Jude separated themselves from the throng and went back home.

'Or the shop could have been torched for insurance reasons.'

'Oh, come on, Carole. What have you been reading?'

'It's quite a common crime. Particularly in recessionary times. People borrow too much, can't pay the mortgage . . . they see a fire as a way out of their liabilities.'

'We don't know that Ricky Le Bonnier had any money problems.'

'No, but he's the kind of man who probably has.'

Jude grinned at her friend. 'You clearly didn't take a shine to him, did you?'

'I thought he was a show-off.' In Carole Seddon's lexicon of bad behaviour there were few more damning descriptions. She had been brought up by her meek and frightened parents to believe that, if you raised your head above the parapet, then getting shot down was completely your own fault.

'We don't know anything about Ricky's finances.'

'Well, I didn't trust him. People who draw attention to themselves like that . . . He's all talk, so far as I'm concerned.'

'Carole, he's been very successful. He must've made a lot of money over the years.'

'And no doubt spent it, paying for all those wives.'

'Well, keep your opinions to yourself, won't you? We don't want rumours going round Fethering that Ricky Le Bonnier torched his wife's shop for the insurance money.'

Carole's thin face grew thinner. 'Jude, you know I'm always the soul of discretion.'

'Yes.'

'Mind you, I do think it's suspicious. And remember the way all the prices in Gallimaufry were discounted . . . it didn't look to me like a thriving business.'

'Very few shops do at the moment. People are battening down their hatches, so far as spending's concerned. Everyone in the retail trade is suffering.'

'Though not everyone is solving the problem by burning

down their premises.'

Jude shook her head in wry weariness. Once her neighbour got an idea into her head, it took a great deal of effort to shift it. 'Well, Carole, I'm sure in time we'll find out more details of what happened.'

They did. On the local news that evening there was an item about the fire. It had taken a while for the building to be made safe, before police and firemen could enter.

And when they got inside, they had found the charred body of a woman.

CHAPTER TEN

Jude's first instinct was to ring the Le Bonniers' house. If there was bad news, she wanted to hear about it straightaway. She never saw any point in prevarication.

Her primary anxiety was allayed as soon as the phone was answered. By Lola. Her voice sounded tight with stress, but at least she was alive.

'I was desperately sorry to hear about what happened at Gallimaufry.'

'Oh well, it was only stuff,' said Lola.

'But you yourself are OK?'

'I'm fine. We were all here when it happened—me, Flora, the kids.'

'And Ricky?'

'Yes, of course, Ricky.' The answer was rather brusque, almost as if she were dismissing the relevance of her husband. 'The first thing we knew about the fire was when the police rang this morning.'

'It must be terrible for you, Lola, after all the work you put into that place.'

'Oh, well . . . Easy come, easy go.' She was trying to sound nonchalant, but couldn't quite carry it off. There was a silence, then Lola went on, 'Presumably you've heard the latest about the fire, have you?'

'You mean that there was a body found there?'

'Yes. A woman's body.'

'Have the police told you who . . . ?'

'No. They're still involved in forensic examination and what have you. They've said they'll let us know as soon as they've got a definite identification.'

'Who lives in the flat over the shop?' Jude just managed to avoid saying 'lived'.

'No one. When we took the place on, because the flat was furnished, I thought we should let it out, so that at least we'd get some income if things got hard—at that time having no idea of quite how hard times would get—but Ricky said no. He never likes thinking about the details of finances, calls all that "penny-pinching". He likes to think in terms of "the bigger economic picture".' There was irony in the way Lola quoted her husband, possibly even veiled criticism.

'So the flat was empty?'

'Empty of people, yes. I used it for storage. There was a lot of stuff up there, piled on top of the furniture and beds.' Her tone was kept determinedly light, but Jude could feel Lola trying to come to terms with the scale of her losses.

'So you haven't any idea who the dead woman is?'

'No. I've checked the obvious people, and there doesn't seem to be anyone missing. My mother-in-law Flora's here with us. Ricky took Polly to Fedborough Station yesterday afternoon to get a train up to London. He's checked she's at home with Piers. I've called Anna and Bex . . . you know, they're two of the assistants.'

'Did they know about the discovery of the body?'

'I don't know. Neither of them mentioned it. And I didn't raise the matter. I don't want to add to the dripfeed of local gossip. Anyway, Anna and Bex're both fine. And I've rung around all the other casual staff. Also fine.'

'So it sounds like whoever died in Gallimaufry, it wasn't

anyone you knew.'

'That's the way it seems,' said Lola Le Bonnier.

Sadly, she was wrong. On the national news the following morning, it was announced that the body found in the burnt-out shop was that of the owner's stepdaughter, Polly Le Bonnier.

CHAPTER ELEVEN

Carole had been ambivalent about getting a Christmas tree. She hadn't done so any other year since she'd been alone in Fethering. But then again she hadn't had Stephen and family coming down any other year since she'd been alone in Fethering. And Lily was getting to the age when she might start to take an interest in pretty lights and shiny baubles. It'd really only be for the hours when they were with her, which was a bit of an unnecessary indulgence . . . but then again . . . She ended up buying a Christmas tree about three feet high, and a set of fairy lights. And a box of assorted glass baubles. And some lametta. And a little silver fairy to perch on the topmost branch.

Carole thought she'd been rather foolish to buy all the stuff, but she did enjoy setting it up. And while she dressed her Christmas tree, she thought about Polly Le Bonnier. She did an action replay in her mind of the conversation they had shared at Jude's open house, and tried to identify anything the girl had said that might be odd. But nothing came. Except that line 'I know where things went wrong for me.' That was intriguing, but now there was no chance of finding out from Polly what she had meant.

A more obvious question was: why, though, when her father had taken the girl to Fedborough Station to catch a train up to London, had she ended up back in Fethering? Carole concluded with some frustration that she didn't have enough information to provide an answer. But the mystery still niggled away at her.

Jude phoned her round five that afternoon. 'I've just had a call from Lola.'

'Oh, any more news about how it happened?'

'No. Well, if she had any, she didn't volunteer it to me. But listen, Lola's got Piers Duncton with her . . .'

'Polly's boyfriend?'

'Exactly. Apparently he's in a terrible state—which is hardly surprising. He feels confused and guilty. I get the impression Lola's finding it difficult to deal with him . . . you know, she's got the children and Ricky and his mother and . . . I think she'd be quite glad to get Piers out of the house for a while.'

'So?'

'So she was suggesting he might come and talk to me.'

'What, you as a healer?'

'No, no. Me as someone who gave a party which Polly attended. Piers is desperate to work out what happened to his girlfriend in the hours before she died. He wonders whether she might have said anything to someone she'd seen at the party, something that might give a clue to what she was feeling, or what she was planning to do.'

'It's funny, I was just thinking the same myself.'

'Well, anyway, I said fine, he was welcome to come here and ask me anything he wanted. Lola sounded so relieved. I gather things are pretty tense up at their place—one of the kids, Mabel, the little girl, is laid up with an ear infection, one of the Dalmatians has just had puppies—and Piers may be just one extra complication she could do without right now. So he's on his way.'

Carole, hypersensitive to any imagined slight, immediately thought that she was being excluded. 'Very well,' she said shortly. 'Let me know if he tells you anything interesting, won't you?'

'Carole . . .' Jude lengthened the name in mild exasperation. 'What I was going to say was why don't you come round and talk to Piers as well? You spent at least as much time at my party with Polly as I did, probably more.'

'Yes,' said Carole. 'That's true.'

He was tall, gangly, with big ears and a big mouth. What would be called 'a mobile face'. There was no surprise that he worked in comedy. But he wasn't smiling that afternoon. He looked tense and was sucking on a cigarette as though his life depended on it.

Piers Duncton refused Jude's offer of an alcoholic drink, opting for a black coffee instead. But she had some Chilean Chardonnay left from her party (the booze never did run out), and she poured glasses for herself and Carole.

'We were desperately sorry,' Jude said, 'to hear about what happened to Polly.'

'Thank you.' Nicely spoken, clearly went to the right schools before Cambridge. 'I still can't really believe it. I feel so guilty about the whole thing. I mean, I had a text from Polly yesterday afternoon, saying she was going to catch the seven-thirty-two train to Victoria . . . and now . . . this.'

He sat uneasily on one of Jude's over-draped armchairs, tense as a cat testing out an unfamiliar surface. She found a glass dish for him to use as an ashtray and said, 'Please, do ask us anything you want. If there's something we can do to help, then just say what it is.'

'Thank you . . . Jude. Was it?'

'That's right.'

'And I gather Polly came to a party here on Sunday . . . ?'

'Yes.'

71

'With her dad?'

'And her famous grandmother.'

The boy nodded. Clearly he'd already encountered the formidable Flora. 'Had you met Polly before?'

'No.'

In response to his quizzical look, Carole said, 'Nor had I.'

'Did you talk to her much?'

Jude shook her head. 'Only really to say hello. I was busy looking after my other guests.'

'Yes, of course.'

'I had quite a chat with her,' Carole volunteered.

'What did you talk about?'

'Her family, a little bit. She mentioned you too, and the fact that you'd be spending Christmas with your parents in Gloucestershire.'

His face registered a new pang of suffering as he said, 'God, I haven't told them what's happened yet. It's like I'm pretending it's all a mistake, like the body in Gallimaufry has been indentified wrongly, and Polly's about to come through that door any minute.'

Emotion seemed momentarily to rob him of words, so Carole thought she might as well continue. 'She also told me that she was an actor—which is, I suppose, what I would call an actress—and that she was finding work hard to come by.' Piers nodded acknowledgement of this. 'She said that you were a comedy writer, and that she was writing something too.'

'Ah. So she mentioned the book?'

'She sounded quite optimistic about it, almost as though its publication might start a turnaround in her life.'

'Polly said that?' He shook his head wryly. 'She always was something of a dreamer.'

'Have you read the book?' asked Jude.

'No. She was very private about her writing.'

Carole was quick to pounce on the inconsistency. 'Polly said you had read it. Said you thought it was wonderful.'

He looked confused for a moment, as if he had been caught in a lie. Though a more innocent explanation might be that he was thrown by these reminders of his dead girlfriend. The confusion in his expressive face gave way to sudden anger, but he managed to curb it. He reached into his pocket for cigarettes, then belatedly appealing to Jude for permission to smoke, lit one up.

'Yes, I did read a few chapters of Polly's book,' he conceded.

'And did you think it was wonderful?'

The question made him look even more uncomfortable. 'It's very difficult to pass comment on the work of someone with whom you're emotionally involved.'

Jude nodded heartfelt agreement. At various times she had shared her life with an actor and a stand-up comedian, so she knew at first hand the level of paranoia in many creative people.

'What kind of book was it?' asked Carole. 'Polly told me it was part fact, part fiction.'

'I'd say it was pure fiction,' said Piers firmly.

'And what was it about?'

'Hard to say. A girl growing up, I suppose, and the difficult time she had doing so.'

'A "Misery Memoir"?' Jude suggested.

'Well, if it were true, you might have called it that. But it was fiction. And Polly kept telling me what a happy childhood she'd had, so I don't think there could have been any autobiographical element in it.'

'From what you say,' said Carole, 'or rather, from what you don't say, I don't get the impression you thought much of Polly's book.'

'Well . . .' He was silent, then a bit tearful as he went on, 'It can't hurt her now for me to say what I really thought.' He took a deep breath before announcing, 'The writing was clumsy and, from what I read of it, the plot just didn't hang together.'

'So you don't think she'd have had any chance of getting it published?'

'God, no.'

'But she said an agent friend had also liked it a lot.'

'Wishful thinking. I know the agent friend in question, Serena. I was up at Cambridge the same time she was. And Serena didn't want to hurt Polly's feelings, so she said what she wanted to hear. It's significant she didn't offer to represent her as an agent once the book was finished. I'm afraid the situation was that . . . well, Polly always wanted to be as good as other people, particularly as good as me. When we first met, we were both in the National Youth Theatre. And she was always a better actor than me, I'd never argue about that. I mean, I can do revue and stuff, funny faces, funny accents, but I'm not really an *actor,* not like Polly. So when we first met, she was kind of the dominant partner. Then I went up to Cambridge and I got involved with the Footlights, so I was writing and appearing in revues and what-have-you . . . and Polly, on the weekends she came up, was consigned to the role of a hanger-on. You know, she'd be down in London during the week, trying to get acting work, and I'd be in Cambridge having a whale of a time, surrounded by lots of extremely bright and privileged people . . .'

'People like Lola?'

'Yes, exactly. People like Lola.' He seemed for a moment to lose the thread of his narrative. 'Anyway, with all that happening . . . the dynamics of me and Polly changed.'

Carole remembered the difficulty Polly had hinted at of maintaining their affair through Piers's time at university.

'And then after Cambridge and after I'd done shows at the Edinburgh Fringe Festival, we moved in together. In a flat just near Warren Street tube station, where we still are, actually. Or were.' He didn't want to dwell on the thought. 'Anyway, I started having some success as a writer and poor Polly was still finding the acting work hard to come by and . . . well, it put even more pressure on the relationship. You know, I was kind of mixing with supposedly glamorous people in the comedy world, and the prospects for me getting my own sitcom away were looking good, and then there's Polly sort of in my wake. She hated being seen as an appendage or a parasite. I think that's what got her thinking about writing something herself.'

' "Anything you can do, I can do better" syndrome,' suggested Jude.

'Exactly that.' The memory seemed to depress him. He sank back into silence.

Carole decided it was time to move into investigative mode. 'You say you got a text from her from Fedborough Station saying she was about to catch the London train . . . ?' He nodded. 'Have you any idea why she might have changed her mind and come back down here to Fethering?'

'None at all. That's why I wanted to talk to you. I thought you might know something.'

'Sadly not,' said Jude.

'Oh well.' He picked up his coffee cup in a shaking hand and downed the remaining contents. 'Thank you for your time. I'm sorry if I've interrupted your evening. It's just I feel so powerless. Polly's dead and I've got to do something to find out why!'

'I know how you feel,' said Jude, her voice sounding even softer after his outburst. 'One thing . . .' she said, as he rose from his chair.

'Yes?'

'You talked about the dynamics of your relationship with Polly changing, the balance changing. How much have they changed?'

'What do you mean?'

75

'One of the first things you said when you came here this evening was that what had happened to Polly made you feel "guilty". You presumably mean you feel guilty because you think you should have been around, protecting her?'

'I suppose so. In a way, yes.'

'I was just wondering whether there might be another reason why you felt guilty . . . ?'

He controlled another flash of instinctive anger, then said, 'Are you suggesting that I might have had something to do with Polly's death? Because I was in London at the time and I do have an alibi for the night of the fire, someone who can vouch for where I was and—'

'Whoa, whoa, whoa.' Jude raised a hand to calm him. 'I'm not making any accusations here. All I was wondering was whether the cause of your feeling guilty might be because your relationship with Polly was coming to an end?'

'I didn't say that.' Piers was blushing furiously.

'No, but was it?'

There was a silence which Carole eventually broke. 'Interesting that you said you had an alibi for the time of the fire . . . someone who could vouch for where you were all night . . .'

Any barrier of defiance Piers might have put up instantly crumbled away. 'Yes, all right. I was with another woman.' He went on, recklessly, 'I've met someone else. One of the cast of the new sitcom I'm writing. This is the real thing. I was going to tell Polly as soon as we got Christmas and New Year out of the way. I didn't want to hurt her over the holiday.'

'Ah,' said Jude.

'How thoughtful of you,' said Carole.

CHAPTER TWELVE

Jude disclosed as little information about her 'clients' as she could, so she hadn't told Carole that her first contact with the owner of Gallimaufry had been professional. Before she'd taken her son Henry along for help with his asthma, Lola herself had needed to call on Jude's healing skills. After the birth of her first child Mabel, she had suffered terrible post-natal depression. Exceptionally intelligent, coming from a high-powered job in music PR, used to having her own way, Lola had found the shock of being stuck at home as a mother totally drained away her self-confidence. Sessions at Woodside Cottage (and with an acupuncturist to whom Jude referred her) had sorted out the problem, and it had not recurred after the birth of Henry. But Jude remained aware of the woman's inner fragility and was worried about how she would be coping with the shock of Polly's death.

So she rang Lola again on the Wednesday morning, Christmas Eve. 'Are you surviving?'

'Yeah, it's not easy, but having the kids around is helping. They don't realize what's happened, so they kind of take my mind off things. Mabel's had an ear infection, but that's better, thanks to good old antibiotics. She's fantastically excited about Father Christmas coming. Henry's still a bit young to take all that in, but he's pretty bouncy too. And one of the Dalmatians has just had puppies, so they add to the feeling of new life about the place. I'm surviving.'

'Good. Just wondered if you'd like to meet. You know, if I could be of any help?'

'Not a bad idea. I've got some last-minute shopping . . . which I could do in Fethering. Apparently the rest of the parade's open now . . . apart, of course, from Gallimaufry,' she added sardonically.

They agreed to meet at the swings by the beach.

Lola, Mabel and Henry looked as though they'd stepped out of a catalogue for upmarket winterwear. The Yummy Mummy and her two adorable kids, the little ones muffled up in so many layers that they looked like multicoloured Michelin men. Mabel was extremely articulate about which swing she wanted to go on, a grown-up one with no restraining cradle. Henry, who couldn't yet speak, made his desire to be put into one of the baby ones equally clear. Having taken an immediate shine to Jude, Mabel wanted to be pushed by her, and Henry seemed happy for his mother to do the job. As they pushed the swings, the women talked.

'How's Ricky taking it all?' asked Jude.

Lola screwed up her face in puzzlement. 'Always hard to know with him. I mean, he's usually so up, so positive about everything, that it takes time for a real disaster to get through to him. I think he is suffering—he must be. But there's always been quite a distance between him and Polly . . . you know, she kind of came in a job lot when Ricky married her mother. They didn't see that much of each other, there was a bit of history from when the marriage broke up, and then her mother dying didn't help.'

'Oh, I didn't know that.'

'It was ugly. Drugs overdose, thought to be accidental, though no one's quite sure. Heroin. It's amazing, actually, that Polly was as sane as she was. Anyway, their relationship could be pretty spiky, but Ricky did care for Polly a lot, in his own way. Mind you, you'd never know it from the way he's behaving now. I asked if he wanted me to pull the plugs on Christmas, you know, minimize the celebrations with a view to what's happened, but he wouldn't hear of it. Wants to leave all our arrangements in place, even through to our New Year's Eve party. I did send you an invitation to that, didn't I, Jude?'

'Yes, thank you, I'll be there.' A sudden thought came to her. 'I say, would you mind if I brought a friend with me?'

'Fine. The more the merrier.'

'It's Carole, my next-door neighbour. You know, you met her in the shop.'

'She'll be very welcome.'

Jude was glad Lola didn't ask why she wanted Carole along on New Year's Eve. Partly, it was because she didn't like thinking of her friend on her own that night, but she had another motive too. There had been an unexplained death in the Le Bonnier family. If any investigation was required, Jude would be glad to have Carole's rational mind helping her on the case.

'So you say Ricky's OK?'

Lola nodded, then sighed with frustration. 'It's strange . . . you can be very close to someone, love someone very much and then suddenly realize that there are whole areas of their personality that you just don't know at all.'

'At the party Polly told Carole that she'd introduced you and Ricky.'

'Sort of, yes. It was through her, well, through Piers, really.'

Jude picked up a subtle flicker of intonation in the voice, and she made a connection with Piers's reaction when he'd talked about their time together at Cambridge. Her brown eyes found the woman's hazel ones. 'You and Piers used to be lovers, didn't you?'

Lola did not hesitate with her reply. 'Yes. It's a long time ago now. When we took a Footlights revue up to the Edinburgh Festival. We were sharing a flat and sort of living in each other's pockets up there and . . . well, it was inevitable.'

'Did the affair continue after Edinburgh?'

'Not for long. We both had other people. Piers was with Polly, as he had been from before he started at Cambridge, and I was with . . . a Classics don at Caius.'

'Another older man,' Jude suggested.

'I do seem to be a sucker for them, you're right.' Lola grinned ruefully. 'And, to save you the trouble of working out the psychological reasons for that . . . yes, my father was a strong presence in my life, and he did die when I was in my early teens.'

'Thank you. Has Ricky talked to you much about Polly's death?'

She shook her head. 'Only about practical things. For someone who seems so open to everyone who meets him, he's surprisingly reticent about saying what he's feeling.'

Jude gestured to the children on the swings. 'And presumably these two haven't shown any reaction to what's happened?'

'I haven't told them anything about it. Mabel adores Polly— Polly goes into a kind of grown-up naughty sister routine when they're together. Or, that is, she did. But she's not here that often, so Mabel, having seen her on Sunday afternoon, won't be aware that she's not around for quite a while. By which time . . .' Lola sighed '. . . I will have worked out something suitable to tell her.'

'So, in spite of the tragedy—the double tragedy—life in the Le Bonnier household continues as normal.'

'As normal as I can make it. Though the real difficulty I'm having is with Ricky's mum.'

'Flora?'

'Yes. She's never been easy. Partly just the actressy temperament. And her disability doesn't help. She can hardly use her hands at all now and Flora is . . . well, let's say she's not the kind of person to make light of adversity. But also she was always on the side of Ricky's previous wife.'

'Polly's mother?'

'No. God, no. She loathed that one, apparently. Regarded her as the evil seductress, luring Flora's precious son into a life of substance abuse. Though, from things Ricky's said, I think it was actually him leading Polly's mother astray.'

'What was her name?'

'Vanessa.'

'But then you said there was another wife before Ricky married you?'

Lola smiled ruefully. 'Mm. Always very generous with his favours, my husband. Yes, he married this woman called Christine, who nobly dragged him out of what the tabloids would call his "drugs hell". Sanctimonious prig, from everything I've heard about her. Organized Ricky to within an inch of his life.'

'And I now know about all of Ricky's wives, do I?' asked Jude.

'All you need to know is that I'm the fourth.' Lola grinned. 'And last. He's not going to get away from me.' There was a lot of love and determination in her words. 'Anyway, Flora and Wife Number Three got on very well together—which I think may be part of the reason why the marriage broke up. Wife Number Three—I'm sorry, I do have great difficulty thinking of her as Christine—got Ricky back on to the path of righteousness. I think he was grateful to her for getting him off the drugs, but as time went on, he began to find the path of righteousness very boring, so the marriage sputtered to a halt.

'Anyway, Flora has never made any secret of the fact that she thinks I'm a very poor substitute for Wife Number Three. Still, she's fond of the children, we don't actually meet that often,

81

and we've worked out a kind of modus vivendi, whereby we're polite to each other and avoid open rows.'

'So what's happened to her now?'

'She's taking Polly's death terribly hard. Seems to have fallen apart completely.'

'Were they very close?'

'Not in recent years, from what I can gather. Flora was apparently all over Polly when Ricky first married Vanessa. Glamorous actress with glamorous little girl accessory. And Polly wasn't actually a grandchild, so she didn't cast too unflattering a light on Flora's age. But then adolescence kicked in with its usual destructive force, and from what Ricky's said, Polly started to cast a more critical eye over her famous "grandmother". So, having once been very close, they became . . . I don't know what you'd say . . . estranged? I mean, Polly can still be polite in Flora's company, though she doesn't find being with her easy, so she tries to avoid it whenever possible and—' Lola's progress was stopped by a sudden thought. 'That is, she *tried*. Did try. I must get used to saying "did".'

'You say Flora's falling apart completely. What do you mean by that?'

'She's staying in her room, doesn't want to eat anything. And the times I've been in to see her, she's actually been crying. That's very unlike her. Flora was always of the "stiff upper lip" persuasion. She's an actress, she can disguise her emotions. So, anyway . . .' Lola sighed wearily—'that's just another thing I have to cope with.'

Jude stopped pushing the swing for a moment and reached across to touch the girl's arm. 'And how are you coping?' she asked.

'With difficulty,' came the reply. And, as Mabel shouted for more pushing on her swing, tears welled up into her mother's eyes.

On the local television news bulletin that evening, as well as the normal Christmas Eve stories about the last-minute rush to the shops, there was a sobering update on the tragedy at Gallimaufry in Fethering. Forensic examination, the police announced, had revealed that the victim, Polly Le Bonnier, had not been killed by the fire. The cause of her death had been a single bullet wound.

An accident investigation had suddenly become a murder inquiry.

CHAPTER THIRTEEN

Of course, Christmas Day, when it happened, was fine. Stephen and family arrived soon after noon, as anticipated. Lily had slept most of the way in the car, but had woken before they reached Fethering, so was at her most wide-eyed and enchanting to greet her grandmother. Gaby said that Father Christmas had left a stocking for her that morning and, as was expected—indeed demanded—of someone her age, when opening its contents, Lily had been much more interested in the wrapping paper than she had been in the presents.

Needless to say, Carole had overcatered in every area of the lunch, particularly the alcohol. Stephen, as the designated driver, wasn't drinking. While his mother saw the wisdom of this, particularly since he now had the additional responsibility of a baby in the car, she did wish he might just have had one glass to celebrate the occasion. But she didn't put any pressure on him; she knew Stephen was doing the right thing. And Gaby, now that Lily had been weaned, was very much up for drinking a lot. So the two women managed to get through a bottle of champagne and most of a Chilean Chardonnay.

The food went down very well. Lily was tried on a bowl of specially puréed turkey and sprouts, but turned her nose up at it, preferring a familiar jar of her Lamb and Tasty Vegetables. But when they got to the mince pies, she was much more enthusiastic, nearly consuming a whole one—or at least spreading its contents over her face and high chair tray.

The adults enjoyed their food, though, and Gaby raised a glass with 'compliments to the chef'. It was a long time since Carole had cooked such an elaborate meal. Going through the process reminded her of dinner parties in her early married life, and of the satisfaction she had sometimes got from seeing David and Stephen well fed. The success of her Christmas lunch gave her confidence a boost. Carole Seddon was actually quite good at cooking. She ought to do more of it. Maybe give the odd dinner party, expand her Fethering social network . . .

The only threat to the harmony of the occasion was a phone call on the dot of one o'clock. Unable to think of anyone likely to ring on Christmas Day, Carole went to the hall and answered the phone in some bewilderment. She was not happy when she recognized the voice at the other end of the line as that of her ex-husband.

'I just . . . erm . . . rang to say "Happy Christmas".'

'Happy Christmas,' his ex-wife replied shortly.

'And I gather that you've got the . . . erm . . . family with you . . . ?'

'Stephen, Gaby and Lily are here, yes. Having drinks, we're just about to have lunch.'

'Could I have a word with them?'

Carole couldn't stop herself from asking, 'Why?'

'Because I want to wish them a Happy Christmas.'

'Stephen,' she called through to the sitting room, 'your father wants to speak to you.'

'Can't you bring the phone through here?'

For some reason she didn't want to do that, she didn't want David intruding into the closed magic circle around Lily. But she knew she was being unreasonable and took the handset through to Stephen.

He seemed to her to spend an unnecessarily long time chatting with his father. Also it was just chat, almost light-hearted banter, the kind of dialogue Stephen very rarely exchanged with her. Then David wanted to speak to Gaby, and he seemed to have plenty to say to her too. From what could be heard at the Fethering end, it sounded as though David was being flirtatious with his daughter-in-law. Carole didn't know why she found the idea of her ex-husband being flirtatious quite so repellent.

Then, to annoy her even further, David apparently insisted the handset should be brought to Lily so that her grandfather could coo at her and hope to prompt some responsive gurgling.

Carole was extremely relieved when the phone call ended. She reckoned it was a simple demonstration of power play from David. All right, she'd won the prize of having the family for Christmas Day, but he was going to ensure that no one forgot about his existence.

'Good,' she said, brightly brittle. 'I think we can go through for lunch now.'

'Dad sounded OK,' said Stephen, 'though it must be a bit lonely for him spending Christmas with strangers.'

'I'm sure he's coping.'

'But, Mother, he doesn't know these people in Swiss Cottage very well.'

'Mother'. And David was 'Dad'. Carole wanted to ask why her son couldn't call her 'Mum', as he sometimes did. But of course she didn't say that. Instead, she just almost snapped, 'I'm sure Christmas lunch is giving him an opportunity to know them better.'

'Yes, but—'

'I think, if we could go through for our lunch . . .'

The awkwardness passed, of course. And once they were into the meal, and Lily was providing the cabaret by smearing her Lamb and Tasty Vegetables all over everything, the atmosphere relaxed. But Carole did not forget what she regarded as David's shabby behaviour.

After lunch it had been thought that Lily might be ready for another sleep, but she seemed to be responding to the occasion and was very wakeful. So Carole led the way through to the sitting room to gather round the tiny tree for the ceremony of present-giving.

Obviously they started with Lily. A lot of her presents were still up in Fulham, but Stephen and Gaby had brought with them what they were giving her. They also produced, to Carole's further irritation, David's present for his granddaughter, which she noted was much bigger than her own.

But Lily avoided a one-upmanship contest between her grandparents. With even-handed tact, she again did what was expected of her, ignoring the presents completely and appearing to find the wrapping paper much more interesting.

Carole was expecting what she usually got from Stephen, which was—though she hadn't dared mention the fact to Jude—Lily of the Valley toilet water. She'd never, before her neighbour raised the issue, thought that it might make her feel old and unglamorous. But then a lot of the time Carole Seddon did feel old and unglamorous.

She was therefore surprised to open a small parcel containing a diamanté brooch in the shape of a snowflake. Carole didn't as a rule wear much jewellery, but she rather liked the look of what she'd been given and immediately pinned it on to her front. She was almost effusive in her thanks, particularly to Gaby, who she felt sure had done the actual shopping.

Then it was her daughter-in-law's turn to open her present. Carole watched with some trepidation as the careful wrapping was dismantled and its contents revealed. 'That is marvellous!' shrieked Gaby, immediately wrapping the boa round her neck, then going to wrap its loose end around Lily's neck too. The baby gurgled and pushed a bit of the feathery stuff into her mouth. Once the choking hazard had been averted, Stephen whipped out his camera to record the photo opportunity.

'It's bloody great!' said Gaby. 'One of those presents where I had no idea what I wanted, but now you've given it to me, I know it's exactly what I wanted. A bit of glamour—God, I need that after the last year. Carole, you must just have seen this in the shop and thought, "That boa has Gaby written all over it!" '

'Well, yes, that's more or less what happened,' her mother-in-law lied.

Then came the moment for Stephen to open his present. Carole had put everything in the same parcel, which inevitably had the bulk and shape of two shirts. He picked it up and weighed it in his hands. 'Now I wonder what this could be . . .' he said archly before starting carefully to undo the ribbon.

The third object had been placed between the two others, so the first thing he saw was a shirt. A Marks and Spencer's shirt, no less. Sober, pale blue, no pattern. And beneath it he could see another shirt. Sober, white, no pattern.

'Oh, Mother, that's great,' he said. 'Just what I wanted.'

'Well, you can never have too many shirts, can you, Stephen?'

'No, that's true.' He made to put them down on the floor.

'There is actually something else.'

'What?'

'Between the shirts. There's something else.'

'Oh.' His brow furrowed as he reached into the space and pulled out the packet containing the Glow-in-the-dark Computer Angel. 'Ah,' he said, his brow furrowing even more. 'What is it?'

'It's what it says, Steve,' his wife prompted him. 'A Glow-in-the-dark Computer Angel.'

'Right.' Puzzled, he turned the packaging over in his hands. 'And what does it do?'

'Read what it says on the front,' Carole suggested.

He looked at the words and slowly read, ' "Your Computer

Angel deals with all your computer problems, glitches and viruses. Just wind her up and her flapping wings will spread her protection over your desktop or laptop. And when you turn the lights off, your Computer Angel will glow in the dark." ' His face turned blankly to his mother's. 'How does it work?'

'What do you mean?'

'Well, is it an anti-virus protection? Because I don't see any software with it.'

'No, no, it's—'

'And there doesn't seem to be a USB connection.'

'No, there isn't.'

'So how can it deal with all my "computer problems, glitches and viruses"?'

'Well, it may not actually be able to do that.'

'But, Mother, it says it can.'

'Yes, but it's more . . . It's just a nice thing to stick on your computer.'

'Why?'

'Well . . . Because, when you wind it up, its wings flap.'

'Why would you want its wings to flap?'

'And it glows in the dark.'

'But what use would that be? You wouldn't be using a computer in the dark, would you?'

'Oh, for heaven's sake, Steve,' said Gaby in some exasperation, 'it's a joke.'

'A what?'

'It's just a fun thing to have on your computer.'

'A fun thing?'

'Yes.'

'Why?'

'Because it *is!*' snapped Carole. And as her son continued to look with befuddlement at his extra gift, she went on, 'Anyway, you can change the shirts if you don't like them.'

And normal Christmas service was resumed. Oh well, you can't get everything right with presents, thought Carole. And Gaby was very pleased with her boa.

They left soon after four. Lily, her mother reckoned, would be asleep before the car reached the end of the road. And as she tidied up the substantial remains of the lavish lunch, Carole reflected that it had really all worked very well. A family Christmas Day, just like proper families had. A perfect day, except for a couple of details.

One was the call from David, which still rankled.

And the other cause of disquiet was the news she had received the day before, about Polly Le Bonnier having been shot. Even when she was at her most relaxed with her enchantingly adorable granddaughter, Carole Seddon had been unable to clear her mind completely of thoughts about the unsolved murder.

Chapter Fourteen

She woke the next morning still glowing with success. The relief that she normally experienced on reaching Boxing Day was a much more positive sensation than she had felt in recent years, and she decided to put into action a plan she had been toying with for the previous twenty-four hours.

Boxing Day might be a fine time for professional policemen to pursue murder inquiries, but amateurs found things more difficult. Everyone battened down their hatches over the Christmas period; it was not the ideal opportunity for casual calling on people by those with investigative intentions.

But certain imperatives overrode seasonal considerations and, as Carole was never left in any doubt by Gulliver, dog-walking was one of them. The rhythm of a dog's life cannot be interrupted by public holidays or international events. When a dog needed to be walked, it very definitely had to be walked.

Carole was banking on the fact that her quarry's dog had the same sense of priorities, and in this conjecture she was proved to be correct. Though she had woken soon after six, she resisted Gulliver's heavy hints that he wanted to go out for his walk at the normal time and waited till just before seven-thirty. At that time, given the fact that it was Boxing Day, she knew the only people on Fethering Beach would be dog-walkers.

And, as she had hoped, one of them was the owner of a West Highland terrier with a Black Watch coat on. It was Anna from Gallimaufry, her blonded hair again hidden by a thick scarf.

Normally, on seeing someone she knew—and even more someone she didn't know—on Fethering Beach, Carole Seddon's reaction would have been to take a route as far away from them as possible. But on this occasion she led Gulliver straight towards the woman. The two dogs circled each other warily.

'Hello. Anna, isn't it?' said Carole.

'Yes, that's right. I recognize you from the shop, but I'm sorry, I don't know your name.' The woman spoke strangely, almost surprised at hearing her own voice. From her own experience, Carole knew this was because she had not spoken to anyone for the last twenty-four hours. Anna had spent Christmas Day on her own.

'Carole Seddon.'

'How nice to meet you properly. And I'm Anna Carter.' She seemed almost pathetically grateful to be talking to someone. Gulliver and the Westie had reached a mutual conclusion that the other dog was no threat. Not even very interesting. They had loped off in different directions to snuffle about in separate piles of shingle.

'I hope you don't mind my just coming up to you like this, Anna, but I did want to say how sorry I was about what happened to . . .' Carole couldn't bring herself to say 'Gallimaufry'—'the shop.'

'It was terrible. God knows where I'll get another job around here.'

Carole hadn't considered that consequence of the fire. 'Oh, I'm sure you'll be able to find something.'

'I don't know. It took me a while to find the vacancy at Gallimaufry. No one's been recruiting much recently, and I'm sure it'll be worse after Christmas.'

'Something'll turn up,' said Carole, doing a passable impression of the kind of person who always looked on the bright side. 'Do you live here in Fethering?'

'Yes, I moved in in September. I haven't met many people yet.'

'Oh, I'm sure you soon will. You'll find we're a friendly bunch.' Carole didn't know why she found herself saying things like that. In her own mind she had formed many descriptions of the denizens of Fethering. The one she had never come up with was 'a friendly bunch'.

'Have you moved here from far away?'

'Quite a distance.' Carole recognized the intonation Anna used on her answer. It was one she'd often resorted to herself and was designed to deflect further questions. Well, that was fine. Carole didn't particularly want to know the woman's life history. She did want to know, however, any information Anna might have that would shed light on the recent tragedy at Gallimaufry.

Without discussing where they were going, they both seemed to agree to walk in the same direction, while the two dogs made ever wider loops around them. The tide was low, the sea a sullen sludge-green with small scummy waves that lapped against the shore. The air was cold enough to give their faces a light scouring. 'I'm sorry to ask you the question that everyone in Fethering must have been asking you for the last few days . . .'

'I haven't seen that many people,' said Anna, confirming Carole's perception of her loneliness.

'Oh. Well, I'm afraid it still is an obvious question. Do you have any idea what started the fire?'

'Not really.'

'I was assuming some of the draping stuff must have caught alight from being too close to all those candles and fairy lights.'

'I'd be surprised if it was that,' said Anna. 'The candles were all put out when we closed up the shop. And those lights are special ones, you know. Passed safety regulations. They give out very little heat.'

'Then do you have any idea what might have started it?'

The woman shrugged under her layers of coat and echoed Gerald Hume's diagnosis. 'Maybe an electrical fault.'

'You don't think it was started deliberately?'

'Why should it be?'

'Insurance? From all accounts the business wasn't doing that well.'

'So who might have started it, then?'

'The owners?'

Anna stopped in her tracks and looked incredulously at Carole. 'Ricky?' Instinctively she added, 'Ricky wouldn't ever do anything like that.' She seemed affronted by the suggestion.

'Or Lola, I suppose.'

'No way. There is just no way either of them would have done that. Ricky's loaded. I think Gallimaufry was almost a game to him, a bauble he tossed the way of his bored young wife to keep her occupied and to stop her nosing into his business. He never expected to make any money out of it.'

'But is he still loaded? I know he has made a lot of money at times but—'

'Ricky will never have any money worries. That's one thing of which I'm absolutely certain.' The woman's conviction was as strong as Flora Le Bonnier's had been on the same subject. 'He's just one of those very blessed, very charismatic people for whom everything always goes right.' Her admiration for him seemed as strong as Flora's, too.

'Well, whatever did cause the fire,' said Carole, 'I'm sure the police investigations will discover it.'

'I wouldn't have thought it was a police matter. There was no criminal involvement. And no one got hurt.'

It was Carole's turn to look incredulous, before the realization came to her that Anna did not actually know about the death in the inferno of Gallimaufry. The murder.

They had now arrived at the top of the beach, where the straggling grass of the dunes gave way to the stretch of pavement which was rather grandly known as 'the Promenade'. Anna was busying herself with reattaching the lead to her Black-Watched Westie. They had nearly reached the parting of the ways.

Carole wished desperately she could suggest they go somewhere for a cup of coffee, but she couldn't have chosen a worse time to put that idea into practice. At eight o'clock on Boxing Day morning there would be very little open in the entire British Isles, certainly nothing in Fethering.

But the Promenade did feature some glass-walled shelters with rusty metal frames. So terrified was she of her recurrent image of an elderly person sitting in one that in normal circumstances Carole kept well clear of them. But these weren't normal circumstances. With uncharacteristic boldness, she took Anna's arm and led her to sit down. 'There's something I must tell you. I'm afraid it's not very good news.'

Gulliver had wandered off down to the shoreline. Perhaps he'd seen the other dog being put back on its lead and was trying to postpone his own similar fate. Anna looked a little surprised at being led into the shelter, but she didn't say anything. Carole asked if she had heard any news on the radio or television the previous couple of days.

'No, I try to avoid the media. It's all bloody Christmas stuff, everyone full of bonhomie, comedians dressed up as Santa Claus. I can't stand it.'

Here was further confirmation of the isolation in which Anna had spent the holiday, but Carole didn't comment. She simply passed on the information about the discovery of Polly's body in the wreckage of Gallimaufry, and the subsequent revelation that the girl had been shot.

There was no doubting that this was all news to Anna. She

went very white, accentuating the bright redness of her lipstick, and it was a moment or two before she could reply. Finally she managed to say, 'How ghastly.'

'Yes. Did you know Polly?'

'I knew of her. I've never met her. Ricky talked about her sometimes. Did you really say she'd been shot?' Carole nodded grimly. 'Ricky must be in a terrible state.' Anna said that almost as though the thought gave her comfort.

'I don't know how he's taking it. My friend Jude—she's the one I was in the shop with last week—she's spoken to Lola, but that was just when we'd heard that Polly's body had been found in the shop. Before we knew she'd been shot.'

'It's ghastly,' Anna repeated, shaking her head as if she could dislodge the unsettling image of the murder.

'What's odd is why Polly came back to Fethering. Ricky had apparently taken her to Fedborough Station to catch a train back to London. You don't have any idea why she might have changed her plans?'

'I told you, Carole, I never met her. All I know is that Ricky had a child from one of his previous marriages.'

'Do you know how many marriages he's had?' Carole knew the answer—Jude had told her—but she thought it might be worth finding out how much Anna knew about Ricky's past.

'Certainly three. There may have been more. He seems to have gone through relationships like an emotional wrecking ball.'

'Three including Lola?'

'Yes. He was married very young to the girl next door, or at least only a few doors away. Can't remember what her name was, but they split up when he moved up to London and started in the music business. Then there was a second wife whose name I don't know either, but I think she was the mother of Polly. Whether Ricky was Polly's father or not, I don't know.

Finally, after, I'm sure, various and diverse entanglements, he met Lola.'

Carole couldn't see any reason to tell Anna about Ricky's other wife. Instead she asked, 'And, from what you can gather, that's a happy marriage?'

The woman's face froze, as it had done when the subject arose of where she had lived before Fethering. 'I have no idea. From what the public sees, everything seems to be fine.'

'But you don't—?'

'I don't know anything more about them than you do!'

Carole took the hint and changed the subject. 'How many people have keys to Gallimaufry?'

'Well, Lola does, obviously. And—' She stopped at the sound of her mobile ringing. The haste with which she snatched it out of her pocket suggested that she was expecting someone to contact her. When she recognized the number, disappointment flickered across her face and she rejected the call. She replaced the phone in her pocket and stretched out her arms. 'I must be getting back.'

'Sorry, you were just telling me who had keys to the shop . . .'

'Yes.' For the first time the look she directed to her interrogator was edged with suspicion. 'Why do you want to know?'

Carole shrugged sheepishly. 'Just natural curiosity.' Before Anna could say anything, she went on, 'I'm sorry, but Fethering's a very nosy place.'

'You don't have to tell me that.'

'No, and with something like this happening . . . a murder . . . well, I'm afraid you're going to get a lot of questions like the one I've just asked you, Anna. So I suppose you have to decide whether you're going to just ignore them all or come up with some answers.'

Carole knew this apparent ingenuousness was a risk, and she waited tensely to see how the woman would react. Fortunately, she'd chosen the right approach. 'You're right,' said Anna. 'I'd better practise my act, hadn't I? All right, let's start with the keys at Gallimaufry . . . Lola has a set, Ricky has a set, I have a set. There's also a spare set hidden at the back of the building, in case of emergencies. But I'm not going to tell anyone where they are.'

'I wouldn't expect you to.'

'No.' Anna was silent for a moment, then said, 'I'm still having difficulty taking this in. You say Polly was shot?'

'It was on the television news.'

'Ricky must be in a dreadful state. I can't begin to think what the situation must be like up at his place.'

'Not the most relaxed it's ever been, I would imagine.'

'He must be totally preoccupied by the tragedy. Not able to think about anything else.' And again there seemed a perverse note of satisfaction in Anna's voice. She shook her head in bewilderment. 'But Polly . . . shot dead . . .'

'Yes.'

'God, that's amazing. I mean, why on earth would anyone do that?'

'The very question all the inhabitants of Fethering—not to mention the investigating police officers—are asking.'

There was a silence. Unaccountably, Carole found herself tempted to ask how Anna had actually spent her Christmas. She felt sure it had been in bleak solitude, as her own had been for the past few years. But the urge towards empathy was stopped by the remembrance that her own Christmas the day before had been enlivened by the presence of Stephen, Gaby and Lily. To probe into Anna's life might be intruding on private grief.

So, instead, she pressed on with another investigative question. 'Did you know either Ricky or Lola before you moved to Fethering?'

For some reason, this was a step too far. With a curt, 'No. Now if you'll excuse me I must be on my way', Anna had gathered herself up, brought her snoozing dog up to its feet, and set off into the village.

Leaving Carole sitting in a rusty shelter on Fethering Promenade, the image of unhappy retirement which she had striven so hard to avoid. She was quickly up and off to collect Gulliver. Then she went straight back to High Tor.

CHAPTER FIFTEEN

Had she spent the previous day on her own like Anna, Carole would have been inhibited from contacting anyone on Boxing Day. Her loneliness would have been too raw, she would once again have been horrified at the idea of provoking pity. But because she had had what she was thinking of increasingly as 'a normal Christmas', she did not hesitate in dialling Jude's number the minute she got home. Another person might have knocked on the door of Woodside Cottage but not Carole Seddon.

Her neighbour sounded bleary and Carole realized it was only half-past eight in the morning, perhaps a little early to contact someone on a public holiday. 'I'm sorry, I hope I didn't wake you.'

'You did, actually, but don't worry about it.'

'Were you late last night?'

'Yes, I was at Georgie's; she and her family always have their Christmas dinner in the evening, and then we were playing party games into the small hours. I didn't get back till about three.'

'Oh,' said Carole, a little worried that a Christmas Day whose celebrations finished at four in the afternoon when Stephen and family had left perhaps didn't match up.

'And how was your Christmas?'

'Oh, you know, quiet.' Realizing that this was precisely the answer she had given to such inquiries in the past, bleak years,

Carole hastened to add, 'It was lovely to see the family. Lily really seems to have caught on to the idea of presents.'

'Oh, good. And were they all appreciated?'

'Yes, very much so. You'll be glad to know that Gaby adored her boa.' No need to dwell on Stephen's bewilderment when he unwrapped his Glow-in-the-dark Computer Angel. Instead, she summarized the conversation she had just had with Anna on Fethering Beach.

'Interesting,' said Jude at the end of the narration. 'Particularly the areas she didn't want to go into.'

'Yes. Extremely cagey when we got on to anything about her past, it seemed. She's a very private person.'

'And you say she was expecting a phone call?'

'Seemed to be. She certainly pounced on the mobile, and looked disappointed when she saw who it was.'

'Waiting for a call from a lover . . .' Jude mused.

'We have no basis for saying that. Could have been a friend, a member of her family, anyone. We know hardly anything about her.'

'No, but we do at least now know who has keys to Gallimaufry.'

'Yes,' Carole agreed, with a modest swell of pride at her investigative achievement.

'So what we want to find out now is—' There was a trilling noise in the background. 'Sorry, that's my mobile going.'

'Call me back.'

Jude phoned back about ten minutes later. 'Interesting,' she said. 'The call on my mobile was from Ricky Le Bonnier.'

'Oh?'

'He wants to come and talk to me.'

'About what?'

'Anything I noticed unusual in Polly's behaviour at my party. He's got an interview with the police coming up later in the morning. I think he's trying to keep one step ahead of them.'

'Get to you before they do, you mean?'

'Yes.'

'Hm.' There was a slightly peeved silence before Carole said, 'Of course, at the party Polly did, in fact, talk to me more than she talked to you.'

'I know that. Which is why I suggested that you should also be here when Ricky comes.'

'Oh. Oh, did you?' Carole couldn't keep the pleasure out of her voice. 'When's he coming?'

'In about half an hour.'

'I'll be there.'

'How's Lola taking it?' asked Jude.

'She's not too bad. Got the kids to keep her occupied; she doesn't have much time to brood. No, it's my mother who's really cut up about what's happened.'

'And you, Ricky? How're you coping?'

He wrinkled his nose. 'I don't think it's really hit me yet. So many practical things need doing. Then there's the police sniffing around. And they're still doing forensic investigations on . . . on . . .' he couldn't bring himself to mention his stepdaughter's body—'you know, so we can't even make funeral plans. It just seems to be one practical thing after the other at the moment. But I think it's going to hit me quite hard when things settle down.'

'Yes,' said Jude.

'Any idea why your mother's taking it so hard?' asked Carole. 'From the brief time I saw the two of them together, she and Polly didn't seem particularly close.'

'No.' Ricky Le Bonnier was silent for quite a long time, dwarfing the draped armchair on which he was sitting. He was dressed in khaki chinos and a brown leather jacket, cut long. The day's choice of glasses were large and owl-like with orange plastic frames. In spite of his adverse circumstances, there was still a compelling energy about the man.

When he finally spoke, it was with caution. 'I think the reason Mother's reacting like she is is because she's kind of got the feeling what's happened to Polly could have happened to her.'

'I'm sorry,' said Carole, 'I don't understand.'

'Look, Mum's generation was a lot less open about depression than we are now.'

'Are you saying Polly was depressed?' asked Jude.

'Of course I am. Look, she had no real reason to top herself. Not now. I mean, she was very affected by my breaking up with her mum, and then her mum dying.'

'A drug overdose, Lola said.'

'Did she?' He grimaced, as though he didn't want his wife passing on that kind of information. 'Well, yes, it was. And, obviously, that affected Polly at the time—or at least I was told it did. And I wasn't there for her then, so maybe I've got to hold my hand up and take a bit of blame. But it's not like she's my own daughter. Not my own flesh and blood. Not like Mabel and Henry.' He couldn't disguise the pride he felt for his new family. 'I mean, I like to think I did my duty by the kid when Vanessa and me were together, but . . .'

He coloured, as if he didn't want to have that claim examined too closely. 'Anyway, we're talking a long time ago. Last few years, Polly's life has been fine. OK, she wasn't getting much acting work and I don't know how healthy her relationship with Piers was, but basically she had no material or logical reason to take her own life. So she must've done it because she was depressed.'

'You're sure she did take her own life?'

'What else is there to think?'

Carole was tempted to reply that there were quite a lot of

other things to think, even tempted to mention the word 'murder', but she restrained herself. And she did feel a little guilty for never having considered the possibility of suicide. 'So what about the fire? You reckon Polly started that?'

'Again, what else can I think?'

'But from what she said to me, she appeared to like Lola. Why would she want to destroy her friend's business?'

'Carole, people suffering from severe depression are not at their most logical. I'm sure it all made some kind of sense to Polly's poor, tortured mind.' For the first time his voice broke. The emotion was getting to him. 'I'm sorry.'

Jude found herself wondering unworthily how much of his reaction was real. She had spent time with a lot of actors, and Ricky Le Bonnier shared with them a flamboyance which could all too easily turn to self-dramatization.

'I still don't quite see,' said Carole, 'why your stepdaughter's committing suicide should have such an effect on your mother.'

'It's relevant,' he replied, 'because Mother has been a depressive all her life. And, as I say, in her generation, it was a hard thing to own up to. You had to hide it. There was a stigma about mental illness, you had to pretend everything was OK. You couldn't succumb to it, then you'd be thought of as "not having any backbone", "letting the side down". You'd be told to "snap out of it". And the kind of medication you could get for depression in those days—assuming you ever plucked up courage to seek medical help—well, it was pretty scary stuff. I mean, I've dabbled in the odd recreational substance in my time . . .' As ever, when he referred to drugs, there was a kind of sheepish pride in his tone—'but I wouldn't have touched any of the prescription drugs they used to dish out for depression in those days. They'd literally blow your mind.

'Anyway, Mum was always terrified that people in the family might be depressives. She even used to worry about me—though she certainly had no need to. I'm glad to say I'm fine. I've never had a depressed thought in my life. I'm too bloody cheerful, if anything, some people would say almost bumptious. But then Polly became part of the family circle. And she was never a relaxed child to have around the house. I think she'd been upset when her parents split up, and then perhaps I didn't give her as much time as I should have done. And I think Mum, you know, having been there herself, recognized that depressive streak in Polly and now feels she should have done more to help the girl before . . . what happened happened. That's why she's so upset.'

'Did Polly seem depressed to you, Ricky, when she came down before Christmas?'

'I don't know, Jude.' He shrugged. 'I'm not really an expert on the subject. I've been told she's a depressive, but I'm not sure what the signs of that are. We've always had quite a sparky relationship—not to say a spiky one. She still blames me for leaving her mother . . . and, as I've said, I'm sorry for that. And maybe there was something I could have done to get her mother off the heroin. After all, I managed to do it. But we were divorced by then, she was kind of out of my life. Anyway, I'm not going to go on beating myself up about stuff like that. Life's too short, you have to move on, you have to get over things. So, in answer to your question, no, I didn't notice anything particularly different about Polly last week. But, you know, I was busy, and I've often been told I'm not very sensitive to other people's feelings.'

He announced this more as if it were a badge of honour than a criticism. 'I mean, I'm not proud of it,' he lied, 'but sometimes going into things with hobnail boots flying can have its advantages. Like when dealing with hypersensitive artistes . . . either you accept their egos at their own evaluation, you know, a lot of people kind of bend over backwards trying to answer their every whim, whereas with me, I'm the original WYSIWYG . . .

"What you see is what you get." I don't act differently with different people, whatever size stars they may be. I'm just Ricky Le Bonnier—take it or leave it. And a lot of supposedly difficult artistes were prepared to take it. I mean, when Elton John was upset, it was always me they used to send in to sort him out. And, though I say it myself, it usually worked out pretty well . . .'

And he was off on another of his name-dropping recollections. Jude asked herself why she didn't find him repellent. However great his egocentricity and habit of blowing his own trumpet, he never quite lost touch with his charm. And he was annoyingly well aware of that fact.

Towards the end of his monologue, when he spoke of Polly, he got a little tearful, and again Jude suspected artifice. But there was no doubting his sincerity when he turned to Carole and asked, 'Was there anything in what she said to you at the party that gave a hint of what she was planning to do?'

In spite of her own doubts, Carole decided this was not the moment to question whether the girl had suicidal intentions, so all she said by way of reply was, 'Nothing specific, no. She seemed a bit cynical about life in general, but I think a lot of young people are. And she seemed quite excited about this book she was writing.'

'Ah.' Ricky nodded. 'The book. Maybe it was something to do with that.'

'In what way, something to do with that?'

'As you say, she was excited about it. I think maybe she'd been investing too much hope in . . .' His fingers mimed quotation marks ' "the book". She thought that it would be the cure-all, the thing that would set her on a level with Piers in terms of success, that would make her enough money so that she didn't have to continue traipsing around auditioning for parts she very rarely got.'

'And you think, maybe,' Jude suggested, 'that she just had

some bad news on the book . . . that a publisher had turned it down, perhaps? And that was what prompted her to take her own life?'

'It could have been that.' He seemed glad to seize on the idea. 'Yes, that might make sense. I'll check with Piers whether she'd had any news on that front.'

'You know that Piers came to see us?' asked Carole.

'I heard that, yes. I think Lola was quite glad to get him out of the house. She'd got enough on her plate, what with Mum in the state she's in and everything else that was going on.'

'Piers told us that he was about to break up with Polly, that he'd found someone else. Did you know that, Ricky?'

He nodded. 'I'd suspected things weren't too rosy between them for some time.'

'Do you think Polly knew she was about to be dumped?'

'She must've done. She must've known it was only a matter of time. Another reason for her to think life wasn't worth living.' His voice broke again, and again Jude couldn't be sure how genuine the emotion was. 'Poor kid.'

'Yes, poor kid,' she echoed.

'Ricky,' said Carole briskly, 'you keep talking about Polly's suicide. Has the possibility occurred to you that she might have been murdered?' Good old Carole, thought Jude, getting straight to the point.

He looked genuinely shocked at the suggestion. 'But why would anyone want to murder her?'

Carole shrugged. 'Why does anyone want to murder anyone? There is a fairly well-known list of traditional motives.'

'Well, I can't think any of them would have been applicable to my stepdaughter!' There was a new harshness in his tone as he said this. 'And, whatever you do, if the police want to talk to you, don't start planting ideas of murder in their minds.'

'Of course we wouldn't,' said Jude at her most palliative.

'Incidentally,' Ricky went on, 'there is quite a strong likelihood that the police will be in touch with you. Lola and I have been interviewed, and, as I told you, Jude, I'll be talking to them again shortly. From what I can work out, they're trying to reconstruct the hours before Polly's . . . death.' He didn't like using the word, but his momentary lapse into grief was quickly replaced by a more businesslike tone. 'Anyway, if they do get in touch, I'd be grateful if you could let me know. We've got each other's mobile and landline numbers, so you can get through to me wherever I am. And please remember—if you do have to say anything to the investigating officers, what we're talking about here is a suicide.'

Ricky Le Bonnier didn't stay much longer. With a look at his watch, he announced that he must get to his own meeting with the police.

From the front door the women watched him stride to his large black Mercedes 4 × 4. 'Would you have described Polly as a lifelong depressive, Jude?'

'No. And Piers told us how she went on about what a happy childhood she had had.'

As Ricky clicked his key fob to open the car, a figure who must have been waiting for him by the gate stepped into view. She looked very small beside Ricky's bulk. Seeing her, his body language changed. He snapped some apparently dismissive remark, got into his car and drove off.

Carole and Jude both recognized the woman as the superannuated hippy they had seen in the Crown and Anchor, and again in the crowd outside the ruins of Gallimaufry. They wanted to talk to her, but by the time they reached the end of the garden path, she had got into an ancient, matt-orange-painted Volkswagen Camper, and was driving away.

CHAPTER SIXTEEN

'Yes, I know who you mean,' said Ted Crisp when Jude rang him. 'She's quite often in the pub. Always has a pint of Guinness.'

'Do you know her name?'

'Not her proper name, no. The Crown and Anchor regulars always refer to her as "the Dippy Hippy".'

'That figures.'

'Of course, that's when they're not calling you the same thing, Jude.'

'Oh, very funny.'

'You think I'm joking?'

'I will retain my dignity and not answer that.'

'Please yourself.'

'Anyway, next time the Dippy Hippy's in, Ted, could you give me a call?'

'All right. It's likely to be a lunchtime.' He sounded a bit bewildered at the request, but then went on, 'Oh, I get it. You and Carole are off on another of your little investigations, aren't you?'

'Well . . .'

'Might have known it. Mysterious death in a shop on the Parade, and Fethering's two favourite sleuths are instantly on the case. Well, I wish you luck if you think the Dippy Hippy's going to be any help to you.'

'Why shouldn't she be?'

'There's the small matter of understanding what she says. They don't give her that nickname for nothing, you know. The lady, I'm afraid, is definitely one chocolate truffle short of the full selection box.'

'Are you saying she won't talk to us?'

'No, she'll do that all right. It's trying to stop her talking that may be a bit of a problem.'

Jude reckoned they had got as far as they could at that moment in investigating the death of Polly Le Bonnier. And since it was Boxing Day, she went to bed for the afternoon and caught up on the sleep she'd missed the night before.

The call from Ted came through the next day, lunchtime on the Saturday (though Jude, like many people during the lull immediately following Christmas, had difficulty working out which day it was). The Dippy Hippy, she was informed, was at that moment nursing a pint of Guinness in the Crown and Anchor.

Jude rang through to High Tor, but there was no reply (Carole had taken Gulliver out for a long walk), so she went down to the pub on her own. It was surprisingly full—a lot of Fethering residents, after forty-eight hours cooped up with their relatives, clearly felt a communal urge to get out of the house.

But the pub's busyness was good for Jude's purposes. The lack of seats made it quite legitimate for her to take her glass of Chilean Chardonnay and sit opposite the Dippy Hippy, first gesturing and asking, 'Do you mind?'

'Be my guest.' There was something childlike about the woman's voice. The shape of her hair was Jean Shrimpton circa 1965, shoulder-length with a deep parted fringe, but its frizzled greyness gave a blurred effect. The flowered dress she wore was very short, revealing a lot of gnarled, white-tighted leg. Her clunky shoes were decorated with little leather flowers. The greenish velvet coat lay scrumpled on the settle beside her.

There was something discomfiting about her mutton-dressed-as-lamb appearance.

As ever, Jude had no problem initiating conversation. 'Quite a relief in some ways to get Christmas over, isn't it?'

'Yes. Good to hang loose.'

'My name's Jude, by the way.'

'Ah.'

The woman didn't volunteer her own name, and Jude didn't want to frighten her off by asking for it. She just said, 'I've seen you in here before.'

'I've seen you too. A few days ago. With your spiky friend.'

Jude wasn't sure that Carole would have liked the description, but she recognized its accuracy. 'Do you live in Fethering?'

The woman gestured with her head towards the river. 'Up in one of the old fisherman's cottages. My parents lived there. And my grandparents. It's been divided into flats now, though. I've got the top floor.'

'Ah. I'm over in the High Street.'

There was a silence. Jude worried whether Ted Crisp had been wrong about the Dippy Hippy's garrulousness. But the silence didn't last long. The woman appeared just to be gathering her thoughts before she launched into a monologue. 'When I last saw you in here, I was sitting in an alcove next to you, so I could hear everything you said. I wasn't eavesdropping or anything, I just couldn't help hearing. And I heard you talking about Ricky. Which some people might think is strange, but I don't think it's strange. I'm a great believer in synchronicity.'

'So am I,' said Jude, glad after all that Carole wasn't with her for the interview. She would manage the conversation better without someone beside her snorting ill-disguised contempt for 'New Age mumbo-jumbo'.

A rather ethereal look came into the woman's eyes as she said, 'Most things are meant.'

'I agree. It's interesting that almost all faiths are based on the premise that nothing is accidental.'

'Right. The tapestry of our lives is woven in the stars.' Jude felt even more glad she hadn't got Carole with her. 'I was meant to be sitting at the table next to you the other day. And you were meant to come and sit opposite me today. I knew when I woke up this morning that I would have a significant encounter with someone who would be important to me. We all have to free up our souls so that we can be open to the promptings of our instincts.'

'So true,' said Jude.

'We want to be open like sea anemones, ready to take in any experience that floats past on the tides of life. Human beings are receptors. We are designed that way. Too many people shut themselves off from experience. And if you do that, you shut off your sensitivity to the crosscurrents of life. You live fixed in the present, you're a slave to time. Whereas, if you open yourself out, time becomes irrelevant. You are released from its shackles. You can see the future just as clearly as you can see the present or the past. You are suspended free in time.'

Even Jude, who was broad-minded in her approach to alternative life theories, found herself remembering a line she had once been told: 'If you keep an open mind, people are going to throw a lot of rubbish into it.' But she suspended her scepticism and said, 'You mentioned that my friend and I talking about Ricky Le Bonnier was a moment of synchronicity . . .'

'Yes.'

'So that means you know him?'

'Know him? Ricky is my soulmate. We have always been destined to be together.'

'Ah.' Jude wondered whether the Dippy Hippy actually knew about Ricky's previous relationships and marriages—including the current one.

'I love him, you see, and love is all that matters. When two people are soulmates, nothing that comes between them really signifies.'

'So have you and Ricky ever actually been an item?' Jude only just stopped herself from adding 'in the real world'.

'Yes,' the woman replied devoutly. 'He is my husband.'

'Your husband in heaven or somewhere like that? Or your real husband?'

'My real husband. Ricky and I were married right here. In Fethering Church.'

'Oh.' This was the last answer Jude had been expecting. 'So you're his first wife?'

'I'm his only wife. We were married in Fethering Church,' she repeated.

'But, I mean, you did get divorced. Ricky has been married three times since that.'

The Dippy Hippy smiled patiently at Jude. 'Marriage is real. A divorce is only a piece of paper. A piece of paper can't stop two people loving each other.'

'It can stop one side of a partnership loving the other,' Jude pointed out. 'In fact, such a piece of paper is frequently issued *because* one side of a partnership has stopped loving the other.'

'It's not like that with Ricky and me,' said the woman firmly. 'Our relationship is for ever.'

'Are you Catholic?' asked Jude.

'I don't have a religion, not like that. I have faith, which is much better. Faith that things are being organized in such a way that everything will turn out all right.'

The woman spoke with such certainty that Jude had to remind herself that the logic of her thesis was highly dubious.

'So are you saying that you and Ricky Le Bonnier will end up together?'

'Oh yes.' There wasn't the smallest nuance of doubt in her

Simon Brett

voice. 'We met here in Fethering, and we'll end up here in Fethering. We were at the village school together here. Ricky was looked after by his aunt, because his mother was always off acting all over the world. He was lonely at school. I was his friend. So we got married. And we still are married.'

'In whose eyes?'

'In the eyes of the Power which arranges such things.'

'Ah,' said Jude, slowly nodding her head. 'I understand. By the way, I don't know your name . . . ?'

'Kath.'

'Right, Kath. So how long were you and Ricky married?'

'We still are married.'

' "In the eyes of the Power which . . ." Yes, I understand that. But how long after you got married did he move out, did you stop living together?'

'Only three years. But we are still together, you know, spiritually . . . on an astral plane. We'll always be together in a cosmic sense.'

Jude found this talk was getting her closer than she had ever anticipated to Carole's views on 'New Age mumbo-jumbo'. Time perhaps to move from the astral plane to a bit of detective work. 'I actually saw you with Ricky this morning. Outside my house. He had just come to see me.'

'Oh, I didn't know who he had been visiting. I just knew the car would be there.'

'Sorry? You knew it would be there?'

'I had a sense when I woke up yesterday morning that Ricky was going to come to Fethering. He has a very strong aura. I can always sense when his aura is close to mine. So I drove out in the camper, knowing I would see his car. And of course I did.' She smiled beatifically. 'It was outside your house.'

'He didn't seem to have a lot to say when he saw you.'

'No, often he doesn't. He isn't ready to be back with me yet.

He's still under the influence.'

'The influence of what?'

'Of the Devil Women.'

Jude nearly spilled her Chilean Chardonnay. 'I beg your pardon?'

'Devil Women took Ricky away from me. But Devil Women cannot win in the long run. The Power is always stronger than the Devil Women.' Jude was beginning to think she'd drifted into some science fiction B-movie, as Kath went on, 'I only have to wait, then Ricky will come back to me.'

'So are you saying that all of the other women with whom Ricky's spent time with are Devil Women?'

'Oh yes.' No flicker of hesitation.

'And when they are finally defeated, he'll come back to you?'

'Oh yes.' With exactly the same certainty.

'Kath,' asked Jude gently, 'did you know Polly?'

'Polly?'

'Ricky's daughter. The one who died in the fire at the shop.'

'She's not my daughter.'

'I know that. Sorry, I should have said "Ricky's stepdaughter". But did you know her?'

Ignoring the question, Kath went on, 'Ricky and I didn't have children. I was on the Pill.' She spoke this with some pride, as if it were an unusual concept, which, Jude reflected, to women of Kath's generation, it probably was. 'Ricky and I were going to have children later. But then the Devil Women got in the way.'

'Have you ever met any of the Devil Women?' It was not a question that Jude had ever in her life anticipated she might have to ask.

'I've seen one or two.'

'Including Lola?'

'I'm not interested in their names.'

'Lola is Ricky's current wife.' Jude hadn't wanted to use such a dismissive adjective, but she couldn't think of another, more appropriate one.

'The one he calls his wife. I am his real wife.'

'And, so far as you're concerned, she's just his latest Devil Woman?'

'If you like, yes. But she's not real.'

'Right.' Jude decided not to take the conversation back into the realms of 'the Power which arranges such things', instead asking, 'So you have met Lola?'

'I've seen her in the shop.'

'But do you feel any resentment towards her?'

Kath gave her a curious look. 'Why should I feel resentment?'

'Well, Ricky is married to her.'

'*Says* he's married to her. I told you—he's really married to me.'

'Either way, you could regard Lola as someone who's taken your man from you. And women in that situation have frequently been known to feel considerable resentment.'

'Well, I don't feel it.'

'Why not?'

'Because it's not the Devil Women's fault that they're Devil Women. There's an Evil Power that gets into them. They can't help it. To blame someone for being a Devil Woman is like blaming someone for being born with red hair.'

'Right,' said Jude. 'I understand.' Which was not strictly true, but probably a more prudent course than asking for further explanations. 'One thing you said interested me, Kath—well, a lot of things you said interested me, but there's one I'd like to ask about.'

A smile spread across the wrinkled face. 'Ask away. It's a free country.'

'You said you have an instinct for when Ricky is close, when he comes to Fethering . . .'

'Yes. That's what I had yesterday morning.'

'And when did you last have it?'

'Last Sunday I knew he was in Fethering.'

'Yes, he was. He actually came to a party at my house.'

Kath smiled again and opened her hands wide, as if to say that her point was proved.

'And did you see him that day?' Kath shook her head. 'And there wasn't another time, between last Sunday and yesterday, when you sensed that Ricky was near you?'

'His car was there on the Sunday,' Kath said slyly.

'Yes, we've just established that.'

'But it was also here later on the Sunday.'

'Could you sense that?' The Dippy Hippy looked at her curiously. 'I mean, did you have an instinct that the car was here?'

'No,' came the prosaic reply. 'I saw it. Parked down by the Yacht Club.'

'What time of day was this?'

'Evening. Eightish, probably.'

'Yes. And did you see Ricky in the car?' Kath nodded vigorously. 'Did you talk to him?'

'No. I wouldn't talk to him under those circumstances.'

'Under what circumstances?'

'He wasn't alone. He had his latest Devil Woman with him.'

'Lola?'

'I told you, I'm not interested in their names. She's the latest Devil Woman to seduce Ricky away from me.'

So it had been Lola. In spite of their denials of the fact, Jude now knew that Ricky Le Bonnier and his young wife had been in Fethering in his Mercedes 4 × 4 on the evening that Gallimaufry had been set on fire.

CHAPTER SEVENTEEN

'From what you say,' Carole observed, as she sipped a cup of coffee in Jude's overfilled sitting room, 'she sounds like Fethering's answer to Miss Havisham—a woman whose entire life stopped when a man let her down.'

'There is an element of that about her,' Jude agreed. 'Except that she's not embittered. She seems to have a very cheerful and benign outlook on life. And she's absolutely convinced that all Ricky's affairs with other women are just aberrations. He's still really hers. To her mind he's never stopped being hers.'

'Which, I would say, is a measure of quite how seriously that mind is disturbed.' Then Carole, ever practical, went on to ask, 'What does she live on? Fresh air, or does she have a private income?'

'She's got a job. Ted filled me in on a few details after she'd left. She does the books for Ayland's, one of the boatyards along the Fether—one of the few that are still in business. Apparently she's had that job for most of her life. Still, from what I gather, she has a fairly frugal lifestyle. So she doesn't need much money.'

'Just enough to keep her in crystals and joss sticks?'

Jude ignored the gibe and went on, 'But I think Kath's a reliable witness.'

'What, because she has *instincts* and can sense people's *auras?*'

'No,' said Jude patiently. 'Because she keeps a very clear division between what you call her "instincts" and things she has actually seen with her own eyes. And she definitely saw Ricky

118

and Lola in the Mercedes 4 × 4 on the evening of the fire.'

'Yes, that's odd, isn't it, because when Ricky came to see us, he implied that he had gone straight home to Fedborough after he left your party. What time did he leave, by the way?'

'I don't know exactly, but everyone had gone by half past six. And so far as we know, the only other time he went out that evening was to take Polly to catch the seven-thirty-two at Fedborough Station.'

'So if your oh-so-reliable witness Kath is right, he's been lying.' Carole drummed her fingers on the arm of her chair. 'The other thing I've been thinking about is the gun.'

'What about the gun?'

'The fact that there was a gun. I mean, if Polly had been found stabbed or strangled, well, all right, there are plenty of suitable murder weapons available anywhere. But a gun—in Fethering? It's not as if we're talking about south London, or the back streets of Manchester, or the slums of Glasgow. I can't think that many people in Fethering have guns—except for legitimate purposes like shooting at targets or pheasants.'

Jude smiled inwardly at the *Daily Mail* sensibility which informed all of her neighbour's views on criminal demographics. But Carole had, nonetheless, raised an interesting point. 'You're right. And the police statement said that Polly was killed by a single bullet wound, which suggests that the weapon used wasn't the kind of shotgun which most people in shooting parties would use. It's a rifle or a pistol.'

'Well, who in Fethering would have one of those? And, more importantly, where is it now? If the murderer had any sense, he would—'

'Or she.'

'Yes, absolutely right. He—or *she*—would have got rid of the weapon as soon as possible.'

'And, given the geography of Fethering, where would you do

that—speaking as a murderer who had some sense?'

'Well, the sea's the obvious place. Except, of course, the coastline's so flat here, you might have to go quite a long way out to find deep enough water. Mind you, the same's not true of the Fether. Even at low tide, in the river there's enough water—not to mention a lot of extremely glutinous mud—to hide a gun very effectively.'

Jude nodded agreement. She looked thoughtful. 'I was just thinking back to that boy who was drowned in the Fether . . .'

'Aaron Spalding? That was the first time we got involved in a murder investigation, wasn't it, Jude?' Carole sounded fondly nostalgic.

'Yes. But remember the interesting thing about what happened to the boy's body. He was what is called locally a "Fethering Floater".'

'That's right. He was swept up on Fethering Beach twenty-four hours after he'd gone into the river. Of course I remember, Jude. I was the one who found him.'

'Yes . . .' Jude mused and unconsciously tapped at her chin.

'What?'

'Well, I was just wondering whether what happens to a body might also happen to something small and heavy like a gun . . . ?'

'That if it was thrown into the Fether, it, too, might get washed up on Fethering Beach?'

'Do you think it would?'

At that moment there was a loud knock on the front door of Woodside Cottage.

There were two detectives, a man and a woman, and they'd clearly attended all the latest training courses on dealing with the public. Their approach was politeness itself, apologizing for interrupting things, but asserting that police work didn't stop because it was a holiday season. They explained they were making general inquiries to try to ascertain the cause of the death at Gallimaufry, and they had been informed that the deceased, Polly Le Bonnier, had been at a party given by Jude on the Sunday, the day—or perhaps the day before—she died.

At this juncture Carole suggested that perhaps she should leave, so that the detectives could question Jude on her own.

'I think you should stay,' said her neighbour. She explained that Carole had also attended the party and had, in fact, spent longer talking to Polly than she had.

The police questioning was courteous and thorough, but if Carole and Jude had been hoping to be brought up to date on the official inquiry into the death, they were doomed to disappointment. Inquiries about how Polly had died were deflected by the information that forensic investigations were still continuing. When there was any news that could be made public, the media would be informed. In the meantime, the detectives would be very grateful if the ladies could just answer the questions to the best of their ability.

So they did. And no amount of prompts—such as Carole's assertion that during their conversation Polly had seemed far from suicidal—made the detectives divert by a millimetre from their party line. They certainly never once mentioned the word 'murder'.

After the detectives' departure, the two women felt rather flat. It was so frustrating to have spent time with people who, undoubtedly, knew infinitely more about the case than they did, and to end the encounter without even the most meagre scrap of new information.

'All we do know,' Carole announced huffily, 'is that their investigation is ongoing. Which means they haven't yet solved the case . . . otherwise they wouldn't have bothered coming to see you.'

This was so self-evident that Jude didn't think it worthy of comment. Instead, she began slowly, 'The only good thing about their visit—'

'Oh, there is a good thing, is there?'

'Yes. They've given me an excuse to ring Lola.'

'What?'

'I can just tell her that the police have been questioning us. I'm sure she'd want to know. And Ricky certainly would, he said so.'

'Well, I think I'll be getting along.' Carole rose to her feet. 'Gulliver was covered in sand when I brought him back from his walk. I came straight round here, so I'd better go and do some sweeping up. Let me know if you hear anything new from Lola.'

'Of course I will,' Jude called out to Carole's retreating back. Then she dialled the Le Bonniers' number. She was relieved it was Lola who answered, and quickly passed on the news of her visit from the police.

'Thanks for letting me know. I must say, their investigations are very thorough. They seem to be contacting everyone who had anything to do with Polly or anyone else in the family.'

'Is that a problem for you?'

'Not really. Well, it's just another thing that takes time, like Mabel's ear infection, and the Dalmatian puppies, and Piers reappearing from his parents' place in Gloucestershire, and Flora needing full-time attention for the last couple of days . . .'

'How is she, by the way?'

'Better today, thank God. She's a tough old bird. The iron discipline she exercises over her emotions has reasserted itself. It's in the genes, you know. If you asked, Flora would tell you that her upper lip has been permanently stiffened by generations of aristocratic in-breeding.'

'How long is she staying with you?'

'Till New Year's Day.' Lola didn't quite manage to prevent this from sounding like a prison sentence.

'Where does she live?'

'Service flat in a big block in St John's Wood in London. Very exclusive, very tasteful, very soigné.' A gloomy thought intruded. 'Though God knows how much longer she'll be able to manage there on her own. Her hands are virtually useless now.'

Apparently casual, Jude changed the topic of conversation. 'The detectives who came to see me were very pleasant.'

'Yes, they all have been. I mean, heaven forbid you should ever be involved in an investigation into an unexplained death, but if you were, you couldn't ask for a more sensitive and efficient bunch of cops in charge.'

'You've seen a lot of them?'

'And how. Well, obviously they're going to be asking us a lot of stuff, since Polly was Ricky's stepdaughter. But they have been as pleasant as their job allows them to be. Mabel's taken a definite shine to one of the young detective constables. And, incidentally, she keeps asking about you too, Jude. You made quite an impression on her when we went to the swings that day.'

'I'm honoured.'

'So you should be. Mabel's very picky about who she favours with her friendship. At the moment the list only includes you, the detective constable and Lisa Simpson.'

'I'm doubly honoured.'

'Well, be careful. Or you could find I'm dragooning you into babysitting duty. There are very few people who Mabel will allow to babysit her.'

'I will await the call. How is her ear infection, by the way?'

'Getting better. Antibiotics finally kicking in.'

'About the police . . .' Jude gently nudged the conversation back on track. 'What kind of stuff have they been asking you?

Checking alibis and things like that?'

'Oh yes. A lot of very gentle probing along the lines of "Where were you on the night of the twenty-first?" But at no point have they suggested that we're suspects in any criminal actions. Instead, they've done a lot of circuitous talk about how important it is to be able to "eliminate you from our inquiries, Madam".' The accent she dropped into for the last few words reminded Jude of Lola's background in Footlights revues.

'And I assume that you and Ricky could both account for yourselves throughout the night of the fire?'

Jude had made the question sound as flippant and unimportant as she could, but still detected a guardedness in Lola's tone as the reply came back, 'No problem. One of the only advantages of Mabel's ear infection—and it wouldn't be an advantage for anyone who wasn't looking for an alibi—is that it makes her sleep very badly. She kept waking up through Sunday night, so Ricky and I could give firmer accounts of our whereabouts than usual.'

'And you weren't in Fethering earlier in the day, you know, on the Sunday?'

'Ricky was. You should know, he came to your party. I was stuck at home, looking after poor little Mabel. She was feeling really sorry for herself. That was the worst day of the ear infection . . . well, that and the Monday. She just lay on the sofa, hardly reacting to anything. She didn't even perk up for Polly, and she adores Polly. That is, adored.' Once again, Lola winced from the pain of bereavement.

'Yes, at my party Polly told Carole she was going back to your place to see "the little ones".'

'Not that she saw much of them. When it comes to parties, Ricky's a great "stayer". He never leaves when he says he's going to. As a result it was after six when they got back here, and Polly only had about half an hour with the kids before Ricky had to take her to the station to catch her London train.'

'The seven-thirty-two?'

'I think it was that one.'

'Except, of course, she never caught it, did she?'

'No.' Again Jude could hear a slight wobble in Lola's voice.

'So you weren't in Fethering at all on that Sunday?'

'I've told you—no.' The answer was almost snappish, but maybe Lola was being extra-vehement to hide her emotional lapse.

Well, thought Jude, somebody's lying. Kath is positive she saw Ricky with Lola in his Mercedes 4 × 4 near Fethering Yacht Club at around eight o'clock on the Sunday evening. Lola denies being there.

And, in spite of the woman's loopiness, Kath's was the version of events Jude was inclined to believe.

Television schedules are over-stuffed at Christmas. The best offerings—and here 'best' is very definitely a relative word—are reserved for the main days of celebration—Christmas Day and New Year's Eve. And the less important parts of the holiday are padded with all kinds of rubbish, particularly lots of superannuated movies.

And so it was that that Saturday evening Carole found herself watching a black and white film, starring Flora Le Bonnier. Entitled *Her Wicked Heart,* it was a typical Gainsborough production, a melodrama set in a vaguely eighteenth-century period with lots of cloaks, knee-breeches and buckles (and quite a lot of swash to go with all the buckling). Flora played Lady Mary Constant and it was her wicked heart that featured in the title. Disappointed by her loveless marriage to the dissolute Sir Jolyon Bastable, she develops a secret life as Black William, a highwayman. In this guise, while holding up his coach, she meets and falls in love with the handsome but penniless

125

aristocrat Lord Henry Deville. Their budding romance is impeded by two obstacles—one, Lord Henry believes her to be a man and, once that situation is clarified, two, she is still married to Sir Jolyon. Only when her husband dies in a fortuitous duel, can Lady Mary and Lord Henry be together. They ride off into a greyish English sunset, determined to 'rid this country of the scourge of highwaymen'.

Carole thought the whole thing was tosh, but quite watchable tosh. What struck her most, though, was the beauty of Flora Le Bonnier, which glowed through the dusty monochrome print. Probably in her early twenties when the film was shot, she had the kind of natural good looks which would have made men do stupid things, like giving up families and careers just to be near her. Carole Seddon, whose looks were never going to cause comparable upheavals, could still appreciate such beauty when she saw it. And she could still wonder how it must feel for someone like that to see the depredations of age on her face and figure. In the film Flora's hands were particularly beautiful, slender and expressive, unlike the ugly claws they had become. Though Flora Le Bonnier remained a fine-looking woman and looked good for her age, she had declined considerably since her glory days.

And although Carole knew there was no genetic link between the two women, she kept being struck by the actress's likeness to her dead granddaughter. Polly's face had more character than sheer beauty, but the two shared an expression of unshakeable determination. And when in the film Lady Mary faced some reverse, the set of her mouth was exactly the same as her granddaughter's look of dogged resentment.

The effect this perception had on Carole was, almost for the first time, to make her confront the reality of Polly Le Bonnier's death. She felt restless and, after she'd completed her bedtime routine, unready for sleep. So, as happened increasingly, she found herself sitting down in front of her laptop.

She started, as so many researchers do these days, with Wikipedia. The entry for Flora Le Bonnier was, like most Wikipedia entries, incomplete and full of unsupported detail. There was an exhaustive listing of the film and television productions in which she had appeared, but very little personal history. Flora Le Bonnier's rule about not speaking directly to the press appeared to have paid off.

The only parts of the entry that alerted Carole were the following sentences: 'Flora Le Bonnier was adopted as a baby by George Melton, a solicitor, and his wife Hilda, but subsequent research revealed her to be a descendant of the long-established Le Bonnier family which became extinct with the death in action of Graham Le Bonnier in the Western Desert in 1941. The accuracy of this link to the aristocracy has been questioned in various press reports.'

And then, just when she got to the interesting bit, there were two words in brackets, printed in blue: '[citation needed]'.

The following morning, Sunday, Carole dropped in at Woodside Cottage on her way back from Gulliver's walk and told Jude of her online findings. They agreed that Flora Le Bonnier's background deserved further investigation.

'Needless to say, when I googled her name there were thousands of references. I suppose I'll have to work through all of them.'

'If you've got the energy, Carole. It may not be that important, anyway. I mean, does it matter these days whether people have an aristocratic background or not?'

'It matters to Flora Le Bonnier.'

CHAPTER EIGHTEEN

After Carole had left, Jude was not really surprised to have a call from Piers Duncton asking if he could come and see her. Ever since Lola had said he was back in Fedborough, she'd been expecting to hear from him. She hadn't yet decided on his motives, but she knew the young writer was as keen as Carole and she were to find out the exact circumstances of Polly Le Bonnier's death.

'Did you manage to have any kind of Christmas?' she asked, once she'd got him settled in the folds of an armchair and supplied him with a cup of black coffee and an ashtray for the cigarette he kept taking nervously in and out of his mouth.

'It wasn't the most relaxed couple of days I've ever spent. My parents are a bit formal at the best of times, and so they wanted all the Christmas rituals observed, even though I was feeling shitty because of what happened to Polly.'

'Did they ask you about it?'

'No. In some ways I was grateful that they didn't. I suppose that made it easier for me to control my emotions. But at the same time I kept wishing that they would say something, acknowledge her death. I mean, they'd known her for over ten years. But I suppose everyone finds their own way of coping with tragedy.'

'And what's your way of coping with it?'

'Finding out what really happened, how Polly actually died. I'm determined to do that. I've told . . .' he baulked at giving

128

the name '. . . this other girl I'm seeing that we're not going to meet up again until I've got to the truth.'

Jude recognized the strategy. Piers was assuaging his guilt by punishing himself. He wanted to close the chapter of life with his previous girlfriend before focusing all his attention on the new one.

'Incidentally,' she asked, 'did your parents approve of Polly?'

'I think they liked her OK. They've always been terrible snobs, so they approved of the Le Bonnier connection. But I think they'd probably have preferred her to be a corporate lawyer rather than an actor. Mind you, they'd have preferred me to be a corporate lawyer rather than a writer.'

'And Lola and Polly got on?' It was the question Jude didn't want to ask. She liked the owner of Gallimaufry and didn't want to think ill of her. But the fact remained that Ricky and his wife had both been seen in Fethering on the night of the fire. Lola was in the frame as a suspect.

'Yes, they always did. Polly and I were an item before I met Lola.'

'I know that. The reason for my question was that Lola told me . . . you and she . . . at the Edinburgh Festival . . .'

He blushed. 'Polly never knew about that, so there was never any awkwardness between the two of them.'

'Good. And what about you and Lola now?'

The blush spread as far as his prominent ears. 'To resort to a cliché, we're just good friends. Nothing more.' Jude's quizzical look demanded amplification. 'Look, she's one of my closest woman friends. I can talk to Lola about stuff I wouldn't dare raise with anyone else, and maybe it's because we were once lovers that we're so relaxed with each other. But I promise you there is nothing more to our relationship than that. Lola is absolutely devoted to Ricky. He's the love of her life. She wouldn't even consider going to bed with anyone else.'

'And do you reckon that Ricky is equally faithful?'

Piers looked awkward as he answered. 'I'm honestly not sure. I mean, I know he had a reputation as a womanizer in the past, but I think marrying Lola has settled him down a lot. Whether a leopard can totally change its spots, though . . . I really don't know.'

'But if you were to hear that Ricky had had an affair, you wouldn't be that surprised?'

Uncomfortably, he confirmed that he wouldn't.

'And you haven't heard any rumours connecting him to anyone in particular?'

'No, and I'm not likely to. Look, I live in London. I don't know anything about the rumour-mill of Fethering.'

'Of course you don't.' Deftly Jude redirected the conversation. 'You know the book Polly was writing, the one she mentioned to Carole?'

'Yes, of course.'

'Well, I just wondered if you knew where it was.'

'Where physically, you mean?'

'Physically, geographically, whatever. Do you have a manuscript of it yourself?'

Piers shook his head. 'I don't know that she ever even printed it out. I've never seen a hard copy. The bits of it I read I read straight off her laptop.'

'And where is her laptop? In your place in London?'

'No. Polly never went anywhere without her laptop. She had it with her when she came down here. It's quite a small one, she put it in her leather rucksack. So I suppose it must have still been with her . . . in Gallimaufry . . . when she . . .' With an effort of will he regained control of himself. 'I asked Lola about it. The police told her they'd found the remains of a laptop in the shop. Totally destroyed by the fire. There's no chance of retrieving any information from it.'

'And that laptop would have contained the only copy of her book that Polly had?'

'I assume so. Certainly she didn't have another computer. I suppose she might have done a printout or backed up the book on to a flash drive or something, but she never mentioned that to me.'

'Just a minute . . . Polly told Carole that she'd shown some of the book to an agent.'

'Serena Fincham, right.'

'Well, she must have had a hard copy to send her, mustn't she?'

'No. She emailed it.'

'So, so far as you know, there's not a single copy of Polly's book anywhere in the world?'

'No. I'm afraid it died with her.'

Was Jude being hypersensitive to detect an undercurrent of relief in his words? But then a new thought came into her head. 'What about Polly's mobile? Do you know if the police found that?'

'Lola didn't mention it. But I assume that would have been destroyed in the blaze too.'

'She would have had it with her?'

'Oh God, yes. Never went anywhere without her mobile. She kept it in one of those phone sock things. Hideous fluorescent pink.'

Remembering this personal detail about the dead girl once again threatened his fragile emotional equilibrium, so Jude moved quickly on. 'Piers, when we last spoke, just before Christmas, you had just heard about Polly's death . . .'

'Yes, that's why I came down here to Fethering.'

'But then you hadn't heard how she died. At that time, presumably, you thought she'd been killed by the fire in Galli-maufry. Of course, we now know she had been shot.'

He shook his head, as though trying to dispel the image her words had created. 'Which really means we can rule out an accidental death. We are talking about either suicide or murder. Piers, you probably knew Polly as well as anyone did. Would you say she was capable of killing herself?'

There was a long silence before he replied. 'I just don't know. You can be very close to someone, think you're sharing every thought, every emotion, and then something happens which makes you realize you never knew them at all. And that's a bit how I've been feeling since Polly . . . since she died. That there are whole areas of her personality that I never knew at all.'

Jude remembered Lola using almost exactly the same words about Ricky. Was it just coincidence, or could it mean that she and Piers had discussed the situation? She listened carefully as the young writer continued, 'I know Polly hadn't been happy in recent months . . . well, for years, possibly. I think she'd expected that finding acting work would prove easier than it did. Maybe she thought her famous surname—even though she'd only got it through her mother's remarriage—would give her an entrée to the West End, but it certainly didn't. And I guess there were other things that might have been upsetting her.'

'Like her relationship with you?'

'Well . . .'

'Piers, you told Carole and me last time we met that you were just about to break off with Polly, as soon as Christmas and the New Year were out of the way. She must've had an inkling that something was in the air. Weren't there any rows or disagreements between you?'

'A few, yes.'

'About what?'

'Mostly about the fact that we were doing less things together. My work was taking me away a lot of the time, so Polly was having to spend more and more evenings in the flat on her own. She didn't like that, so sometimes when I got back late we'd have fights—particularly if I'd been drinking, and, given the nature of the work in which I'm involved, I usually had been drinking. Television's a very sociable business,' he pleaded in mitigation.

'When you talk of having "fights",' asked Carole sternly, 'do you mean actual physical violence?'

'God, no,' Piers protested. 'I'd never hit anyone—and certainly not a woman.'

'Did Polly know about your new girlfriend, the one from the sitcom?'

'No, I'm sure she didn't.'

'She wasn't even suspicious that you had someone else?'

'I don't think so.' But he didn't sound very sure about it.

Jude picked up the interrogation, moving off on a sudden tangent. 'Presumably Ricky and Lola know more about the progress of the police enquiry than you or I do?'

'Probably, yes. They certainly seem to have spent a lot of time talking to various detectives.'

'But have they passed any details on to you?'

He shrugged. 'Bits and pieces. Lola usually tells me most things.'

As soon as he'd said the words, he wished he hadn't, but Jude didn't pick him up on them. 'Has she said whether the police have found the gun which killed Polly yet?'

'I don't think so. I can't recall her mentioning it. Why would that be important?'

For someone with a Cambridge education, Piers Duncton could sometimes be surprisingly dense. Or so wrapped up in his own concerns that he couldn't see the bigger picture. 'Because,' Jude explained patiently, 'if they did find a weapon, then the death could be either suicide or murder. If they didn't, suicide becomes much less likely. It's quite tricky to dispose of a gun after you've shot yourself.'

Piers acknowledged the truth of this, then said, 'Oh yes, I think Lola did mention something about the police having found a gun in the ruins of the shop.'

Jude found this sudden access of memory somewhat suspicious and her scepticism didn't decrease as Piers went on, 'Actually, the more I think about it, the more I think Polly may have taken her own life. There were signs in the last few months, signs I can only recognize in retrospect. God, if only I'd picked up on them and got help for her, Polly might still be alive today!'

His outburst of emotion also seemed suspect to Jude. 'So why do you think she killed herself?'

He shrugged hopelessly. 'Depression. It's a very cruel illness. Insidious. And Polly had suffered from it all her life.'

He now seemed to be echoing exactly what Ricky Le Bonnier had said about his daughter's death. 'Just a minute,' Jude remonstrated. 'Only a few days ago, you sat here in this very room telling me Polly was always talking about how happy her childhood had been.'

'I know,' said Piers. 'But when I said that I was thinking she had died in an accident, and I didn't think I needed to tell comparative strangers about her history of depression. Now, though, now that we know she committed suicide, we don't have to maintain the pretence anymore.'

We don't *know* she committed suicide, thought Jude, but no amount of further argument would shift Piers Duncton from his stated belief that his girlfriend had killed herself. Jude felt certain he was behaving like that because he suspected murder and was trying to protect the person who he thought might have done it.

She also was beginning to think that Ricky had supported the suicide theory for exactly the same reasons.

And that the person they both wanted to protect was Lola.

CHAPTER NINETEEN

Now knowing that Piers Duncton shared everything with his ex-lover, Jude was unsurprised the next morning, the Monday, to have a call from Lola Le Bonnier. But the reason for her making contact had nothing to do with Polly's death. She wanted Jude's help in her professional capacity.

'It's Flora,' said Lola. 'You know she's been in a terrible state since . . . since what happened.'

'Yes. Has she taken a turn for the worse?'

'I don't really know. But she's now manifesting physical symptoms, which she wasn't before. Basically, her back's packed in and she doesn't seem able to get out of bed.'

'Have you called the doctor?'

'That was my first thought, but Flora won't hear of it. She doesn't trust "those damned money-grabbing quacks".' Lola's impersonation of her mother-in-law was uncannily accurate. 'She's always relied on what are now called "alternative therapies"—long before they were fashionable. In London, she's got a network of acupuncturists and reiki healers, but down here . . .'

'I'm the nearest thing to an alternative therapist?'

'Exactly.' There was a slight giggle in Lola's voice. Again Jude felt strong empathy with the girl, an attitude that clashed uncomfortably with the suspicions she'd been harbouring overnight. 'I know it's supposed to be holiday time, but would you mind coming to have a look at Flora?'

'Of course. I'll be with you in as long as it takes.'

'I may have to go out, and I know Ricky has a lunch somewhere, and I'm not sure where Piers is, but Varya will be here. She's the au pair.'

Jude knew that Carole would happily give her a lift in her immaculate Renault to the Le Bonniers', but she didn't ask the favour. She never liked to impose on her neighbour's generosity when it was for work.

Fedingham Court House had Elizabethan origins, still evident in the redbrick frontage and high chimneys of the main part of the house. But generations of owners had renovated and improved (according to their lights) the structure, so that the house had become a compendium of three centuries' architectural styles. Jude's taxi deposited her in front of elaborate, high wrought-iron gates which opened automatically after she had announced herself into the entryphone.

Though Fedingham Court House was impressive in size, there was nothing daunting about it. At the back of the grounds was farmland, which melted upwards into the soft hazy grey undulations of the South Downs. The gravel circle in front, on which stood the Mercedes 4 × 4 and a brand-new Mini, was a little untidy. The garden too was welcomingly unkempt, and a child's swing hanging from a tree emphasized the homely impression. For the kind of person who could afford it—which presumably Ricky Le Bonnier could—it was the perfect family house.

The front door was opened before Jude reached it by a young dark-haired woman she didn't recognize but assumed correctly must be Varya. The au pair held a sleeping Henry in her arms and round one side of her legs peered the mischievous face of Mabel, excited to see one of the few people to whom she vouchsafed the great honour of her friendship. Round the other

137

side of the au pair peered an equally curious Dalmatian.

'Hello, Mabel,' said Jude. 'And what's the dog called?'

'Spot the Dog.' The girl spoke with the seriousness of a child who'd spent more time with adults than with her own generation. Not hooded and scarfed as she had been at the swings by Fethering Beach, she was revealed to have wispy hair so blond as to be almost white, a striking contrast to her bright brown eyes.

'And is Spot the Dog the one who's just had puppies?'

'No, he's a boy dog. Boy dogs can't have babies. Nor can boy men.'

'Ah, thank you for telling me that. So what's the name of the lady dog?'

'You don't say "lady dog". You say "bitch".'

Jude stood corrected and exchanged a grin with the au pair. 'So what is the name of the bitch who's had the puppies, Mabel?'

'She's called Spotted Dick.'

'But isn't Dick a boy's name?'

'Yes, it is. So she shouldn't be called Spotted Dick. Daddy chose the name. Daddy's sometimes very silly.' But it was clear from her tone that Mabel approved of her father's silliness. 'Would you like to see Spotted Dick's puppies?'

'Yes, please.'

Jude was led from the hall, which was heavily garlanded with decorations and featured a ceiling-high Christmas tree, into a huge farmhouse kitchen, off which, in a small scullery, the proud mother lay in a nest of rugs. Six small white puppies were feeding vigorously from her.

'They're four boys and two girls,' Mabel announced authoritatively. 'But we can't keep them all. When they're bigger, most of them will go to good homes. And the spots don't show at first, but they will all be spotty.' She clearly took in and retained any information she was given.

After a few moments admiring the puppies, Mabel announced that they could go now. 'Are you feeling better?' asked Jude as they passed through the kitchen. 'Because I hear you've been poorly.'

'Yes, I've had an ear infection.' She produced a perfect parroting of the phrase. 'I have lots of ear infections. I may have to have grommets,' she concluded proudly.

'But you are feeling better?'

'Yes. That's because of the . . .' it was an adult word too far 'antibibotics.'

'Good,' said Jude, trying hard to keep a straight face and not catch Varya's eye. As they arrived in the hall they met Ricky, who was just putting on a Drizabone riding coat.

At the sight of Mabel, he crouched down and welcomed her into his arms. 'Ooh, Daddy,' she squealed, 'can we play a game? Can we play Hiding Things.'

'Sorry, lovely. Daddy's got to go out to lunch, and then he's got meetings in London for a couple of days, but he'll be back on Wednesday afternoon. That's only two days away, gorgeous. We can play Hiding Things then.'

'Is this going to be a "boozy lunch", Daddy?' Another phrase she'd clearly picked up from adult conversation.

'Almost definitely, sweetie.' He stood up, with Mabel still in his arms. 'Oh, hi, Jude. Very good of you to come and see Mother.'

'No problem.'

'I think it's her back. Just stress, probably, you know, after what happened. She's a tough old bird, but I'm afraid she's not as strong as she'd like to think she is. And, as Lola probably told you, she's never trusted doctors.'

'I'll see what I can do for her.'

'Very good of you. I've told her you're coming. If you don't mind, I must be off, but she's in the bedroom right opposite the top of the stairs.'

'I'll find her.'

'Mm . . .' He hesitated for a moment, as if about to say something, but thought better of it. 'I see Henry's fast asleep, Varya.'

'Yes, Ricky. I was just taking him up to put him in his cot when Jude arrived.'

'Oh well, you'd better take him now.' He put Mabel down and planted a kiss on the top of her head. 'You go up and help Varya tuck Henry in.'

'All right, Daddy.' She followed the au pair. Halfway up the stairs she turned and waved at him formally. 'See you later, aggelater.'

'In a while, crocodile,' he responded, his seriousness matching hers. Then he turned to Jude. 'She's right, of course. It will be a boozy lunch.'

'Are you going somewhere local?'

'No, up to London. Drive to Fedborough, get the train to Victoria, boozy lunch today and a few more boozy meetings in the next couple of days. Hope I've sobered up by the time I have to drive back from the station on Wednesday.'

'Will this be the first time you've been to Fedborough Station since you took Polly there on that Sunday?'

'I suppose it will.' He grimaced. 'I hadn't thought of that.'

'Sorry, I shouldn't have mentioned it.'

'No, no, don't worry. Just something I'm going to have to come to terms with.' He still didn't sound like a man whose stepdaughter had been killed only a week before. But, as Lola had said, it was hard to work out what someone as positive as Ricky was actually feeling.

'I hope you don't mind my asking, but have the police got any nearer to explaining what happened?'

'Don't apologize. Everyone's asking the same questions. And

I don't blame them. We want to get to the bottom of it as much as anyone else. But I'm afraid the police haven't told us anything definite yet.'

Jude thought there was no harm in repeating the question she'd put to Piers about the whereabouts of Polly's mobile phone. Ricky said he had no idea. 'I would assume that it was destroyed in the inferno at the shop.'

'Probably, I expect you're right. I was just thinking, if the phone was found, it might explain a few things.'

'How so?'

'There'd be a record on it of the calls and texts Polly had received, maybe even the message that had made her change her mind and go back to Fethering.'

'I suppose that's possible. But since the phone is now probably an unrecognizable melted blob of plastic and metal . . .' He didn't need to finish the sentence. 'Anyway, I must get off to this lunch.' He made a childish stomach-rubbing gesture. 'Lovely lunch. Best meal of the day. Except nobody lunches properly these days. Back in the sixties, early seventies, we'd have these proper lunches every day. Start with two or three Camparis and orange, have at least a bottle of wine per head and round it off with a couple of brandies. Lunch was part of the creative process back then, bloody good ideas came out of lunch. That's why the current state of the music business is so formulaic and anodyne. None of the bloody accountants who run things these days ever have a proper lunch. Sandwiches at the desk, a bottle of fizzy water . . . no surprise no original ideas come out of that. Oh, don't get me started.'

Jude could have observed that she hadn't got him started, that he seemed quite capable of self-starting without any help from anyone. But she didn't. Instead, she asked, 'Ricky, thinking back to that Sunday, the one before the fire, could you—?'

He looked at his watch. 'Got to be on my way or I'll miss the train. Good luck with Mother. Oh, by the way . . .' He stepped closer to Jude and spoke with a new earnestness. 'Don't worry if she says anything odd.'

'What kind of odd?'

'Well, if she starts making accusations about anyone. She's a wonderful woman, in very good nick for her age, but occasionally she does get confused. Usually when she's had a shock of some kind. And what's happened with Polly has really knocked her sideways. As a result, Mother may say some strange things. Just ignore it. As I say, she's confused. I'm sure she'll soon be back on an even keel.'

'But what kind of—?'

'Sorry, Jude, must be off. Just don't take any notice of anything Mother may say about Polly's death.'

CHAPTER TWENTY

Even on her bed of pain Flora Le Bonnier did look rather magnificent. Though the white hair was ruffled from her attempts to get into a comfortable position amidst the piled-up pillows, nothing could spoil the fine bone structure of her face. There remained a theatrical grandeur about her.

Jude had been fully prepared for the old woman's attitude to be imperious, but in fact it came closer to humility. 'It's so good of you to come and interrupt what is, I'm sure, a well-deserved break for you.'

'It's absolutely fine, don't worry about it.' Jude's voice had taken on a soothing tone, already part of the healing process. 'Now, let's just find where the source of the pain is.'

In spite of Flora's assertion 'I can tell you that—it's in the small of my back', Jude ran her hands over the woman's whole body. She didn't touch, didn't even remove the duvet, just let her fingers flow up and down an inch or two above the bedclothes. When she stopped, she said, 'Yes, I can understand where you're feeling the pain, but, in fact, the tension that's causing it is in your shoulders. Our bodies have an amazing ability to refer pain, just as our minds can refer anxiety.'

'What do you mean by that?' asked Flora, intrigued.

'Often when we're worried about something, we refer that worry to something else.' Jude had done enough acting in her life to risk a professional parallel. 'Like when you're going on stage. What you're afraid of is exposing your skills in front of a large audience, but that's very rarely what you worry about in the moments before curtain up. Instead, you worry about throwing up, having an attack of diarrhoea, bringing the most primitive kind of shame on yourself. You worry about the possible symptom, rather than the real cause.'

Flora Le Bonnier was silent for a moment while she assessed this claim. Then she said, 'You're right. And in the same way, when you're really, genuinely ill and you have to give a performance, suddenly you stop feeling pain for the duration of the show, and it all comes crashing in again the moment the curtain's down.'

' "Doctor Theatre",' Jude agreed, knowing that her use of the actor's phrase would increase the bond between them. 'So, right now your body is reacting to the tension in your shoulders by giving you a pain in the small of your back.'

Flora seemed to accept the logic of that. She shifted in the bed and winced. 'More importantly, though, can you do something to relieve that pain?'

'Yes, I think I can. If you get into the least uncomfortable position you can find and just slip your nightie down off your shoulders . . .'

Having been used to the constant attention of dressers in theatres and on film sets all over the world, the old woman showed no coyness about revealing her bony body with its skin the texture of muslin. Jude anointed the shoulders with the smallest amount of oil, and let her fingers flicker gently against the flesh. There was no physical strength required for what she was doing, just immense mental energy and concentration. Jude could sense the heat emanating from the woman's body and focused her mind on melting away the tight knot of pain that was causing it.

After about twenty minutes both women felt the same flood of relaxation as the pain ebbed away. Flora sank back on to the pillows and Jude, totally drained, as ever, by the effort of heal-ing, subsided into a bedside chair. A long, relieved silence stretched between them.

Then Jude said, very gently, 'And of course our bodies and our minds go on playing tricks on us all the time, don't they? Something that's troubling the mind expresses itself in a bodily ailment.'

'Yes. Something which doctors—in the days when I still fool-ishly wasted my money consulting doctors—never seemed to understand. They seemed to regard the body and the mind as totally separate.'

'I think they've got a bit better about that kind of thing over recent years.'

'Huh. Well, I've yet to meet the traditional doctor who could do what you've just done for me.'

'Luck, I think. It seemed to work this morning.'

'Are you suggesting that your healing doesn't always work?'

'I certainly am. Sometimes the magic's just not there. I rarely know the reason . . . some fault in my concentration, scepticism from the patient . . . ? I'll never fully understand it. Still, so long as it works sometimes . . .' There was another silence, then Jude continued, 'Well, then, Flora, what was it in your mind that was so dreadful it could completely immobilize your body?'

'Obviously it's related to Polly's death.' Flora seemed to feel some relief from making that statement. Jude didn't prompt her, she let the old woman take her own time. 'I think for me what happened was the culmination of many years of anxiety.' Another silence, while she gathered more of her thoughts. 'What I'm going to say now may sound rather fanciful, but it is true. As you may know, the Le Bonnier family has a long history in this country dating back to the Norman Conquest.'

'I had heard that, yes.'

'And amongst the inheritances of that long history are certain

145

advantages, of looks, of intelligence, of resilience, of bravery even. But there are also less welcome family characteristics which have been passed on. It may sound melodramatic, but in this context I cannot avoid the expression "Bad Blood". Bad luck, anyway.'

Jude maintained the silence until Flora Le Bonnier felt able to continue. 'I refer to what in earlier days might have gone under the blanket description of "madness". In these supposedly more enlightened days we speak of "manic depression" or what's that new phrase they've come up with? "Bipolar Disorder"? Whatever you call it, I'm referring to a tendency, all too common amongst creative people, towards violent fits of self-loathing, a self-loathing which in its most extreme manifestations can lead to self-destruction.

'There has been a suicidal streak, a flaw, whatever you want to call it, in the Le Bonnier family. Some people have even been melodramatic enough to refer to it as "the Le Bonnier Curse" . . . anyway, it's been mentioned for as far back as their history is recorded. And the fact that those family records are incomplete is due to that very flaw. In the early nineteenth century a certain Giles Le Bonnier not only killed himself but also destroyed the ancestral family home in Yorkshire when he burnt the place to the ground. Invaluable family records were also lost in the inferno. Because of that tragedy a contemporary historian would have trouble piecing together the distant history of the Le Bonnier family.'

Remembering what Carole had discovered through Wikipedia, Jude rather daringly said, 'It has been suggested that the more recent history of the family is also hard to piece together.'

'I don't understand what you mean.'

'I gather that some newspapers have actually questioned whether you have any connection with the Le Bonnier family.'

It was a bold thing to say, and the icy hauteur with which

Flora greeted it would have convinced most people of her aristocratic credentials. 'I don't read newspapers,' she announced imperiously. 'I never have. Journalists have no interest in the truth; they look only for character assassination and sensation.'

'But don't you even read reviews of your performances?'

'No, I never have. What possible benefit can one gain from reading them? A good notice makes you question yourself to such an extent about what it was you did that was worthy of praise that you become self-conscious; while a bad notice depresses you so much that you never want to work again.'

'Ah, right,' said Jude, deciding not to pursue that particular line of enquiry further. 'You were talking about the "Le Bonnier Curse" . . .'

'Yes. The suicidal streak, I am glad to say, does not manifest itself in every bearer of the Le Bonnier name. I myself, though occasionally prone to black moods of despair, have generally managed to keep the demon at bay by concentrating on my professional work. Though I have always worried inordinately about being a transmitter of the family curse, my son Ricky, mercifully, seems untouched by it. I sometimes wonder whether he has ever had a negative thought in his entire life and, of course, his robust self-confidence has enabled him to make the enormous success of that life that he has.

'But his daughter Polly, I fear, was not so fortunate. As a small child, she was adorable, a blithe little lass without a care in the world. But as she got older, the shadows of her inheritance began to close in on her. The depression started to take over her life.'

'Just a minute,' Jude objected. 'You talk about "the shadows of her inheritance", but Polly has absolutely no connection to the Le Bonnier family. She was Ricky's *step*daughter, not his genetic daughter.'

147

'I know that,' Flora replied patiently. 'But I'm talking about "the Curse of the Le Bonniers". It doesn't just affect people who carry the "Bad Blood" of the Le Bonniers in their veins. It affects everyone who becomes involved in the family.'

Jude's credulity was being rather stretched by all this. Though Flora Le Bonnier's narrative carried undoubted dramatic conviction, its contact with logic seemed very tenuous.

'So Polly,' the old actress went on, 'became infected with bad luck as soon as she became part of the Le Bonnier clan. The Curse took its toll on her mother, too. It killed her.'

'Polly's mother died of a drug overdose.'

'That was the means by which she died. What killed her was "the Curse of the Le Bonniers". And then it reached out its tentacles to Polly, crushing her with depression, driving her into madness, and forcing her to follow the awful precedent of Giles Le Bonnier.'

After assimilating this, Jude said quietly, 'So you think Polly started the fire at Gallimaufry?'

'What else is there to think?'

There was obviously quite a lot else to think, but Jude wondered whether there was any point in troubling Flora Le Bonnier with any of it. The old actress had made her mind up about her granddaughter's death and, though the initial shock of her conclusions had hit her hard, she now was on the road to recovery. Until a definitive explanation of what had happened to Polly emerged, was there any necessity to mention the anomaly of the girl's having been shot before the fire at Gallimaufry had been started? Jude decided that, on balance, there wasn't. For the time being, she would allow Flora Le Bonnier to go along with her son's suicide explanation of his stepdaughter's death.

But as to the business about 'the Le Bonnier Curse', Jude didn't believe a word of it. And, in spite of the compelling way Flora had spoken on the subject, Jude wondered whether the old actress really believed a word of it either.

She looked at the large watch strapped to her wrist by a wide ribbon. It was nearly one o'clock. As ever, when she was performing her healing routines, she had lost sense of time. 'I must be off,' she said, rising and looking down at the old woman, whose body lay relaxed on the bed and whose eyelids were drooping. 'I think you'll sleep now. And I think when you wake up, you will feel hungry. Have something to eat then. You need to keep your strength up.'

'I can't thank you enough for what you've done.'

'No problem. Pleased to help.'

Flora Le Bonnier raised herself on her pillows and reached across to the bedside table. 'Ricky'll sort out what we owe you. But, please, take this.'

She picked up a copy of her autobiography, *One Classy Lady*, in two arthritic hands, using them as a seal might use its flippers. 'Sadly, I am unable to inscribe this for you. My hands can't grip a pen these days, which is a source of enormous frustration to me. But if I could write in the book, I would put: "To Jude, an infinitely welcome saviour in time of need, with love, Flora Le Bonnier." '

Jude thanked her and left the room, knowing that by the time she reached the foot of the stairs, the old lady would be asleep.

As ever, when dealing with actors, Jude was aware of the potential for duplicity, and yet by the time she left Fedingham Court House she had become more convinced by Flora's performance. Talk of 'the Le Bonnier Curse' was—to any outside scrutiny—complete nonsense, but the old actress had expressed what she believed to be the truth. In the taxi back to Fethering, however, Jude remembered Ricky warning her against believing Flora's opinions about Polly's death. What had he been afraid his mother would say? Something that might betray him?

Because, in spite of their mutual alibi about tending the wakeful Mabel with her ear infection, Ricky Le Bonnier headed Jude's current list of suspects. And, regrettably, Lola was not far behind him.

CHAPTER TWENTY-ONE

Normally Carole discouraged Gulliver from bringing anything back from Fethering Beach, fearing the introduction of unwanted 'mess' into the sacred precincts of High Tor. But the stick he had found that morning, and to which he'd shown such obvious attachment, seemed a harmless enough trophy. Scoured pale and smooth by long immersion in the sea and about a foot in length, it could have been purpose-built for 'fetching' games. Having scrutinized its every surface for the smallest fleck of tar, Carole allowed him to walk proudly home with the stick held in his jaws, and even to lie down and chew it in his favourite spot beside the Aga. Meanwhile, she busied herself around the house removing any motes of dust that might have dared to settle during the previous twenty-four hours.

The whine that brought her hurrying back to the kitchen was more aggrieved than distressed, but the sight that greeted her was not a pretty one. There seemed to be a disproportionate amount of blood over everything and it took her some time to locate the part of Gulliver's body that was its source. Mopping with tea towels and kitchen roll eventually revealed that the blood was coming out of his mouth, prompting an immediate panic about an internal haemorrhage. This was assuaged when Carole spotted that the wound was actually on his gum, but seeing what had caused it gave rise to renewed anxiety.

The remains of Gulliver's perfect stick lay bloodstained on the floor. His assiduous chewing had split the wood open, revealing the rusty rivets which held it together. It was one of those that had gashed the dog's gum.

Within minutes Gulliver was sitting on a dirty rug on the backseat of Carole's immaculate Renault on an emergency rush to the vet's in Fedborough.

'He'll have to have a general anaesthetic,' said Saira Sherjan.

'Oh dear, is it very serious?'

'No, Carole, it's not very serious. Simply that dogs don't like having their mouths fiddled about with. And while I could say to a human patient, "Now I'm just going to give you an injection of local anaesthetic so that you won't feel a thing when I stitch up your gum", it's difficult to get a dog to take that information on board.'

'Yes, of course, I take your point,' said Carole, feeling rather stupid.

But the vet's grin cheered her. 'Simplest if we keep him in overnight. You could take him home later today, but he'll be a bit woozy and we'd rather have a look at him in the morning, if that's OK with you . . . ?'

'Fine,' said Carole. She prided herself on not being one of those people who got sentimental about animals. But she was still surprised to feel a small pang at the thought of spending a night in High Tor without Gulliver.

'I'll just give him an injection now to calm him down—not that he looks too much as if he needs calming down . . . Would you mind just holding him?'

Carole did as requested and Gulliver, docile as ever, submitted to the injection. Saira led him out of the surgery and returned a moment later. 'By the way, do pass on my thanks to Jude for her party last week. I will get around to sending her a card, but you know how it is over Christmas.'

For a moment Carole was tempted to ask how Saira had

come to meet her neighbour, but she decided that the question would be sheer nosiness. Instead, she enquired, 'Have you been busy over the holiday?'

The vet's fine eyebrows rose ruefully. 'And how! I know human beings tend to have a lot of illness over Christmas, and I can understand that, because for many people it is a very stressful time, though how that anxiety communicates itself to animals I don't know. But it does. It's been emergency call after emergency call for the whole of the last week. And because I don't have kids like most of the partners, guess who tends to get lumbered with most of those emergency calls? Rhetorical question.'

'So you haven't had any problem in keeping to your no-alcohol routine?'

'No, I haven't. I tell you, I've forgotten what alcohol smells like. And I've forgotten what my bed looks like too. So, Carole, tell me all the Fethering gossip.'

'I don't think there is any, really.'

'Oh, come on. You must have heard some dirt. You're one of the Fethering Beach dog-walkers, aren't you?'

'Yes.'

'Well, I know for a fact that dog-walkers constitute one of the most efficient gossip grapevines in the world. Members of the Fethering Beach Dog-walking Mafia exchange all kinds of secrets on their early morning walks.'

Oh dear, thought Carole, something else I'm missing out on. The most she usually exchanged with another dog-walker was a curt 'Fethering nod'. To avoid making herself sound completely anti-social (which, it occurred to her, perhaps she was), she told Saira Sherjan that the only topic of conversation in Fethering was still the tragedy at Gallimaufry. 'But I expect you'll have seen all about that on the news.'

'No. I've forgotten what my television looks like, as well as my bed.' She was unable to prevent a large yawn. 'Sorry, Carole, but, God, it's been insanely busy this last week. And actually, I don't really mind, because I love the animals and I love the work, but . . .' she mimed propping her eyes open—'I'd be quite glad of an uninterrupted night's sleep.'

'I remember,' said Carole, 'you said you were going to be on duty the evening of Jude's party. Was that a busy night?'

The question was random, merely a politeness, but by serendipity it had been exactly the right thing to ask. 'That was one of the worst nights of the lot,' Saira replied. 'At least with Gulliver you'll never have the problem of puppies.'

'No, he's the wrong gender, for a start, and then again whatever gender he might once have had has been surgically removed.' When Carole had decided on having a dog for her new life in Fethering, she'd done everything to ensure the minimum of complications.

'Well, most bitches whelp as easily as shelling peas. They know what to do, they follow their instincts, there's really no need for a vet to be involved until you get to the point of injections for the puppies. But every now and then you get a really complicated birth, and the one I had that Sunday was the most difficult I've ever encountered. I was up all night that night.'

'What, here in the surgery?'

'God, no, you can't move a whelping dog, particularly one who was in as bad a state as this one was.'

'Did she survive?'

'Yes, I'm glad to say she did. As did her six puppies. She's now the proud mother of four dogs and two bitches. All doing well. But it was a long night.'

'Did you have to go far?'

'No, just outside Fedborough. It's . . . You probably know them. Ricky was at Jude's party.'

'Ricky Le Bonnier?'

'Right. It was their Dalmatian, Spotted Dick—which is a bloody stupid name for a bitch.'

'So you were actually at their place—Fedingham Court House—all through that Sunday night.'

'Yes, the call came in from Lola—that's Ricky's wife—around five-thirty. I was there within half an hour, and finally left just before eight the following morning.'

'And was Lola there all the time?'

'Yes. Poor girl, I felt so sorry for her, because she'd got the problem with the dog whelping, and then one of her kids had an ear infection . . . between the two of them, she didn't get a wink of sleep.'

'And you were with her right through?'

'Pretty much, yes.'

'She didn't leave the house, didn't go out anywhere?'

Saira Sherjan was starting to look at Carole rather curiously. Casual conversation seemed to be transforming into interrogation. 'She didn't leave the house all night,' she replied almost brusquely.

No power on earth could have stopped Carole from asking the next question. 'And was Ricky there all the time as well?'

'No,' said Saira Sherjan. 'He went out a few times.'

CHAPTER TWENTY-TWO

'But Saira had no reason to lie,' protested Carole, irritated to find Jude in one of her rare nit-picking devil's advocate moods.

'No reason that we know of.'

'What do you mean by that?'

'Simply that neither of us knows Saira that well. She may have history with the Le Bonniers about which we have no idea. She could have been another of Lola's Cambridge contemporaries . . . or one of Ricky's many flings with younger women.'

'Well, the way she talked about the birth of those Dalmatian puppies, I believed every word she said.'

Jude grinned. 'You're probably right.'

'I'm sure I am.' Carole was feeling irritable. Partly she was hungry. In the panic of Gulliver's injury and the rush to the vet's, she'd missed lunch and the sugar from the buttered teacake she was eating in the sitting room of High Tor hadn't yet got into her system. Also, though she would never have admitted it even to Jude, she was uncomfortably aware of Gulliver's absence. More than that, she was actually worried about him. However minor the operation, he was having a general anaesthetic. And anaesthetics could go wrong with dogs just as they could with humans. She couldn't wait till ten o'clock tomorrow morning when she was due to go back into Fedborough to collect him.

'So . . .' Jude mused, 'if Saira was telling the truth . . .' she caught the look in Carole's eye—'which I'm sure she was, Lola could not possibly have been in the Mercedes 4 × 4 near Fethering Yacht Club around eight o'clock on that Sunday evening.'

'Whereas Ricky very definitely could have been.'

'Yes, but Kath said he was with Lola. So either Kath's lying or—'

'From the account you gave of her conversation, I'd be disinclined to trust a single word she said.'

'Yes, all right, Carole, she *was* sounding extremely loopy, but there seemed to be a logic—albeit a strange one—in most of what she told me.'

'Think back to her exact words, Jude. Did Kath actually mention Lola by name?'

'No, she said she wasn't interested in the names of Ricky's Devil Women.'

Carole snorted. 'And you describe her as someone capable of logic.'

'But she must have been talking about Lola. Kath said she was the latest Devil Woman to seduce Ricky away from her.'

'Well, maybe, given his reputation as a philanderer, he's moved on to another Devil Woman since he's been married to Lola.' Carole sniffed contemptuously; she'd made the suggestion as a bitter joke against the male gender. But when she thought about what she'd said . . . Carole's blue eyes fixed on her friend's brown ones and she came to the realization first. 'Do you think he might have started up an affair with someone else?'

'It's possible, I suppose. But who . . . ?'

'I think I know,' said Carole with quiet confidence.

'Who?'

'Anna.'

'What do you base that on?'

'The way she behaved, things she said when I talked to her on the beach on Boxing Day. I didn't really notice at the time,

Simon Brett

but she kept defending Ricky. She said he had talked to her about Polly. Somehow, the way she said it implied she talked to him quite a lot. And then when her mobile rang, she grabbed it like she was desperate for a call. And when I told her about Polly having been shot, she said that must have got Ricky very preoccupied. She seemed obscurely pleased about that . . . maybe because it explained why he hadn't called her.'

Jude looked sceptical. 'You're making a few rather big leaps of logic, Carole.'

'No, I'm convinced I'm on the right track.'

'I wonder if there's any way of confirming your thesis . . .' Jude tapped her chin as she tried to think of something.

'You don't have a phone number for Kath?' asked Carole suddenly. 'She'd be able to tell us who was with Ricky in the car, wouldn't she?'

'Yes, but I don't have a number for her.'

'Might Ted have one?'

'I doubt it. Can't think of any reason why he should. I suppose I could ask him to alert me again next time she's in the Crown and Anchor, but I think she's mostly there at lunchtime, so there's no chance till tomorrow.'

'What about contacting her at work?'

'Well, I know she does the books for Ayland's, the boatyard. But they would shut up for the full Christmas break, wouldn't they, Carole?'

'I don't know. A lot of people keep their boats there, people who don't like all the snobbery attached to the Fethering Yacht Club, so there must be someone on duty over the holiday.'

Carole found the number of Ayland's and passed the handset to Jude. They were in luck. The call was answered by Kath herself. She seemed unsurprised by the enquiry, and confirmed that the Devil Woman she had seen with Ricky in his car at the relevant time had heavy lipstick and peroxide blond hair. Jude asked whether she knew if the two of them were having an affair, but all Kath would say was, 'She's his latest Devil Woman, the one from the shop.'

As soon as Jude switched the phone off, Carole, who had pieced the conversation together from her end, announced triumphantly, 'I knew it. That Anna is far too glammed up for her age.'

'Are you suggesting that a woman who makes herself look like that deserves everything that's coming to her?' suggested Jude mischievously.

'Yes,' said Carole, unaware of any irony. 'That's exactly what I'm saying.' She rubbed her thin hands up and down against each other. 'Hm . . . well, I know a fairly foolproof way of making sure my path crosses with Anna's.' An expression of irritation crossed her face. 'Or I would if I had Gulliver with me. I'll have to wait till he's back from the vet's.'

'Carole,' said Jude gently, 'it is possible for a person to take a walk on Fethering Beach without a dog, you know.'

'Oh, is it?'

'Yes, I've done it many times myself.'

'Have you really?' said Carole, bemused by the alien concept.

When she got back to Woodside Cottage Jude found a couple of messages on her answering machine from clients who needed her services. In both cases a back problem had recurred, and in both cases Jude felt pretty confident that the relapse had the same cause. The tensions of family Christmases were reflected by increases not only in consultations with lawyers about divorce, but also in stress-related illness.

Knowing the level of neurosis in the two clients who'd left messages, Jude realized that the sessions would be long and arduous, and she would have to expend at least as much energy in listening as she did in healing.

As a result, by the time she made it back to Woodside Cottage she was totally washed out. She cooked a self-indulgent fry-up for supper, had a couple of glasses of wine and contemplated watching something mindless on television before falling into bed. But, as she reached for the remote, she noticed and picked up the copy of *One Classy Lady* that Flora Le Bonnier had given her.

Jude looked first at the title page. No ghost writer was acknowledged, which possibly (though by no means definitely) meant that Flora had written the book herself.

She flicked through the first chapter, which made much of Flora's connection with the aristocratic Le Bonnier family. Without positively stating that she was the illegitimate daughter of the Graham Le Bonnier who was killed in the Western Desert, the implication was definitely there. It was also implied that Flora had been unaware of her ancestry during her girlhood. Only when she joined the Rank Charm School did she become interested in her family background, and it was then that her connection with the Le Bonniers was proved. Though what the nature of that proof was, the autobiography did not specify.

Jude moved on to the pages of photographs, of which, given the range of their subject's career, there were many. Jude was struck, as Carole had been when watching *Her Wicked Heart,* by how stunningly beautiful Flora Le Bonnier had been in her prime. Most of the photographs were either posed studio portraits, official production publicity shots or movie stills. Almost none of them gave any insight into Flora Le Bonnier's private life.

There was just one, showing her with a two-year-old Ricky and that, too, was a highly professional piece of work in black and white, mother and child artfully displayed on a metal bench in some lavish garden. That was it; nothing else of a personal nature. There were no family album snaps, none which might show their subject in an unguarded moment. Having spent the morning with Flora, Jude concluded that the actress's life had contained very few unguarded moments.

Moving to the index, she found a mere half-dozen references to 'Ricky'. None to 'Richard', so maybe the child had been christened with the shortened name, or maybe he had just always been called that. The mentions of him in the book were all similar in tone. Ricky was 'a delightful child', 'the greatest joy that life had brought me', 'a prodigiously talented musician'. Like the photograph in the garden, there was something posed and sanitized about the references.

Only on one occasion did what could have been genuine emotion break through the carefully written text. Flora Le Bonnier was about to begin a six-month tour to Australia, playing Mrs Erlynne in *Lady Windermere's Fan*. She wrote:

The thought of leaving three-year-old Ricky for such a long time stabbed through my heart like a sliver of ice. No amount of public adulation from antipodean audiences could make up for the sense of bleak bereavement I felt at that moment.

It sounded heartfelt, but the extravagance of the language still made Jude ambivalent about the sincerity of the sentiments expressed.

She tried to analyse what she knew about the relationship between Ricky and his mother. The only time she had seen them together, at her open house, Flora had seemed almost to worship her son. But then, when she'd talked to Kath, she'd been told: 'Ricky was looked after by his aunt, because his mother was always off acting all over the world.' Given the fact that Ricky and Kath had gone to the same village school, that aunt must have lived near to Fethering. Jude wondered idly whether she'd been Flora's sister. Or indeed whether she was

161

still alive. And, if so, where?

She scoured the index and flicked through the text, but could find no reference in *One Classy Lady* to Polly Le Bonnier. There was no mention of any of Ricky's marriages. All Jude could find in the book which related to his adult career was the one sentence: 'My son's artistic talents developed in a different way from my own, and he made a huge success developing new talents in the heady "pop music" scene of the late sixties and early seventies.'

More interesting, from Jude's point of view, was the fact that there was no mention at all of who Ricky's father had been. No reference, so far as a fairly exhaustive flick through the pages of *One Classy Lady* could establish, to any husbands or lovers in the life of Flora Le Bonnier.

CHAPTER TWENTY-THREE

Carole Seddon woke early the following morning, denying to herself that she was feeling the absence of Gulliver from his usual base in front of the Aga. She washed and dressed briskly, determined to put into action her revolutionary plan of taking a walk on Fethering Beach without the excuse of a dog.

The timing was, of course, pivotal and, being Carole, she reached the Promenade at seven-twenty, even though she knew there was no chance of Anna appearing with her Black-Watch-clad Westie until half past. Risking the ever-present danger of looking like a sad old pensioner, Carole sat in one of the sea-front shelters and waited.

It was a cold day, the weather seeming to reflect the general feeling that everyone had had enough of Christmas jollity, and couldn't wait to get back to the normality of the forthcoming year.

Seven-thirty came and went, and there was no sign of Anna or her dog. Carole recognized that not everyone was such a fetishist about punctuality as she was and gave the woman the benefit of the doubt. She sat waiting in the shelter, willing herself not to look lonely and decrepit, wishing she had brought *The Times* crossword with her, both to while away the time and also to give the illusion of purpose.

She let eight o'clock pass, but by a quarter past reconciled herself to the fact that she wasn't going to see Anna that morning. Her first thought was that maybe the woman realized she and Jude were on to her and had taken evasive action, but she soon realized what a ridiculous idea that was. Anna was probably unaware of any interest they might have in her and had changed her morning routine for reasons that they could not begin to guess at.

Carole stood up and stretched her frozen limbs, about to go straight back to High Tor. It would soon be time to get in the Renault and drive to Fedborough. The thought of having Gulliver back brought her a disproportionally warm glow which she tried unsuccessfully to suppress.

But as she started back along the Promenade, she saw coming towards her a woman with a dog. Not Anna, the dog-walker she had been hoping to meet, but a dog-walker nonetheless. The words of Saira Sherjan came back to her. 'I know for a fact that dog-walkers constitute one of the most efficient gossip grapevines in the world. Members of the Fethering Beach Dog-walking Mafia exchange all kinds of secrets on their early morning walks.' Carole changed direction and advanced towards the woman.

Her luck was in. The dog the woman was walking—and had just let off the lead—was a Labrador. Younger than Gulliver, but definitely a Labrador. Conversational opening gambits did not come better gift-wrapped than this.

'Good morning. She's a lovely girl, isn't she?'

Nothing could go wrong that morning—Carole had got the gender right. 'Yes, she's adorable,' said the woman. 'But where's yours?'

So much for Carole's image of herself surrounded in a carapace of anonymity. Someone had noticed that she was in the habit of taking Gulliver on to Fethering Beach for a walk every day for the last God-knew-how-many years. Now she looked at the woman, Carole realized that they had passed most mornings with no more than a 'Fethering nod'.

'Oh, I'm afraid he's had an accident.' And with no difficulty at all, Carole found herself relating Gulliver's encounter with the rusty staple, and his hasty removal to the vet's in Fedborough.

'Saira looked after him, did she? Well, he's in good hands there. She's easily the most sympathetic in that surgery. She sorted out Kerry when she had a growth on her leg.'

'My name's Carole Seddon, by the way.'

'Oh, yes, I know.' Another proof that it was impossible to be anonymous in a village the size of Fethering.

'But I'm afraid I don't know yours.'

'Ruby. Ruby Tallis. Me and my husband Derek live up on Sea Road.'

'Oh, I'm in the High Street.'

'Yes. High Tor, isn't it?'

To Carole's surprise, the fact that everything about her seemed to be public property did not feel like an invasion of privacy. On the contrary, it felt rather comforting, almost as though she were something she never thought she would be— 'part of the community'. In no time at all, she and Ruby were having quite a voluble conversation about canine ailments and the vagaries of vets. Neither woman suggested sitting down. While Kerry the Labrador snuffled amongst the smells of the shoreline, they just stood and chatted. Yes, chatted. Carole Seddon was actually *chatting*.

Moving the subject on from vets to recent events at Gallimaufry required no effort at all. Like everyone else in Fethering, Ruby Tallis had plenty of views and opinions about the death of Polly Le Bonnier. Or it might be more accurate to say that her husband Derek had plenty of views and opinions about the death of Polly Le Bonnier, and Ruby just parroted them.

'Derek reckons it was a burglary gone wrong.'

'Oh, does he?'

'Yes, he reckons it was probably a drug addict, keen to get some money for his next fix, and the girl surprised him in the shop and he shot her and then set the place on fire to cover his tracks.'

'But why would Polly have gone there?'

Clearly this was not a subject on which Derek had an opinion. His wife reasserted that he thought the killing had been done by a drug addict, 'keen to get some money for his next fix'. She seemed to relish saying the phrase.

'Do you know the Le Bonniers?' asked Carole.

No, neither Ruby nor Derek actually knew the family, but that didn't stop her husband from having opinions about them. 'Derek wouldn't be surprised if that Ricky didn't have something to do with it too.'

'To do with the murder?'

'Probably not that. But something to do with the burglary.'

'What sort of something?'

Ruby Tallis looked around slyly, as if afraid of being overheard in the empty expanses of Fethering Beach. Then, touching a gloved finger to her nose, she whispered, 'Drugs.'

'Oh?'

'That Ricky Le Bonnier works in pop music,' she confided, 'and Derek says that everyone who works in pop music has a connection to drugs. Hard drugs.' She nodded sagely to emphasize the point.

'So, even if he had taken drugs, what would Ricky Le Bonnier's connection be to the burglary at his shop?'

'Ah well, you see, Derek has this theory . . . he thinks the drug addict who broke into the shop was someone Ricky Le Bonnier knew . . . someone he used to work with in a pop group, and they used to take drugs together. Derek thinks the man was probably a groupie.' Seeing Carole's curious expression, Ruby corrected herself. 'A *roadie*. That's what Derek thinks. And he thinks that Ricky Le Bonnier may have set up this roadie to rob the shop and set fire to it, because it was doing bad business and he wanted to claim on the insurance.'

At last, a part of the Tallis theory which Carole and Jude had also considered.

'Anyway, that's what Derek thinks, and he thinks it was just bad luck that Ricky Le Bonnier's daughter was in the shop when the roadie broke in—otherwise she'd still be alive. And Derek reckons Ricky Le Bonnier must be feeling absolutely terrible, because, in a way, it was his fault that his daughter got killed.'

Well . . . Carole couldn't have asked for a better demonstration of Saira Sherjan's concept of the gossip grapevine amongst dog-walkers. She wondered whether everything that happened in Fethering was subjected to the same conjectural analysis—and she rather feared that it might be. What theories had been propounded on Fethering Beach about herself and Jude she didn't dare to contemplate. No doubt her Home Office background had been transmogrified into working as a spy in the Eastern Bloc, Jude's theatrical past had converted her into a *Playboy* centrefold, and the two of them were universally recognized as Fethering's premier lesbian couple. Carole would have found the idea funny if she hadn't suspected that comparable fanciful elaborations were actually current in the village.

She felt a bit ungenerous when she asked, 'And does Derek have any proof to back up his theories?'

'Not proof as such,' Ruby confided knowingly, 'but Derek does have a very profound understanding of human nature.'

Yes, I bet he does, thought Carole. 'And you yourself didn't see anything odd, did you?'

'Odd? When?'

'Well, I was just thinking that you walk Kerry every morning along the beach, don't you?' Ruby admitted that she did. 'So you would have walked along here the morning after the fire at Gallimaufry . . . ?'

'Certainly. There were still flames at the back of the building when I walked Kerry that morning.'

'But you didn't see anything or anyone doing anything odd?'

'What, like a drug addict running from the building with a gun and throwing it into the sea—something like that?'

'Yes,' said Carole eagerly.

'No,' Ruby replied. 'I didn't see anything like that.'

'And have you asked other people in—' Carole just stopped herself from saying 'the dog-walking Mafia'—'any other dog-walkers . . . you know, if they saw anything unusual?'

'Oh yes. I've talked about it with lots of people, and they've all put in their two penn'orth.' The woman raised a sceptical eyebrow. 'Mind you, some of the theories they put forward were pretty far-fetched.'

And your Derek's *isn't?* thought Carole. 'But none of them', she asked, 'had any proof either . . . you know, something they might have seen to back up their far-fetched theories?'

'No. Well, except for Old Garge. And it's never wise to believe anything Old Garge tells you.'

'Old Garge? I'm not sure that I know who you mean.'

'Of course you do. Old Garge with the Jack Russell. The original Fethering beachcomber.'

These details were enough for Carole to know whom Ruby meant. She had frequently seen an old boy who seemed to live on Fethering Beach and was unfailingly accompanied by a Jack Russell. He had grubby white whiskers and hair, on top of which he always wore a faded peaked cap which must once have been blue. Habitually dressed in a canvas coat and torn jeans, his feet were encased in dilapidated trainers which, even at the distance Carole normally kept from him, she felt sure smelt disgusting.

Gulliver and the Jack Russell had had a few barking matches, but Carole's instinct was always to divert her route away from the man. She found something about him unsettling, and reacted as she might to a person talking to themselves in the street. Still, she now had a name for him: Old Garge.

Ruby observed her looking around the expanse of beach and said, 'I haven't seen him the last couple of days. Maybe there's somewhere he goes at Christmas. Be pretty miserable if he just stayed here in his hut.'

'Are you saying that Old Garge actually lives here on the beach?'

'Oh, yes. Most of the time. He watches everything. Old Garge is the eyes and ears of Fethering Beach.'

Carole felt a little surge of excitement. 'And where does he actually live?'

Ruby Tallis gestured across to the mouth of the Fether, where there were a few fishermen's sheds and tumbledown beach huts. 'Over there. Old Garge's is the one called "Pequod", though goodness knows what that means.' Clearly she had never read *Moby Dick*.

Carole looked at her watch and announced, 'I must be getting back. Got to pick poor old Gulliver up.'

'Of course. Hope he's all right.'

'I'm sure he will be. As you say, he couldn't be in better hands than Saira's.'

'Well, nice to talk to you, Carole. See you again, no doubt.'

In some moods Carole would have been deterred by this suggestion. Could she no longer restrict her morning meetings with Ruby Tallis to a 'Fethering nod'? Was she bound to engage in daily conversation and listen to Derek's opinions for the rest of her life?

But on this occasion she was too excited by having become a fully signed-up member of the 'dog-walking Mafia' to indulge such anxieties. After a brief moment of confusion when she looked around for Gulliver, Carole walked back along the Promenade towards Fethering. But she went the long way round, the way that took her past the huts at the mouth of the Fether.

Pequod was the most dilapidated of all of them. It smelt of brine and tar, and its paint had long been stripped away by salty winds.

On a rusty ring fixed to the door hung a large rusty padlock. The door was closed but not locked. Strains of classical music could be heard from inside. Plucking up the new courage given her by being a member of the 'dog-walking Mafia', Carole knocked on the door. She felt more than ready to meet 'the eyes and ears of Fethering Beach'.

CHAPTER TWENTY-FOUR

'Come in,' said a voice, old but remarkably resonant.

Mentally holding her nose in anticipation of squalor, Carole stepped into Pequod. The first surprise was the cosy warmth that hit her. The second was the lack of unpleasant smells; only a slight resinous aroma from logs on a wood-burning stove and the smoky tang from oil lamps. Their friendly light flickered on the spines of the books with which the whole space seemed to be walled.

In the centre of it Old Garge, dressed in usual down-at-heel style, sat in a subsiding leather armchair. On a small table beside him stood a mug of coffee and, facedown, a paperback book of John Clare's poetry. The piece of classical music ended and was followed by speech, suggesting that his portable was tuned to Radio 3. Curled up on a rug at the man's feet sat his Jack Russell, ears pricked at the arrival of a newcomer, but otherwise welcoming.

'So . . .' said Old Garge. 'Carole Seddon. And what brings you here?'

'How do you know my name?'

'Most people in Fethering know most people's names, even if they never speak to each other. I'm afraid the cloak of invisibility in which you imagine you walk around just isn't very efficient. Where's Gulliver? You've usually got Gulliver with you.'

'He's at the vet's.'

'Nothing serious, I hope.'

171

'Just a couple of stitches in his gums. I'm picking him up later.'

Remembering his manners, Old Garge gestured to an elderly campaign chair. 'Please. Would you like some coffee?'

Carole was suddenly struck by the thought that there was nothing she would like more. Standing on the beach and talking to Ruby Tallis had chilled her to the marrow. She accepted the offer and Old Garge moved across to the stove on which an enamel coffeepot stood. He poured a cup of black for her, as requested, and replenished his own. Then, when they were both sitting with drinks in hand, he smiled at her and said, 'No doubt it was Ruby Tallis who sent you across here?'

'Yes, it was. How do you know all this?'

'That bit I knew just by using my eyes.' He gestured to a small window which Carole had not noticed before, but which she could see offered a perfect view of the Promenade and most of the beach.

She took a sip of her drink. Contrary to expectations, it was excellent coffee. In fact, everything about Old Garge seemed contrary to her expectations. Because of his appearance, Carole had written him off as some kind of tramp, unwholesome and probably not right in the head. As they talked, she discovered he was intelligent, even cultured.

She couldn't curb her curiosity about him, and asked whether the hut was his permanent home.

'I have a room rented up in Downside for post and official stuff, but mostly I'm here.'

Carole looked around the space. 'I didn't think the authorities allowed anyone to live permanently in a beach hut.'

'You're absolutely right, they don't. Any number of Health and Safety reasons why nobody's allowed to live in one.'

'But—'

'But I'm good at finding out things. I've got a friend who

works for the Fether District Council. He tips me off when there's an inspection due, with the result that when the inspectors arrive, I'm in my rented room. I just pop in here for the odd hour, that's all, so far as the authorities are concerned.'

Carole was surprised how snug and relaxed she felt in Old Garge's company. He seemed to have his life sorted. Covertly, as she took a sip of coffee, she scrutinized him. In spite of its whiskery roughness, his face was rather distinguished and must once have been handsome. And though his clothes were torn and discoloured, they seemed perfectly clean. He looked not so much like a tramp as like someone playing the part of a tramp. He also seemed to be aware of—and rather amused by—her scrutiny.

'Seen everything you want to see?' he asked, and she blushed furiously. 'Oh, don't worry. I don't mind people looking at me. It's quite rare these days. Most of them avert their eyes when they walk past me, or change direction to avoid walking past me. Best I usually get is a Fethering nod.'

Carole knew he was teasing her, by giving such an exact description of her own behaviour.

'Doesn't worry me,' said Old Garge. 'There're plenty of people who do talk to me, so I keep my gossip reserves well stocked up. So what was Ruby Tallis telling you about this morning? Or rather, which of her husband Derek's opinions was she telling you about this morning?'

'We talked a bit about dogs.'

'And . . . ?'

'And . . . local events.'

'Local events, right.' He nodded, still just slightly making fun of her. 'And which local events were you talking about?'

'Oh, you know, Christmas and—'

'I wouldn't have described Christmas as a local event. I would have said it was very much an international event.'

173

'Yes, well, but how people spend their individual Christmases, that's of local interest.'

'And how did you spend yours, Carole?'

She was glad to be able to have a normal-sounding answer to give him. 'My son and daughter-in-law and granddaughter came down for lunch on Christmas Day.'

'Very nice too.' He paused for a ruminative sip of coffee. 'So you didn't spend Christmas Day on your own, like you have the last few?'

Carole turned her face away, unwilling to meet his gaze. The 'eyes and ears of Fethering Beach' were proving far too well at-tuned for her taste. Without looking at Old Garge, she asked, 'And how did you spend yours?'

'None of my days are very different from each other. Christmas Day I spent here, just like usual. Walked on the beach with Petrarch—that's the dog—doing my usual "Care in the Community" impression, listened to Radio 3, read some poetry. Do you know, quite often I read poetry out loud in here. No problem this time of year. This time of year I can read away all through the night, if I want to—sleep not being something I'm very good at these days. In the summer, though, when I've got the doors open and I'm reading poetry, I do get some funny looks. Parents putting protective arms round children, hurrying them away.' He seemed embarrassed for a moment, as though an unwanted memory had invaded his mind, before hurrying on, 'They seem to feel that there's something unnatural about poetry being read aloud. Makes them think I'm some kind of weirdo.'

'It sounds as if you don't mind them getting that impression.'

'Well,' he said, rubbing a scaly hand through his white whiskers, 'never does any harm to have a bit of mystique, does it?'

'What did you do,' asked Carole boldly, 'before you started

on your current way of life?'

'What makes you think I haven't always done this?'

'Something in your manner.'

'Ah, but what?'

'That I can't currently say.'

The man turned an intense gaze on her. Through the layers of wrinkles around them, his eyes were a pale blue, not unlike her own. He seemed to be assessing whether or not to give her the information she had asked for. After a moment, Old Garge decided in Carole's favour.

'I used to be an actor,' he said. 'In the view of many people, I might still be an actor.'

'Playing the part of Old Garge?'

'Exactly. How very perceptive of you. A role which suits me, possibly the most comfortable piece of casting I've ever encountered. Old Garge fits me like a glove.' He gave her another piercing look. 'Do you have anything to do with "the business"?'

Carole felt very proud that she recognized the expression from conversations with Gaby. 'My daughter-in-law is a theatrical agent. Well, that is, she was, until she had her baby. I dare say she'll go back to it soon.' And yet Carole couldn't really see that happening in the near future. Gaby seemed so happy and fulfilled with Lily that more babies and full-time motherhood might well keep her away from the agency for quite a while. To her surprise, Carole found the prospect appealing.

'So when,' she went on, 'did you give up acting?'

'I thought we'd just established that I haven't given it up.'

'When did you give up being paid for acting?'

'A better question, but one which I fear I find rather difficult to answer. It's not so much that I gave up acting as that acting gave up me. Calls from my agent dwindled, reflecting a comparable dwindling in enquiries for my professional services.

Then I received the news that my agent had died, and I was faced with the question of whether I should endeavour to get a replacement or not. I fairly quickly decided there wasn't much point. So I moved out of London and down here, to an area which I have known and loved since my childhood. That would be . . . some three years ago . . . probably more. I've reached the age where, in discussions of the past, I have to double the number I first thought of. And it may have been some years before that when I last had a professional booking. I still receive occasional minuscule repeat fees for long-dead television series being sold to Mongolian cable networks, but the last occasion when I received a fee for a current project is lost in the mists of time.'

'Presumably you didn't act under the name of "Old Garge"?'

'No, that would have been a trifle fanciful, wouldn't it? Going way beyond the demands of having a mystique.' He rose from his seat, reached up to exactly the right spot in his shelves, and pulled down a fat book jacketed in two shades of green. '*Spotlight*,' he announced. 'The actors' directory. This volume dates from 1974, which is perhaps the nearest my career experienced to a "heyday".'

From much usage, the book opened immediately at a page revealing the photographs and agent details of four actors. 'I graced the "Leading Man" section in those days. Later I was downgraded to "Character".'

He held the book across to Carole. In spite of the changes wrought by time, she had no difficulty in identifying the right actor. With dark hair and eyebrows, a long, rather delicate face, Old Garge was still recognizable. Very good-looking in a dated, matinee idol way. The name beneath the photograph was 'Rupert Sonning'.

Its owner looked fondly at the image. 'Yes, me just about "on the turn," I would say. Even then the photograph was a good seven years younger than I was. By that time the waist had thickened, the face spread, the veins in the nose become more visible. No longer in the market for romantic leads, moving towards seedy aristocrats, venal politicians and child molesters.' The thought seemed to cause him pain.

Remembering what she had thought after seeing Flora Le Bonnier in *Her Wicked Heart,* Carole couldn't stop herself from asking, 'Is it as depressing for a man to lose his looks as it is a woman?'

Old Garge—or Rupert Sonning—burst into laughter. 'Full marks for tact, Carole. I know you used to be a civil servant, I think I can now rule out the possibility that you worked in the Diplomatic Service.'

'I'm sorry.' She was flustered both by her social gaffe and also again by his detailed knowledge of her life story.

'Don't worry, I've always favoured the direct approach myself. And the answer to your question is probably yes. In my young days my face was—literally—my fortune. "You want a handsome young devil—call for Rupert Sonning!" Oh yes, I was put through the Rank Charm School, learned how to deal with the press, not to tell them anything except the stories the publicity department had dreamed up for me. Then I did a few of those Gainsborough costume dramas, had a very nice time, thank you very much. And, looking like I did, I was also rather successful as a ladies' man.' He chuckled, but there was sadness in the expression with which he looked again at his *Spotlight* photograph. 'Still, those times are gone, and I suppose life now has other compensations. Though, inevitably . . . lesser compensations . . .'

There was a silence, then Carole asked, 'In your acting career, did your path ever cross with that of Flora Le Bonnier?'

He grinned. 'Ah, the lovely Flora. Lady Muck herself. Oh yes, our paths crossed. And how.' He chuckled at some fond reminiscence.

'Have you seen her recently?'

A hint of caution came into his pale blue eyes. 'Why should I have done?'

'She spent Christmas not far away from here. Near Fedborough. With her son and family.'

'Ah, did she?'

Carole couldn't tell if this was news to him, but she rather thought it wasn't. For the first time in their conversation Old Garge had become cagey. But, she reasoned, there was no way he couldn't know the Le Bonnier connection with Fethering. If he could summon up so many details of her own life—even embarrassing ones about how she'd spent recent Christmases—he must have been aware of Gallimaufry's opening and of Lola's connection to Flora Le Bonnier.

'I think you know she did,' said Carole firmly.

The actor spread his hands wide to indicate the end of his small subterfuge. 'Yes, all right, I knew that.'

'So have you seen Flora recently? In the last few days?'

'You're very persistent, Carole, aren't you?'

'I can be.'

'Hm.' He thought about this. 'I don't think I ever had that quality. Of being persistent. Something lacking in my genetic make-up. Perhaps, had I been more persistent, I might have sustained a more enduring career as an actor.' He shrugged. 'Still, one cannot change one's nature, can one?'

'One can try.'

He considered this assertion, then asked, 'Have you tried, Carole? Have you tried to change your nature?'

'At times, yes.'

'Didn't work, did it?'

Carole would have liked to challenge that, but came to the rueful realization that he was probably right. Time to move back into investigative mode. 'Old Garge . . . I feel a fool calling you Old Garge. As if I'm in some third-rate stage play.'

'But you are.' The old man gestured around the hut. 'Look, we're on the set of a third-rate stage play.'

'Well, I'd rather call you Rupert, if that's all right with you?'

He inclined his head graciously. 'I would be honoured.'

'Rupert, you still haven't answered my question about whether you've seen Flora Le Bonnier recently.'

'True, I haven't.' He was silent for a moment, teasing her. 'But I will answer it now. No. It's years since I've seen Flora.'

'Though at one stage you did see quite a lot of her?'

'We worked together on a few films, just after the war, in the late forties.'

'But was your relationship . . .'

He grinned, as he repeated firmly, 'We worked together on a few films, just after the war, in the late forties. Inevitably, we saw a lot of each other.'

It was the practised 'We are just good friends' answer from someone who knew a bit about talking to the press. He did, however, manage to incorporate into it the practised cheeky implication that they might have been more than good friends. Carole recognized she wasn't going to get anything else out of him on the subject, so she changed tack. 'Do you know that Ruby Tallis describes you as "the eyes and ears of Fethering Beach"?'

'I wasn't actually aware of that, but it doesn't surprise me.'

'Well, having talked to you, I'd say it was a pretty accurate description.' He nodded acknowledgement of the compliment. 'So I would have thought you know more than anyone else about what happened the night Gallimaufry burnt down.'

' "More than anyone else"? I don't think you can be taking account of the sterling efforts of the official investigators into the incident, the British police. For the sake of our country's security, I would like to believe that they know more about what happened than I do.'

'Yes, maybe, but . . . Just a minute, have the police actually questioned you?'

'We did have a brief conversation. Up in my room in Downside.'

'Why not here?'

'As I may have indicated, my presence here may not conform to every last detail of certain regulations. I wouldn't wish to add to the constabulary's not inconsiderable workload by forcing them to investigate my circumstances. So I thought it would save trouble all round were I to tell them I had spent very little time here over the Christmas period.'

'So you said you weren't here the night Gallimaufry burnt down?'

'That was exactly what I told them, yes. They had no reason to disbelieve me.'

'Whereas, in actual fact, you were here?'

'You're a woman of very acute perception, Carole.'

She knew she was being sent up, but was too excited to let it worry her. 'Why did you lie to the police?'

Her question seemed to pain him. 'It has been my experience that it is always wise to minimize one's contact with them.'

Had she been less preoccupied by the details of Gallimaufry's incineration, Carole might have enquired into the reasons behind his reply, but instead, breathlessly, she asked, 'Did you see anything that night, Rupert?'

He gestured once again towards the window, through which the blackened ruins of Gallimaufry were clearly visible. 'Hard to miss a major conflagration at this distance.'

'So what did you see?'

He was silent and looked at her. The shrewdness in his eyes was so penetrating she once again had to turn away. 'Why should I tell you, Carole?'

'You must have told other people. Surely it's impossible to talk to any of the Fethering Beach Dog-walking Mafia without the subject coming up?'

'The subject certainly comes up and I'm certainly prepared to listen to other people's theories about it—mostly the theories of Derek Tallis, it has to be said—but I haven't as yet contributed much of my own to the debate.'

'But there must have been things you saw that night.'

'I'm not denying it. All I'm saying is that I'm very selective about who I'm prepared to share that information with.' Their eyes locked. Yet again it was Carole who looked away first.

'Why are you so selective?' she asked meekly.

'Because the stakes are quite high, aren't they? When there might be a murder involved. I mean, say I have information that could send someone down for life?'

Carole couldn't stop herself from asking, 'Have you?'

'Let's keep our discussion in the world of hypothesis for the moment, shall we? But say I did have such information. Whether I share it or not raises rather a substantial moral dilemma.'

'There's really no dilemma. Relevant information should be passed on to the investigating authorities,' said Carole with the pious rectitude of someone who'd spent all her working life in the Home Office.

'No, I'm sorry, I don't hold with moral absolutes like that. The question I ask myself is: "Who's likely to be harmed by my passing on this information?" Is it someone who I think deserves to suffer, or is it someone for whom I feel sympathy?'

'You mean someone who you feel you should protect?'

'Yes, Carole, exactly. That is the question that is currently exercising my mind—and my conscience, and—'

'But if you actually saw—'

'*And*', he continued firmly, 'I haven't yet decided whether my

181

instinct to protect someone is stronger than the call of my civic duty.'

'But can't you at least tell me *who* you're feeling the instinct to protect?'

'Oh, Carole . . .' He shook his head pityingly. 'You'll have to do better than that. Were I to tell you the name of the person who might need protection, you'd know almost the whole story, wouldn't you?'

'Yes, but a young woman has died here and everyone has a moral duty to—'

Her appeal was interrupted by a brisk rapping on the hut door. As they looked towards it, Piers Duncton entered, the habitual cigarette dangling from the corner of his mouth. He reacted with a narrowing of the eyes to Carole's presence, but his words were for the benefit of Old Garge—or maybe Rupert Sonning.

'I've just come from Lola's,' he said. 'The police are on their way to interview you.'

CHAPTER TWENTY-FIVE

As she drove to the vet's, Carole tried to find explanations for what had happened at the beach hut after Piers's arrival. She had been unceremoniously sent on her way, and, when she left, the young man was also chivvying Old Garge to gather up his belongings and leave. The actor raised no objections, evidently as keen as Piers was that he should get out of the place. Presumably the reason for his departure was to avoid further interrogation from the police. And he had dropped that clue about trying to minimize his contact with the constabulary—was that because he'd had uncomfortable experiences with them in the past? Everything that had happened in Pequod again raised the intriguing questions of how much Old Garge knew and whom he was trying to protect. Carole, having come so close to hearing the actor's account of Gallimaufry's burning-down, felt acutely frustrated at being denied her breakthrough on the case.

She didn't see Saira Sherjan at the vet's. Gulliver was brought out by one of the green-clad nurses while Carole paid the receptionist the usual eye-watering bill. The dog seemed none the worse for his hospitalization, and greeted his mistress with heart-warming enthusiasm. She was advised that he should have no adverse reactions to the surgery, but she should try for a week to keep him from eating dried food and chewing bones or sticks, to give the gum a chance to heal.

Gulliver seemed very pleased to be back in High Tor and wolfed down the plate of (soft) dog meat that Carole put in front of him. He then sat up, his tail thumping on the floor, with an expectant look which she knew well. The dog was telling her that he hadn't had a decent walk in the last twenty-four hours, and she had a moral duty to rectify that state of affairs as soon as possible.

Carole was sorry to disappoint him, but telling Jude about her morning's encounters was a more pressing priority. So pressing that she even went round to Woodside Cottage without ringing first to say she was coming.

Jude tapped her chin thoughtfully. 'I wonder . . .'

'What?'

'Well, it's fanciful . . . and it would probably be too neat to have happened in real life . . . but wouldn't it be great if we found out that Rupert Sonning was Ricky Le Bonnier's father?'

'He admitted that he and Flora had worked together,' said Carole cautiously.

'Yes, though as we well know, women don't have babies by all the men they work with. Even in the theatre, where a certain laxity of moral standards has always been the norm. But the timing could be about right.' And Jude told Carole about the relevant movie history she had read in *One Classy Lady*. 'You say Old Garge mentioned being in some Gainsborough costume movies after the war. Late nineteen-forties—that'd be about the time Ricky was born. Hm . . . Pity you didn't ask whether he and Flora had ever been an item.'

'I virtually did, though not at the time realizing quite how important the question might be. I wasn't contemplating the possibility that he might be Ricky's father. Anyway, the only answer I got from him on the subject was a diplomatic one, which admitted nothing.'

'Oh, it'd probably be too much of a coincidence.' Jude sounded almost dispirited. 'But it all comes back to Fethering, somehow. Ricky was brought up around here by an aunt. He went to school here, which is where he met Kath. And now he comes back to live near here. Then you say Old Garge also has long-term connections with the place. What about Flora? She must have come here sometimes to visit Ricky as a child. And if the aunt who looked after him was her sister . . .'

'Have we any means of checking up on this aunt, Jude? Whether she's still alive, even?'

'Well, I doubt if we'd get anything out of Flora. The person who definitely would know is Ricky himself. But he's in London. I heard that when I was over at Fedingham Court House yesterday. Not back till tomorrow. I suppose that Lola might know, but . . .' She snapped her fingers. 'Oh, just a minute, of course! Kath! She would have known about his aunt.'

Jude rang through to Ayland's. Again it was Kath who answered the phone, and again she seemed unsurprised by being questioned about Ricky. She remembered instantly. 'His Auntie Vi. That's what she was called—Auntie Vi.'

'And is she still here in Fethering?'

'Oh no. She's long dead now. Even when she came to our wedding, she was quite doddery. She went into a home soon after, and I don't think she lasted there very long.'

A new thought came to Jude. 'Was Flora Le Bonnier at your wedding? Surely she would have been there to see her son married?'

'No, she couldn't come. Making a film somewhere, I think she was. But she sent us a very generous present. A silver tea set. I've still got that at home.'

'Going back to Auntie Vi . . . you knew her, didn't you?'

'Oh yes. I often used to go back to her place after school. With Ricky. For tea.'

'And do you know what relation she was to him? Was she Flora Le Bonnier's sister?'

'I don't think she was a relation.'

'But he called her Auntie Vi.'

'That's what she liked to be called. By all the kids. She looked after other kids, you see, as well as Ricky.'

'What, she was a kind of paid child minder?'

'More a foster parent, I think you'd call it. All the kids loved her.'

Jude's mind was having difficulty keeping track of the new information, and the new thoughts that led from it. 'Did Ricky talk much about his mother when you knew him?'

'No. Very little.'

'Or his father?'

'He never mentioned a father.'

'But people . . . other children at school, they must have asked if he was related to Flora Le Bonnier?'

'Why should they have done?'

'Well, it's not a very usual surname, is it?'

'Le Bonnier?'

'Yes.'

'But Ricky wasn't called Le Bonnier at school.'

'What was he called?'

'He was just "Ricky Brown" then.'

'So when did he start calling himself Le Bonnier?'

'When he went up to London. When he pretended he wasn't married to me. When he came under the influence of the first Devil Woman.'

Oh, thought Jude, here we go again.

Gulliver finally got his walk, with his mistress and her neighbour. Because she didn't want him chewing unsavoury things on the beach with his injured gums, Carole kept him on the lead. He took a very dim view of that.

Carole and Jude had agreed that they had to pay a visit to

Old Garge. He was the only one who had potentially new information, which might untangle some of the confusions that were building up around their investigation.

The padlock was in place on the hut's door, locking the hasp on to its ring. Knocking produced no reaction. No classical music wafted from the interior. The place was empty and, though Carole had only been there a few hours before, it felt as though it had been empty for a long time. And that it might stay that way for a long time, too.

As the two women walked back up the beach, they were aware of the scrutiny of two uniformed officers sitting in a Panda car by the Promenade. The men had clearly been watching their approach to the hut. Carole and Jude were not the only people interested in the whereabouts of Old Garge.

CHAPTER TWENTY-SIX

If it hadn't been for Gulliver, they would have had a drink at the Crown and Anchor. But he wasn't allowed in the pub, and leaving him tied up outside on a winter's day would have been sheer cruelty. So they returned to High Tor and while the dog settled down in front of the Aga, Carole opened another of the Chilean Chardonnays. 'Most people still think it's Christmas, after all,' she said.

The Aga's heat was cosy, so they stayed in the kitchen.

'I've just realized,' Carole announced, 'that we've been very stupid.'

'In what way?'

'Well, there's one question we should have asked ourselves much earlier, as soon as we met Ricky Le Bonnier.'

'And what is that question?'

'Why he's called Le Bonnier.'

Jude caught on immediately. 'Yes, of course. Le Bonnier is Flora's maiden name, and the way she went on about her family history, it's one she's very proud of.'

'And it's common, I believe, for actresses to retain their maiden names for professional purposes.'

'Particularly if they don't marry.'

'True. Though we've no idea whether Flora ever did marry.'

'No mention of any weddings in her autobiography. Which, of course, takes us straight back to the question of who Ricky's father was.'

'Yes.' Carole felt acutely frustrated. If only she'd realized the importance of the information at the time, she might have pressed Old Garge on the subject of possible paternity. But then Piers had interrupted their discussions. And, come to that, why had Piers suddenly arrived at that moment? What was his connection with the former Rupert Sonning?

'Well,' said Jude, 'we know that at school Ricky was known as Ricky Brown. So the logical answer might be that he was the son of Flora Le Bonnier and a "Mr Brown".'

'Do you think Kath'd know more about that?'

'I doubt it. She said Ricky never mentioned his father. What she did talk about, though, which might be relevant, was the time when Ricky left her to go and work in the music business in London, when he was seduced away by the first of his "Devil Women".' Carole's eyes looked up to the ceiling in exasperation. 'I was wondering if that was when he changed his name. Realizing, perhaps, that Le Bonnier was a name that might carry some weight in the world of show business?'

'It's possible,' Carole conceded, 'and clearly at some point there was a big change in Ricky's relationship with his mother. During his childhood she appears almost to have denied his existence, but when she was here at your party she seemed close to hero-worshipping him.'

'Yes.' It was Jude's turn to look frustrated now. 'If only I'd thought to ask these questions when I went to sort out Flora's back.'

'Maybe she'll have a relapse and summon you again.'

'Maybe . . .' A new thought came to Jude, spreading a beam across her rounded face. 'But of course we will be seeing both Ricky and Flora on tomorrow evening.' Carole looked puzzled. 'Their New Year's Eve Party at Fedingham Court House.'

'Oh yes.' Puzzlement gave way to anxiety on Carole's face.

'Are you sure I'm invited to that? I mean, I haven't received an invitation.'

'Of course you're invited. I asked specially. And, given the number of questions to which we need answers, it'll be a good thing to have us both there.'

'Yes, it will.' Carole drummed her fingers impatiently on the kitchen table. 'So what can we do till then? In terms of investigation?'

'Well, I suppose tomorrow morning you can have another attempt to talk to the Devil Woman who Kath saw in Ricky's car on the evening of the fire.'

'Anna. Yes, I'll try that. And at least tomorrow morning I'll have Gulliver with me, so I won't look such an idiot.'

Jude smiled inwardly at this latest of her neighbour's neuroses as she said, 'The other thing we can do is try to find Old Garge again.'

CHAPTER TWENTY-SEVEN

The Wednesday morning was not so cold. The entire country was still in its state of holiday torpor, but for Carole Seddon Christmas seemed a distant memory. She had survived—even enjoyed—the day itself, but now normal life had to continue. She wanted to put the last week behind her. Going to the Le Bonniers' New Year's Eve Party would be an incongruous reminder of the season.

Gulliver, who appeared to have suffered no ill effects from his surgery, watched the well-practised preparations for a walk with tremendous tail-wagging enthusiasm. When they reached Fethering Beach, Carole didn't have the heart not to let him roam free. The tide was low. Gulliver lolloped off to practise emergency stops in the sand. Carole sat in the shelter where she had last talked with Anna, and waited. Her timing was precise again; it was twenty past seven.

And this time she got a result. Anna must have started her walk a little earlier than usual, because she and her Westie appeared round the corner of a weed-covered wooden groyne way down on the beach. Gulliver gambolled towards them, had a momentary exchange of sniffs with the other dog and then returned to his high-speed braking exercises. What a useful herald he is, thought his mistress, alerting Anna to my presence.

It seemed quite natural for Carole to rise from the shelter and walk down across the shingle towards her dog, and what she could almost call her dog-walking friend. Except that what she had to talk to Anna about might put a severe strain on their embryonic friendship.

After mutual greetings and an exchange of very English sentences about the comparative mildness of the weather, Carole decided she had to leap straight in. 'You remember last time we met, we talked about the fire at Gallimaufry . . . ?'

'Yes.'

'Have the police talked to you about it?'

'They asked me about security arrangements at the shop.'

'Not about anything else?'

'Why on earth should they ask me about anything else?'

'Just because you were seen with Ricky in his car near Fethering Yacht Club earlier that evening.'

The approach had been clumsy, but Carole couldn't have asked for a more dramatic reaction. All the colour left Anna's cheeks, making the red of her lipstick, by contrast, brighter than ever. She swayed as if she might be about to faint, and Carole reached out a hand to steady her. As soon as Anna felt the touch on her sleeve, she burst into tears. Not slow tears, but hysterical ones that shook her entire body as though electric shocks were coursing through her veins.

'Come on,' said Carole, uncharacteristically gentle. 'Come and sit down.'

Leading the way up to the shelter on the Promenade with an arm over Anna's shoulders, she could feel her body's uncontrollable shuddering. Blackie, her West Highland terrier, uninterested in human suffering, trotted off to nose his way through piles of seaweed.

It took a while before Anna was calm enough to speak coherently, and her first intelligible words were: 'I've been terrified of this happening. I knew it'd all come out one day.'

'All what?' asked Carole. Feeling awkward, she detached her arm from Anna's shoulders.

'About me and Ricky. Why would the police want to know about us being there?'

'They are investigating a suspicious death. They're bound to be checking everyone who has a connection with Gallimaufry.'

'God, then it'll all come out.'

Patiently, Carole repeated, 'All what?' There was a silence, broken only by Anna's rasping breaths. 'You don't deny you were in the Mercedes with Ricky?'

'I don't deny anything. I knew it'd all end in disaster. But I do love him.' That prompted a renewed burst of weeping.

As it subsided, Carole asked, 'Are you saying that you and Ricky Le Bonnier were having an affair?' Anna nodded miserably. 'Had it been going on for long?'

'A couple of months. No, nearly three. I started working at Gallimaufry as soon as the place opened in September. I was there on the first day at the gala celebration. And it was early October when . . .' The memory was too painful for her to supply more details. 'Oh, I was very stupid, I know, but very vulnerable. It had been so long since any man had shown any interest in me, in that way . . . I thought, coming here to Fethering, I could make a fresh start, be someone new. But you can never get away from who you really are.'

'And the hair and the make-up,' asked Carole gently, 'was that part of being someone new?'

Another sad nod. 'Yes, and that probably just made me look ridiculous. But it gave me confidence for a time when I first came here. I thought I'd really got away from . . . the situation I was in before. But then the first thing I do when I arrive in Fethering is to screw up totally and start having an affair with a married man.'

Carole couldn't stop herself from saying, 'In this case, a much-married man.'

'Yes, but it seemed to *work*,' Anna protested. 'Ricky and me. I mean, he was totally up front. It's not like he pretended that he wasn't married.'

'Be rather difficult to do that, wouldn't it,' Carole observed tartly, 'given the fact that you were working for his wife, and she presumably introduced you to him?'

Anna nodded abjectly. Carole felt some pity for her, but stronger than that—in fact, she was surprised by its strength— was the anger she felt towards Ricky Le Bonnier. Why was it that some men were incapable of fidelity? There he was, settled with a new glamorous young wife, two small children, idyllic life, and he still couldn't stop himself from groping any other woman who looked like she was available.

'Did Lola know what was going on?'

'No, no. We were very discreet.'

'So discreet that you were spotted in a car together the evening before Gallimaufry burnt down.'

'That was unusual. Nobody would have thought twice about it, if ghastly things hadn't happened afterwards. Otherwise it could have been completely innocent—the owner's husband giving a staff member a lift back after work.'

'On a Sunday?'

Hearing the scepticism in Carole's voice, Anna buried her head in her hands, quietly sobbing.

'And was it at the shop that you and Ricky had your assignations?'

An almost inaudible 'Yes.'

'Why not at your place?'

'I'm in rented rooms. The landlady lives on the premises. She's a nosy cow.'

'Right. And of course there was a furnished flat upstairs at Gallimaufry, wasn't there? Which no doubt had a convenient bed available. Oh yes, I remember. Lola had wanted to rent out the flat, but Ricky wasn't keen on the idea. Now we know why, don't we?' Carole couldn't keep the scorn out of her voice. 'Didn't you ever stop and think what you were doing to Lola? Didn't you think you had any loyalty to her?'

'Nothing we were doing was hurting Lola.'

'Only because she didn't know.'

'Ricky would never do anything to threaten his marriage.'

'Oh no?'

'No. He's just one of those men who's capable of loving two women at the same time.'

'I've heard of them,' Carole snorted. 'And no doubt he told you that he was like that because he was a creative person, and creative people have to be judged by different moral standards from the rest of the world?' The way Anna evaded her eye told Carole that her conjecture had been correct. She felt even more furious with Ricky Le Bonnier, and her anger spilled over towards Anna. 'Well, you'll have to find somewhere else for your trysts now. Your little love-nest has sadly been burnt down, hasn't it?'

Her victim offered no resistance as verbal blows thudded in. 'And have you seen Ricky since that assignation, since the Sunday before Christmas?' Carole continued harshly.

'No. We had a bit of a tiff that evening and I was worried he was trying to end our relationship. But it turned out all right— that's what we were talking about in the car. We were making up, saying that we'd got too much going to stop it just like that. Ricky promised he'd ring me over Christmas, but now all this has happened, it must be very difficult for him to . . .'

There was no need for Carole to ask. She now knew that when they'd last been in the same shelter and the mobile had rung, Anna had been hoping for a call from Ricky. Her expression of disappointment at the time was explained.

Carole moved quickly on to details of timing. 'You were seen in Ricky's car about eight o'clock that Sunday evening . . .'

195

'Who saw us?'

'That doesn't matter. Now, according to Ricky himself—and Lola, come to that—he had gone to take his daughter Polly to catch the seven-thirty-two London train from Fedborough Station. Had he already made the assignation to meet you after he'd done that?'

'No. He called me at about seven-fifteen that evening. He said he couldn't stop thinking about me and he'd suddenly got half an hour free . . . and he could pick me up on the corner of my road and . . .' Her words petered out as she realized how shabby the arrangements sounded.

'You *were* honoured, weren't you? A whole half-hour.'

'You don't know what our relationship was like, Carole,' Anna protested.

'It seems to me I'm getting a pretty fair impression of it. From what you've just said, it was like any other hole-in-the-corner adulterous affair. So, you both got back to the shop in his car at about eight, enjoyed half an hour of . . . each other's company—and then what? Did Ricky do the gentlemanly thing and drive you back to the end of your road?'

'No, I walked.'

'So he didn't do the gentlemanly thing. How gallant.'

'Carole, we are in love.'

That plea got the contemptuous snort it deserved. 'Tell me, Anna—and this is important—did you see Ricky leave Gallimaufry that evening?'

'No, he was still in the shop when I left.'

'Right. And you say you haven't seen him since?'

'Haven't seen him, haven't heard from him.' The woman was on the verge of further tears. 'Do you think the police are likely to question me again?'

Carole shrugged. 'If they're doing their job properly, I think they should.'

'So Lola will find out about Ricky and me?'

Anna's scarf had slipped down, revealing peroxide blond hair whose roots needed doing. Tears had spread her mascara and her scarlet lipstick was smudged. She looked so crushed and feeble that Carole couldn't help feeling a surge of pity. 'Maybe not,' she replied, with no knowledge to justify the assertion. 'It may not be necessary for Lola to be told.'

There was a silence. While they were talking, they hadn't noticed a thin, cold rain begin to fall. Down at the water's edge Gulliver and Blackie were engaged in their own independent but vitally important manoeuvres.

'And, Anna, you don't have an idea why anyone might have wanted to murder Polly Le Bonnier?'

'No idea at all.'

Carole thought it was probably the truth. She had found out everything relevant to the investigation that she was going to find out from Anna Carter. The natural moment had arrived for them to collect their dogs and go their separate ways. But there was still something that was intriguing Carole.

'You keep talking about having come to Fethering to make a new start. What was it you were trying to get away from? A divorce?'

'Something rather more permanent than that,' Anna replied quietly. 'My husband died.'

'Oh, I am sorry.'

'Don't worry. It was nearly four years ago. I've . . . I don't know what the best expression is . . . Not "got over it"—well, you don't get over it—"I've come to terms with it." Yes, that's probably right. So I'd rather it hadn't happened, but I can cope with the rest of my life. Or at least cope with most of it. The bit I couldn't cope with was being treated like a widow. My husband and I had quite a close circle of friends, and of course they all knew . . . and it wasn't that they weren't kind to me, but whatever they did, I got the feeling they could never forget that "poor old Jo's a widow".'

'Jo?'

'Yes. Another part of the makeover. The hair, the make-up, the name. I was Joanna Carter-Fulbright. So I chopped off the ends of my old name and made myself into "Anna Carter". And I moved down from Carlisle to Fethering, and I cut off all communication with my old friends. To start a new life. And then the first thing I do in that new life . . .' tears threatened again— 'is to begin having an affair with Ricky Bloody Le Bonnier.'

'I'll be seeing him tonight,' said Carole. She felt calmer now; the flames of anger had subsided to glowing embers. 'I've been invited to their New Year's Eve party.'

'Oh, so have I!' The thought seemed to excite Anna.

'But will you be going?'

'Yes, I must.' She turned her tired, tear-washed face to Carole as she murmured intensely, 'I can't not see him.'

CHAPTER TWENTY-EIGHT

That New Year's Eve you would not have known that Feding-ham Court House was a place of mourning. The display of Christmas decorations which Jude had observed on her last visit had been doubled in size, and black-dressed waitresses worked assiduously to see that no one spent a moment without food or drink. From the huge sitting room music blared, and through the door could be seen the live band who were playing.

There was also a huge number of people. A few familiar Fethering and Fedborough faces, but not many. There was a good scattering of older men with gorgeously attired younger wives or girlfriends, who somehow looked as if they must be Ricky's contacts from the music industry. There were even stars from the world of rock whom Carole could recognize from the media but not put names to. It was clearly a very glamorous party. Carole was glad they'd agreed to leave their coats in the Renault; that made a quick getaway possible if required. All her insecurities about being somewhere where she didn't know anyone rose immediately to the surface. Her atavistic instinct was to stay very close to her neighbour.

Jude intuitively sensed her unease, and whispered as they entered the hall. 'Don't think of it as a social occasion. Think of it as a stage in our investigation. There's a lot of information we need to get from the various Le Bonniers.'

Though at that stage finding a Le Bonnier looked like being something of a challenge. No sign of Ricky or Lola. There were so many guests that they must have been off somewhere in the noisy throng doing their hostly duty. The party wasn't going to offer the most conducive atmosphere for interrogation of murder suspects.

Looking around at the milling guests, Carole also felt sure she'd got the dress code wrong. All the other women were so colourful and flamboyant that she feared her trusty Marks & Spencer's little black number looked absurdly dingy by comparison. Its eternal aim—to make her look anonymous and invisible—might be having the opposite effect of making her look conspicuous. Even the sparkly snowflake brooch Gaby had given her felt cheap and inappropriate in this environment.

Jude, needless to say, had got her ensemble just right. Without changing her habitual style of a long skirt and wafty tops, she had added a sparkling stole and shimmering glass beads to give the overall impression that she had dressed for a special occasion.

Both women took the proffered glasses of champagne, and Jude sailed boldly forward towards a room where there wasn't music playing. 'Let's look for somewhere with seats.'

'Why do you want to sit down?'

'I don't, Carole, but I know there's one person in this household who will be sitting down.'

'Flora. Of course.'

Through the crush they did manage to find the old lady. She was sitting in a high-winged armchair which, with her in it, looked like a throne. Her hair had been expertly remoulded into shape and she wore a dress of glittering silver. The diamonds round her neck and hanging from her ears were undoubtedly the real thing (making Carole feel that her brooch was even more tawdry). If ever there was an illustration for ageing gracefully, Flora Le Bonnier was providing it. Only her crippled hands, immobile fingers pressed together as she lifted a champagne glass to her lips, let down the image.

When the two women reached her chair, she was alone, surveying the scene with all the grandeur of a monarch reviewing her troops. She recognized Jude instantly and inclined her head graciously to Carole.

'You're looking magnificent,' said Jude. 'I do hope this means that you're feeling better.'

'My dear girl,' Flora Le Bonnier trilled, 'I cannot thank you enough for what you have done for me. From the moment you finished your healing, the pain disappeared and, thank the Lord, has stayed away. No professional doctor, however many letters he might have after his name, could have begun to do what you did for me.'

Jude decided that when it came to investigation, there was no time like the present. 'I've been reading your book, Flora,' she said, 'which I found absolutely riveting.'

'Oh, it's just a pot-boiler.' In spite of her modest words, Flora was clearly very pleased by the compliment.

'One thing that really interested me,' Jude went on, 'was about Ricky.'

'Oh?' There was a new alertness in the old woman's eyes.

'For a start, there doesn't seem to be a lot about him in the book.'

Flora sighed. 'I know. I so wanted to put in more about my dear boy—I'd even written a lot of it—but I had this very stubborn editor at the publisher's. She kept saying, "The book is about *you*, your career, not your family life." So, I'm afraid, if I wanted to get the book published, I had to go along with her recommendations. I kept telling her that Ricky was famous in his own right, that his involvement in pop music might spread the potential readership for the book, but she wouldn't budge.'

'Oh well, maybe he'll write his own biography in time.'

A gracious smile greeted this. Flora clearly had no objection to the idea. She looked at Carole. 'And have you read the book?'

The expression was so imperious that Carole felt as if she was up in front of a headmistress for not having done her homework. 'No, I haven't yet, but I'm looking forward to borrowing it from Jude and reading it.' She was, too. A second mind applied to the text might deduce more about the Le Bonnier family secrets.

Jude was still in investigative mode. 'There was something in the book which I found rather strange . . .'

'Oh?'

'Well, I hadn't thought about it before, but I found I was suddenly asking myself why Ricky's surname was Le Bonnier.'

'Why shouldn't it be? It's my surname. It's a name with a great deal of history.'

'Yes, I'm not questioning that, but there is a tradition in this country that children take the surname of their father.'

'Traditions,' Flora Le Bonnier announced magisterially, 'are there to be broken. Ricky's father had no relevance in his life.'

'But who was—?'

That was as far as Jude was allowed to get. 'My dear girl, you are not the first person to have asked me that question. Over the decades many journalists have tried by various means to winkle a name out of me. None has been successful, and I'm afraid you won't be either. Le Bonnier is a fine and time-honoured name. My son has always been proud to bear it.'

'If that's the case,' Carole chipped in, 'why did he go to school under the name of Ricky Brown?'

The look that travelled down Flora Le Bonnier's finely sculpted nose was very nearly a glare. Then, remembering her manners, she converted it into a cold smile. 'I would gather,' she said, 'that you have never been troubled by the inconveniences of celebrity.' Carole was forced to admit that she hadn't. 'Well, let me explain to you. When Ricky was young, I was—

there's no point in false modesty—very famous indeed. The media make a great fuss nowadays about the hounding of celebrities by the paparazzi, by door-stepping journalists, by stalkers even, but let me tell you that kind of thing was very much up and running in the post-war years. Before the major expansion of television, the cinema played an even more important role in people's lives, and its stars were subjects of intense popular speculation. For my son to have gone to a local school down here in Fethering under the name of Ricky Le Bonnier would have been to condemn him to a nightmare of intrusive interest and teasing. For that reason he was known as Ricky Brown.'

'So Brown wasn't his father's surname?'

Carole's suggestion was greeted by a sardonic smile. 'A nice try, but I think you'll have to be a bit subtler than that. As I said, the identity of Ricky's father is something I have never revealed and I firmly intend to take that secret with me to the grave.'

'So when did he start calling himself Ricky Le Bonnier?' asked Jude.

'That was when he began to work in the music business. His feeling was—and it was one with which I heartily agreed—that having a famous name might help to get his career under way. Which is exactly what happened.' She smiled complacently, as if her words had ended that particular topic of conversation.

But Jude persisted. 'When he was a boy down here in Fethering, he was looked after by someone called "Auntie Vi". I was wondering—'

But wondering was as far as she got. With a flamboyant squeal of 'Flora—darling!' an elderly man with a rather beautiful younger one in tow swooped down on the actress to initiate an exchange of scurrilous theatrical gossip. After a few minutes

Carole and Jude drifted away, their departure unacknowledged by the grande dame of British theatre.

CHAPTER TWENTY-NINE

Their champagne glasses recharged and delicious nibbles supplied by the black-clad waitresses, the two women wandered towards the source of the music. In the hall Ricky Le Bonnier, his arm round Lola's waist, was, as ever, the centre of attention, regaling the group around him with more of his stories. Seeing him there and seeing the look of adoration in his wife's eyes, Carole felt another surge of anger. She thought of her conversation with Anna, the details of which she had told Jude on the drive over to Fedborough. What was it with men, particularly men of Ricky's age, that stopped them from being content with what they had? Why would men like him betray a beautiful, intelligent girl like Lola with a sad, neurotic widow like Anna? Was it the galloping approach of death that motivated them? Was it a feeling that in some conjectural heaven their score would be marked down for not having bedded enough women? Carole Seddon would never understand men.

From what Ricky was saying, the band performing in his sitting room were extremely famous. Carole hadn't heard of them, but Jude had and was suitably impressed to find them playing in a private house. Their host was talking about the band as the two women joined the circle around him.

'Of course, I knew them when they were just five pimply-faced lads from Droitwich. Sent a demo and I summoned them up to my office in . . . I think it was Chrysalis I was working for then. Anyway, I could see they had potential, and I could see that Jed was going to be one hell of a charismatic front man . . . as soon as he had run a brush through his hair and done a major bombardment of his mush with Clearasil. The girls in the office were drooling at him even with the state he was in then. So I gave the lads a bit of advice on their repertoire. They were still too much folk-influenced then to chart in a major way, but I got them to move more into the soft-rock world. I also had the disagreeable task of telling them their keyboard player wasn't up to the job. Always nasty doing that, particularly when you've got a group who've been together since school. But if you want to hit the top, you can't carry passengers. Just the same with the Beatles. I remember telling my old mate Ringo that he was the luckiest bugger in the entire world and, you know, he said . . .'

So Ricky Le Bonnier continued his routine. From his demeanour no one would ever have known that he'd lost a stepdaughter only ten days before. Jude looked at Carole, who immediately understood her rueful grimace. It wasn't going to be easy to get Ricky on his own that evening. So far as grilling him was concerned, their investigation might have to be put on hold.

The same would probably be true of Lola, but just as Carole and Jude were edging away from Ricky's circle, she detached herself from her husband and hurried up to them. 'Jude, you know I talked to you about possibly babysitting Mabel and Henry one day . . .'

'Sure.'

'Well, it might be sooner rather than later.'

'When?'

Lola grimaced apologetically. 'Tomorrow afternoon. It may not happen, but Flora's suddenly announcing that she has to go back to her flat tomorrow. I hope we'll be able to persuade her to stay a little longer, but she can be stubborn and if she insists, Ricky'll have to drive her back up to London and I may have to go too . . . and Varya's seeing in the New Year with some Russians and copious amounts of vodka in Southampton and I'm not sure when she'll be back . . .'

'I'd be happy to do it.'

'As I say, it may not happen.'

'Call me on the mobile in the morning if you need me.'

'OK. Bless you, Jude.' And Lola slipped back to join her husband, whose arm instinctively once again encircled her waist.

Jude announced she wanted to see the famous group at closer quarters, so they drifted into the sitting room. There were people dancing. A lot of young people and, to Carole's distaste, a lot of old people too. She didn't enjoy seeing her contemporaries gyrating and waving their arms about in the air, it was undignified. Beside her, Jude's body was already swaying to the heavy rock beat. Carole, who was too inhibited ever to have ventured on to a dance floor, felt even more envious of her neighbour's instinctive responses.

A tall man with long grey hair in a ponytail moved towards Jude and grinned at her. She grinned back and without any words they started dancing together. They didn't actually touch, but the way their bodies mirrored each other's movements seemed somehow more intimate than touching. Carole edged her way back to the hall. A waitress offered to top up her glass, but she put her hand over it. She had to navigate the Renault safely back to Fethering, and the Sussex police were notoriously vigilant on New Year's Eve.

From long experience, Carole knew there were two available options at a party where you didn't know anyone. One was to stand alone with your drink, possibly showing excessive interest in the contents of your host's bookshelves, but still looking like a social outcast. The other was to stride purposely about the place, as if you were looking for someone. The larger the gathering and the more rooms it took place in, the better this second approach worked. Because if you kept doing circuits of the entire party, you didn't keep walking past the same people, and when you did see them a second time you could pretend that you'd just finished talking to one very interesting person you knew, and you were making your way to talk to another even more interesting person you knew.

There was no contest. Carole Seddon opted for the second approach. Wearing a look of intense intellectual concentration, she sallied forth through the throng in the hall to a room which she had not yet explored. There was a considerable crush inside, which suited her purposes admirably. Squeezing past people reinforced the false impression of having somewhere to go to. And apologizing to them as she squeezed past produced the illusion of conversation.

At the end of the room an archway led into another, equally heaving with guests, and from this one glass doors opened on to a garden terrace. In spite of the winter cold, there were a few people standing there, so Carole, arguing to herself that the fictional person she was looking for was as likely to be on the terrace as anywhere else, went out to join them.

And, contrary to her expectation, she saw someone she did know: Piers Duncton. No great surprise that he should have gone out into the open air to have a cigarette. He was on his own, his angular figure propped against the terrace railings, looking into the garden. Out there strings of fairy lights cascaded from tall trees, lending an aura of magic to the scene.

Carole had no hesitation in going straight up to him and saying, 'Good evening, Piers.'

He turned, squinting against the light from the room she had just left, and it took him a moment to identify her. 'Ah, Carole,' he said eventually.

'How are you, Piers?'

'Oh, you know.' He took a swig from the wineglass in his

hand and looked disappointed to find it was already empty. There was something glassy about his stare, and Carole realized that he was very drunk.

'I suppose I should say: Happy New Year,' she said conventionally.

'Happy New Year?' He thought about it. 'I don't see much happiness in this New Year, I must say.' He raised his empty glass. 'Look, I've got to find some more booze.'

Fortunately, at that moment one of the diligent waitresses appeared on the terrace armed with bottles, so Carole didn't immediately lose her quarry. Piers took a long swig from his refilled glass and looked at her. 'Happy New Year,' he repeated. 'Polly's dead, and you're wishing me a happy New Year.'

'It's very sad, I know, but you said your relationship was about to end.'

'Yes, but I didn't want it to end like this, not with her remains lying in some police morgue being picked over by forensic pathologists.' Spurred on by drunkenness, Piers Duncton was wallowing in his grief. 'Nobody deserves that, least of all a bright, lovely girl like Polly.'

'No. I was surprised to see you at Old Garge's hut yesterday.'

'I wasn't expecting to find you there either.'

'Can I ask why you went there, Piers?'

'You don't have to ask. You heard what I told the old fart. That the police wanted to talk to him. For reasons of his own, he wasn't keen on the idea of that, so he decided he'd make himself scarce.'

'But why did you take it upon yourself to tell him? Do you know him well?'

'I'd met him once before. On the beach with Ricky.'

'And it was your idea to go and warn Old Garge about the police coming?'

Piers looked uncomfortable. 'No. Ricky wanted me to.'

'Wasn't Ricky in London on Tuesday?'

'Yes, but Lola had apparently rung him to tell him about the police being keen on interviewing Old Garge, and she said Ricky wanted me to go and warn him.'

Carole mentally squirrelled away that information. Her suspicious mind registered that Lola could have made up the instruction from her husband. It could have been her own initiative to send Piers down to the hut on Fethering Beach.

'So do you know where Old Garge is now?' Carole asked directly.

The young man's glazed eyes narrowed and he looked rather sly as he replied, 'Oh, he's quite safe for the time being. Out of the way in a nice little flat. It'll take the police a while to find him there.' He smiled complacently as he downed the remains of his wine. 'Ex-wives have their uses.'

'What do you mean? Whose ex-wife are you—?'

But she'd lost him. Muttering that he needed to get more wine, Piers Duncton brushed past her and was quickly absorbed by the throng inside.

Carole stayed on the terrace for a moment, piecing together the information she had just received. And the more she thought about it, the more excited she became. Her suspicion had been proved right. Old Garge—back in his Rupert Sonning days—must have been married to Flora Le Bonnier. He was Ricky's father. And he was now safely ensconced in his ex-wife's flat up in St John's Wood.

Which was maybe why Flora was so keen to get back to London.

Carole looked for the old actress as she went back through the house, but there was no sign of her. She asked Lola, who happened to be passing and was told that Flora had gone up to bed. She was too tired to stay up and see the New Year in.

Carole checked her watch. Only eleven-twenty. The thought

of staying in Fedingham Court House till midnight, and then enduring the excesses of 'Auld Lang Syne' and everyone hugging and kissing each other and . . . She wouldn't mind slipping away before all that happened. Was there a chance that Jude would be equally keen to leave?

She found her neighbour still in the room with the music. Still dancing with the same tall man, though dancing rather closer now. As Jude caught her eye, Carole mouthed, 'Think I might be off. Do you want to come?'

'Oh, I'm not sure . . .'

'Is this your lift?' asked the man, looking at Carole as though she were an unlicensed minicab driver. He winked at her. 'Don't worry, love. I'll see Jude gets back home safely.'

Carole looked around for her host and hostess, but didn't try that hard. Better just to slip away and then thank them in a day or two. Not on the phone. She was sure they wouldn't even recognize her name if she rang to thank them. No, she'd post a well-chosen card saying something like: 'it was such a wonderfully lively party that I simply couldn't find you to say thank you at the end, but I did want to say how much . . .' She'd done it many times before.

She also wondered for a moment whether Anna had fulfilled her intention of attending. There hadn't been any sign of her, but in a crush like that it would have been easy to miss someone. On reflection, though, Carole thought that actually facing the prospect of seeing Ricky and Lola together in their home, Anna would have chickened out.

On the gravel outside the house a minivan was decanting a small band of men with kilts and bagpipes. Carole felt even more relieved that she was escaping the midnight rituals.

As celebratory fireworks from Fedingham Court House garden illuminated the West Sussex sky, it was a very stony-

211

faced Carole Seddon who drove back to Fethering and High Tor.

CHAPTER THIRTY

Waking up to a new year did not improve Carole's mood. When she passed Woodside Cottage on her way to Fethering Beach for Gulliver's early morning walk, there was no sign of life. Nor was there when she came back.

She felt terrible. And what made everything more terrible was the ancient familiarity of the feeling. She remembered the sheer awfulness of school dances, where you'd gone with a friend and then, when a half-decent-looking boy had come on the scene, the friend's loyalty had immediately gone straight out of the window. And though the two of you had agreed to travel back together, somehow you ended up going home on your own.

She couldn't settle to anything that morning and took her bad temper out on the house, cleaning High Tor to within an inch of its life.

After considerable indecision, at eleven o'clock she rang Jude's home number. There was no reply. She didn't even contemplate ringing her mobile.

It was not until a quarter to one in the afternoon that a rather smart BMW sports car drew up outside Woodside Cottage. Jude bounced out with a cheery wave to her escort. What compounded the awfulness of the situation was that Carole hadn't moved back from the bedroom window quickly enough, and she, too, received the blessing of a wave from her neighbour.

★ ★ ★ ★ ★

Moments later, the phone rang. She knew it would be Jude. And it was—a bouncy, bubbly Jude, full of good wishes for the new year, with no hint of apology in her voice. She seemed completely unaware of the purgatory she had inflicted on her friend.

'I just wondered, Carole . . . I know it's late, and you've probably had lunch . . .'

'No, I haven't, actually. I didn't feel like anything.'

'Well, I'm starving and I feel like a huge big, self-indulgent fry-up. Do you fancy joining me?'

Carole was faced with a moral dilemma. Declining the offer might be a way of expressing her disapproval, but accepting was the only way she was going to find out how her neighbour had spent the previous night. Obviously, accepting won.

There was a tantalizing smell of bacon when she arrived in the sitting room of Woodside Cottage. Jude had changed out of her party attire and wore a long Arran cardigan draped over a long denim skirt. She supplied a Chilean Chardonnay for Carole, but poured a glass of Argentinian Cabernet Sauvignon for herself. 'I always find red works better as a "hair of the dog" than white. Now, you just sit down, and I'll bring the food through in a minute.'

Carole did as she was told, and listened to Jude bustling about cheerfully in the kitchen. Something had certainly put a smile on her face. Carole was damned if she was going to ask what.

The fry-up was particularly delicious. Jude's approach to cooking was eclectic, depending on her mood. She was just as likely to offer guests dishes with brown rice and bean sprouts as she was *steak frites*. But the Full English she delivered that afternoon was perfect for a bleak English New Year's Day.

Both women were very hungry (though Carole didn't like to

speculate what had given Jude her appetite). They were silent as they wolfed down their food and only when they'd reached the stage of mopping up the remaining bits of egg and fat with crusts of fried bread did Jude speak. 'Interesting, last night, wasn't it?'

It may have been interesting for *you*, Carole was tempted to say, but she curbed the instinct. If Jude wished to volunteer details of how she'd spent the night, then fine. If not . . . well, Carole was not going to demean herself by asking (though she was afire with curiosity). 'In what way?' she asked uncontroversially.

'Seeing Ricky Le Bonnier in his pomp. That was one hell of a glitzy party.'

'Yes, and hardly appropriate in the circumstances.'

'What do you mean?'

'Well, Jude, I'm not in favour of people going into deep mourning or anything like that, but it is less than a fortnight since his stepdaughter died. You'd have thought he'd have made some concession to her memory.'

'Don't you think, though, that Ricky's the kind of man who's always going to be presenting an upbeat image of himself? I wouldn't imagine many people get through to what he's really thinking.'

'Probably not much,' said Carole waspishly. 'He's one of the shallowest people I've ever met.'

'And yet Lola clearly sees something in him.'

Carole sniffed. 'Without denigrating our gender, I'm afraid it's true that few of us have ever shown much taste when it comes to men.'

Jude giggled. Annoyingly, in her neighbour's view. 'Well, Carole, at least we have made some advance in our investigation. We do now know that Lola's lied to protect Ricky. She gave him an alibi for all of the night of the fire, and what you heard from Anna has broken that.'

'To be fair, Anna left him in the shop at . . . what . . . half-past eight? He may have gone straight back home after that.'

'But Lola said he didn't leave the house again after he'd come back from taking Polly to Fedborough Station.'

'Though I got a different story from Saira Sherjan.'

A new idea struck Jude and her brown eyes sparkled as she said, 'Suppose Lola actually knows about Ricky's affair with Anna, and she gave him the alibi because she didn't want anyone else to find out?'

'The way she was cuddling up to him last night didn't look like the behaviour of a woman who knows her husband's having an affair.'

'Don't you believe it, Carole. Remember how many people were there at that party. Public displays of affection are no guide to the real state of a marriage. And don't forget that Lola used to be quite a good actress.'

'Hm . . .' Carole took a sip of Chardonnay. 'Do you think we're ever going to get more out of Flora Le Bonnier?'

Jude grimaced. 'I think we've had our ration of information there. One thing's for sure, she's never going to reveal the identity of Ricky's father. As she said—rather gleefully, I thought—that secret will go to the grave with her.'

'Do you think Ricky himself knows?'

'I wonder. Flora's will is so strong she's quite capable of having kept it a secret from him too.'

'But what Piers said to me virtually proved that Ricky's father was Rupert Sonning.'

'What?' demanded a thunderstruck Jude. 'Could you run that past me again?'

'Oh, of course, I haven't told you, have I?' And Carole gave a quick résumé of her conversation on the terrace with the drunken writer, concluding, 'So what else do you think he meant?'

Jude nodded thoughtfully. 'You could be right.'

'Of course I'm right!' Carole snapped. 'I wonder if we could get another chance to talk to Flora?'

'Doubt it. I think she's already suspicious of us. And, anyway, she's probably going back up to London this afternoon, so we'd have to find some reason to beard her in her den in St John's Wood. She'd be—Oh, damn!' said Jude suddenly and shot out into the hall, calling back as she went, 'Lola asked me about babysitting, didn't she? Said she'd call me in the morning. And I've had my mobile switched off since last night.'

Iron strength of will was required to stop Carole from asking, 'Why?' Jude reappeared, holding the mobile and tapping through the buttons to check for messages. 'Oh, no! She does want me to. Sorry, Carole, I must ring her back.'

From the Woodside Cottage end of the conversation it was clear that Flora was insisting on being taken back to St John's Wood, and that she required both her son and daughter-in-law to escort her there. Varya had not returned from her vodka-steeped night in Southampton, and if Jude could possibly . . . ?

'I'll get a cab. Be with you in as long as it takes.'

When the call had ended, Carole said, 'Don't bother about a cab. I'll take you.'

'Are you sure?'

'Of course I'm sure,' said Carole, adding frostily, 'I'm not in the habit of making offers I don't intend to carry through.'

'No, well, thank you. I would very much appreciate it.' Jude hesitated. 'Though it just might be a bit awkward if you wanted to join me for the babysitting.'

Carole looked frostier than ever. 'I have no desire to join you for the babysitting.'

They were in the Renault on the way to Fedingham Court

House. Jude had been silently musing away to herself for a while when suddenly she said, 'Piers could have meant something else.'

'What do you mean?'

'When he talked about "ex-wives" and "a flat", you assumed he meant Flora.'

'Yes, of course.'

'But suppose he wasn't talking about her . . . ?'

'How many ex-wives is Rupert Sonning supposed to have?'

'Not Rupert Sonning. Ricky.'

'Ricky's ex-wife? Are you talking about Kath?'

'That's exactly who I'm talking about, Carole.'

As Jude smiled across at her friend, a huge yawn took over her face. Which Carole found very annoying.

CHAPTER THIRTY-ONE

The handover to Jude in the hall of Fedingham Court House was quickly achieved. Mabel made no fuss; she was delighted to see one of her approved babysitters. Ricky was out the front, settling his mother into the Mercedes 4 × 4, as a harassed-looking Lola gave instructions.

'Henry's asleep. The baby monitor's switched through to the playroom and the sitting room, so you'll hear him when he wakes up. If you take Mabel up with you, he'll be quite happy about you taking him out of the cot. And he'll want some milk when he wakes up, his bottle's in the kitchen. Mabel knows where it is. He may need a nappy changing, but it shouldn't be dirty this time of day. Mabel'll show you where everything is.'

Lola looked at her watch. It was just after half past two. 'I don't know what the traffic'll be like, but with a following wind, Ricky and I should be back by seven, which is their bathtime. That is assuming Flora lets us just deliver her and turn straight round.'

'Is she likely to?'

'I don't know, Jude. She's in one of her particularly imperious moods today. Insisting that I travel up in the car with her and Ricky. "I just don't feel I've had a proper *talk* to you, Lola, while I've been down here. What with everything that's been going on, we haven't had a proper *talk*." ' Once again her impression of her mother-in-law was spot-on. 'It's totally unnecessary, but Ricky always gives in to her whims. Anyway, hopefully we'll be able to turn straight round. If we're not back by seven—'

'I'll show Jude where everything is,' said Mabel, solemnly responsible.

Lola grinned. 'She will. She's much more organized than I am. I sometimes think I'm the one who needs a babysitter. And I've put their supper out on top of the fridge. Henry's a bit picky at the moment. If he doesn't like the pasta, try him with a slice of apple or some raisins. Don't worry if he doesn't eat much. He evens up over the day.'

Ricky Le Bonnier came bustling in through the front door. 'Better be off, love. The old girl's champing at the bit.' Lola went off to grab her coat as her husband scooped Mabel up into his arms. 'You'll be a good girl for Jude, won't you?'

'Yes, Daddy. Mummy says she needs a babysitter, not me.'

'And your Mummy is dead right, as ever.' He put the girl down and planted a kiss on top of her white-blonde curls. 'Look after Henry, won't you, and we'll see you at bathtime.'

'If you're back in time.'

'Yes, Mabel, if we're back in time. Which we will try to be.'

'But that'll depend on Grandma. Mummy says she's in one of her imp . . .' Mabel struggled with the word—'impish moods.'

'Something like that.' Ricky ruffled her hair, as if he didn't want to leave her, then looked up to see Lola approaching, grabbed her arm and set off for the car. 'Bless you for looking after them, Jude.'

'No problem.'

' 'Bye.' And the large front door closed.

First Mabel insisted on showing Jude all her dolls and cuddly toys in the playroom. They were arrayed in a long line on the windowsill. 'They're here so that Henry can't reach them when he crawls. He can't crawl yet, but when he can crawl he won't be able to reach my dolls and cuddlies.'

Mabel introduced each of her collection by name. Then she announced that they must play a game.

'What game do you want to play?'

'I want to play Grandmother's Footsteps.'

'But can you play that with just two?'

'Oh yes,' Mabel assured her.

So they played. One of them—'Grandmother'—faced the wall while the other crept across the room towards her. If, when 'Grandmother' whirled round, she caught a glimpse of movement, then the other had to go back to the beginning and start again. Mabel had clearly played the game many times and had become expert at taking tiny steps and then freezing.

They played for so long that Jude was beginning to feel a little weary (and not only from her late night), but fortunately, just when her acolyte thought she could take no more, the Mistress of the Revels decided it was time for a different game. 'This is not a real game, not like Grandmother's Footsteps. This is a game my Daddy made up,' she said proudly.

'What's it called?'

'It's called Hiding Things.'

'Oh yes, I heard you and your Daddy talking about it another time I was here.'

Mabel nodded. 'That was when you came to make Grandma's back better.'

'You're absolutely right.' The little girl had an excellent memory.

'How you play Hiding Things,' she went on, 'is one person hides things and the other person has to find them.'

'That sounds good. What things do you hide?'

'Well, Daddy says there's a game where people hide slippers, but his game is better than that. We hide Woolly Monkey.' And from her array of dolls she took down a toy whose name described him perfectly. He was about six inches high and knitted from dark and light brown wools. Attached to one hand was a knitted banana. 'This is Woolly Monkey,' said Mabel unnecessarily.

'Right, so what do we do? One person closes their eyes and counts to a hundred?'

'I can't count to a hundred. I can only count to twenty. So we count to twenty. And then we say "Coming, ready or not". And then we have to find Woolly Monkey. And the person who's hidden him has to say "warm" if you're near him.'

'All right, I think I understand the rules. And do we just do it in this room?'

'No, in this room and the hall and the sitting room.'

'So who's going to hide Woolly Monkey first?'

'You do, because you're a guest,' said Mabel, who had clearly studied protocol. 'So I close my eyes and you hide Woolly Monkey. One . . . two . . . three . . .'

Fortunately, Mabel counted slowly. Jude decided that her best policy might be to hide Woolly Monkey in full sight, so she put him in a different position amongst the toys on the window-sill.

'Twenty!' Mabel crowed. 'Coming, ready or not!' She looked at Jude, sitting innocently on the sofa. 'I wonder if it's in this room or—'

'Yes, it's—'

'No, you mustn't make clues. You just say if I'm warm.'

Mabel set off towards the hall. 'You're getting colder.' She came back into the room. 'You're getting warmer.' To the toy cupboard. 'Colder again.' Towards Jude. 'Still cold.' Then in the direction of the window. 'Warm. Warmer. Ooh, very warm. You're going to burn your fingers.'

Triumphantly, Mabel picked Woolly Monkey off the window-sill. Then, patiently, she explained to Jude, 'He doesn't go there. His place is between Fluffy Ted and Pollyanna.'

'Oh, I'm sorry.'

'He doesn't like sitting anywhere else.'

'I'm doubly sorry.'

'It's all right,' said Mabel magnanimously. 'You didn't know. Now it's my turn to do Hiding Things.'

'I'll stay here and close my eyes and count up to twenty.'

'Don't do it fast. Daddy sometimes does it too fast, and that's cheating.'

'I won't do it too fast.' Jude closed her eyes and started to count, very slowly. She heard Mabel's footsteps scampering off into the hall. When she reached twenty, Jude shouted, 'Coming, ready or not!'

She made a great play of walking around the playroom, saying, 'Ooh, I wonder if Woolly Monkey could be under the sofa . . . or could he be in the toy cupboard?'

Mabel appeared in the doorway. 'He's not in here,' she announced.

'I thought he might be.'

'I'm not in here. Daddy says there's a clue in where the person who's hidden Woolly Monkey is when you stop counting.'

'I see. Because they might have only just hidden him and not had time to go anywhere else?'

Mabel nodded gravely. 'Yes. So I was in the sitting room. That's a clue.'

Taking the hint that had been proffered, Jude went through into the sitting room. In the crush of the party the night before she hadn't taken in its full splendour. It was a tall room, panelled and roofed in old, dark oak, which was studded with carved wooden roses. A large fireplace in what looked like Cotswold stone dominated the space. Huge logs flared in the grate, in front of which stood a fire guard with the dimensions of a portcullis.

As Jude moved towards the fire, Mabel said, 'Warm . . .

warmer . . . very warm . . .'

'Well, I know that, because the fire's warm.'

The child didn't approve of any part of her game being treated with such levity. 'That's not what I mean. I mean, you're warmer because you're near Woolly Monkey.'

'Yes, I'm sorry.' The heat from the fire was intense. Jude made a cursory examination of the log basket and the coal scuttle, but there was no sign of the hidden toy.

She moved away from the fireplace. 'Colder, colder,' crowed Mabel.

'Well, I can't think where . . . You didn't throw Woolly Monkey on the fire, did you?'

'No, I didn't. I love Woolly Monkey.'

'Then I've no idea . . .'

'It's a very good Hiding Things place. A special Hiding Things place. Daddy's used it.'

'What, when Daddy was playing Hiding Things with you?'

'No, we weren't playing the game.'

'Oh?' Jude was suddenly alert.

'But Daddy used it as a Hiding Things place. I don't think he knew I was watching. I think he thought I was asleep on the sofa. Mummy had brought me down to sleep on the sofa, because I was uncomfy in my bed. And I was asleep, but I kept waking up, because I was hot and my head hurt.'

'When was this, Mabel?'

'It was when I had *my ear infection*.' As before, she said the words correctly, and with pride. 'Before the doctor gave me the . . . anti-things.'

'Which day? Do you remember which day it was?'

'It was before Christmas Day.'

'Do you remember anything about the day? Did Mummy and Daddy go to a party that day?' asked Jude, trying to keep the tension she was feeling out of her voice.

Mabel shook her head. 'No, they didn't go to a party.' Jude's level of excitement plummeted, but Mabel continued solemnly, 'Daddy went to an open house. But Mummy didn't go to the open house because I had an ear infection.'

'So it was the evening after he'd been to the open house,' said Jude, keeping her voice as even as she could, 'and you saw Daddy come and use his special Hiding Things place?' The girl nodded deliberately. 'Can you show me where it is, Mabel?'

'You give up?'

'Yes, I give up. You've won this game. You'll have to show me where you've hidden Woolly Monkey.'

'All right. That means I've won twice. Because I found Woolly Monkey where you'd hidden him in the playroom.'

'Yes, you did, Mabel.' Jude was having great difficulty in not trying to speed up the child's revelation. 'Well done. And where is he now?'

Mabel pointed to the panelling to the right of the fireplace. 'The rose there. That rose. No, the one under.'

Jude touched the smooth old wood of the carved Tudor rose. 'This one?'

'Yes. Daddy turned it and there was a little Hiding Things place.'

Jude turned it. The mechanism moved smoothly. A section of dark skirting board projected into the room, revealing a drawer about the size of a shoebox.

Inside, as anticipated, was Woolly Monkey.

But beneath him was something Jude could not have anticipated—a fluorescent pink mobile phone sock.

CHAPTER THIRTY-TWO

Carole had dropped Jude a little way up the road from the Le Bonniers' house. She didn't want to be seen as she delivered their babysitter. Driving back to Fethering in the Renault she was weighed down by a deep sense of frustration. She felt sure the secrets that might unlock the case lay with the inhabitants of Fedingham Court House, and she feared she was being excluded from a vital stage of the investigation.

Back at High Tor Gulliver, the eternal optimist, looked up at her in hope of a walk, but he was unlucky. His mistress didn't seem even to see him as she sat with a coffee at the kitchen table, her brows furrowed with concentration.

It wasn't that she didn't have another lead to follow up. Jude's conjecture in the car meant that the next port of call had to be Kath. The idea that Ricky's loopy ex-wife was harbouring Old Garge in her flat might be nonsense, but all other investigative routes passed through Fedingham Court House. Jude might well be making great advances there, but, for Carole, Kath offered the only way forward.

Short of sitting in the Crown and Anchor every lunchtime on the off-chance that the woman might turn up, the only potential contact they had was through Kath's work at Ayland's. And was there anyone in this idle and benighted country, thought Carole, who still worked on New Year's Day?

On the other hand, though very few people worked between Christmas and New Year, Ayland's bookkeeper had been there on the Monday. Keen sailors would need access to the boatyard on New Year's Day—indeed, it might be quite busy on a public holiday—so there was a reasonable chance that Kath might be on duty again. The problem was: what cover story could Carole invent to justify her enquiries? This worried her, because the only solutions she could think of involved lying, and Carole Seddon didn't have her neighbour's glib facility in that dark art.

Still, if it came to a choice between lying and making no further progress on the case . . . All she needed was the woman's address. Carole picked up the phone.

Her luck was in, at first. The phone at Ayland's was answered, and it was answered by a woman. *We haven't talked to each other, so she won't recognize my voice*, Carole reassured herself. *A 'Kath' must be short for Katherine, mustn't it? But it might not be, so safer not to take the risk.* From Jude's reports of the woman's continuing attachment to her ex-husband, she was bound to have kept his surname. Carole took a deep breath and went into unfamiliar lying mode.

'Is that Mrs Le Bonnier?'

'Yes.'

'I'm sorry to trouble you on a public holiday . . .'

'Don't worry. As you can gather, I'm in at work.'

'Yes.' Time for the big lie (though it was something that had once been true). 'I'm from the Home Office . . .' Time for the even bigger lie—'and I'm running a check on an asylum seeker.'

'I don't know any asylum seekers.'

'No, I thought you probably wouldn't, but I'm running this check because the man in question, who comes from Somalia, has given your address as where he will be staying in the UK.'

'That's absurd. I've never met anyone from Somalia. How on earth would he have got my name and address?'

'From the phone book. It's quite a common trick. They just pick a name and address in the area where they hope to settle.

Some chancers got away with it a few years back, but we're wise to them now.' Carole sighed wearily. 'But we still have to run these checks. Even on public holidays.'

'Well, as I say, I have never offered shelter to an asylum seeker—from Somalia or anywhere else. Is that all you need me to say?'

'Yes, thank you. All I have to do now is confirm your address.'

'Flat two, seventy-three River Road, Fethering. I can never remember the post code.'

'Don't worry. I can check that out to complete the paperwork. Well, thank you very much for your co-operation, Mrs Le Bonnier. And may I wish you a happy New Year.'

She'd done it! She'd lied at least as successfully as Jude would have done. Now a trip to River Road was in order.

Ignoring Gulliver's pathetic pleas to be taken with her, Carole went into the hall to get her coat. Replacing the handset on the telephone table, she had a thought. If a fictional Somalian asylum seeker could find Kath's address in the phonebook . . .

'K Le Bonnier' and her address were listed in the Worthing telephone directory. As she left High Tor Carole Seddon felt rather sheepish.

River Road, as its name might suggest, ran along the side of the Fether. Though defended by a highly embanked towpath, the roadway occasionally got flooded at times of heavy rain and freak tides. Acknowledging this danger, some of the houses had protective low stone barriers across their front gateways.

Carole eased the Renault into a parking space a little way away from number seventy-three, and looked across at the building. It had a thatched roof, and many layers of whitewash had smoothed the irregularities of what were almost definitely flint walls. The building was very low and Carole was struck by how cramped the two flats into which it had been divided must be.

Fine, perhaps, for Kath, who was very short, but less comfortable for people of standard size.

As she had this thought, she saw the shadow of someone cross in front of one of the cottage's tiny upstairs windows.

The question Carole hadn't considered was, if Old Garge was in Kath's flat, was he there of his own volition or was he a prisoner? The windows looked too small to let a grown man's body through, so maybe he was locked in.

Only one way to find out. She got out of the Renault, wrapped her coat firmly round her, and marched across the road to the entrance of seventy-three River Road. Stepping over the flood defence, she found herself faced by two identical black doors, both with well-polished brass knockers. She raised the one belonging to Flat Two and heard the reverberations of her summons echo through the cottage.

There was a long silence, so long that she thought maybe her quarry had been given instructions to lie low. But then she heard the creaking thud of heavy footsteps coming down the stairs. The door opened and Old Garge stood facing her.

'Carole, we meet again. Am I to assume that you want our conversation to pick up from when we were so rudely interrupted?'

'If that's agreeable to you, Rupert,' she said, deciding that she'd had enough of the Old Garge business.

'That would rather depend, Carole, on the reason for your interest.'

'What do you mean?'

'I would be breaking the terms of my residence here if you were anything to do with the police.'

'I can assure you I have nothing to do with the police.'

'I was assuming that was the case, but I had to be certain.' He backed away from the small doorway, through which he could not have passed without stooping, and gestured to Carole to precede him on the way upstairs.

Going through the open door of the flat and a small hall, she found herself in a low, black-raftered room which seemed to be a shrine to Ricky Le Bonnier. The walls were covered with blown-up photographs of him, but not of the Ricky Le Bonnier of recent years. All of them dated back to the late sixties, the time when he had been married to Kath, the time of her greatest happiness, the time in which she had been stuck ever since. For the first time, as she looked around that room, Carole thought her joking reference to Miss Havisham might not be so far from the truth.

Her entrance into the room was greeted by a low growl, followed by ferocious barking from Rupert Sonning's Jack Russell.

'Be quiet, Petrarch,' said his owner as he closed the door behind him. 'I'm sorry, Carole. He doesn't like being cooped up in here, with only Kath's handkerchief-sized bit of garden to roam around. He misses the freedom of Fethering Beach.'

Carole's first impression of the room had been of all the Ricky Le Bonnier memorabilia, but now she realized that Rupert Sonning had adapted Kath's space to recreate as nearly as possible the interior of his hut. On the table next to where he had been sitting stood a pile of poetry books, on top of which an open copy of Dryden's *Poetical Works* lay facedown. He'd brought his radio with him and classical music filled the room. So did the aroma from a coffeepot.

He offered her a cup, and she accepted. When they were settled down with their drinks, Rupert Sonning asked how she'd tracked him down. 'Did Ricky tell you I was here? Or Kath?'

'I found you through Kath,' said Carole, congratulating herself on not quite adding to her list of lies. 'Presumably it was Ricky who organized your being here?'

'Oh yes, Mr Fixit himself. He saw I was in a spot and he offered to help me out.'

'In what way were you in a spot?'

'Oh, come on, Carole, you were there when Piers came in and told me.'

She felt she was being very obtuse. 'Told you what?'

'Told me that the police wanted to interview me. Well, I couldn't be having that, obviously.'

'Because you knew too much about the murder?'

The old actor gave her a curious look before replying. 'No, not because I knew too much about the murder. Because I wanted to avoid enquiries about whether I'd been living illegally in Pequod, in my beach hut.'

'What?'

'I mentioned this when we spoke before. The Fether District Council are very hot on their Fethering Beach regulations. You're not allowed to stay in a caravan overnight in the Promenade car park, nor are you allowed to sleep overnight in a beach hut. The good folks at the Fedborough offices get very worried about the dangers of Fethering turning into a "shanty town". They say there is insufficient water supply and toilet facilities for people to live in beach huts.'

'And that's what you thought the police wanted to talk to you about?'

'Of course. Why else would they have wanted to see me?'

'They might have wanted to ask you about what you witnessed the night Gallimaufry burnt down.'

'Oh, I wouldn't think so. Ricky said he was sure it was about my residency of Pequod. So he arranged for me to be put safely out of the way up here for a while. Just for a few days, until the police lose interest in what hours I spend in my beach hut.'

Carole's opinion of Ricky Le Bonnier plumbed new depths. Was there any lie the man wasn't capable of telling?

Rupert Sonning, however, didn't share her opinion. 'He's a good man, Ricky,' he said. 'Generous to a fault.'

Carole knew it was the moment for her to take a leap into the unknown. 'And do you think he gets that characteristic from you?'

'From me? Why on earth do you think he should get anything from me?'

'Because,' said Carole coolly, 'you are his father.'

The one reaction she hadn't been expecting was riotous laughter, but that was what she got. Waves of hilarity shuddered through Rupert Sonning's great frame till he was choking and incoherent. Eventually, he managed to gasp out, 'His father? Where on earth did you get that idea from?'

Carole was disquieted, but not completely abashed. 'You don't deny that you worked with Flora Le Bonnier in Gainsborough films after the war?'

'No, I don't, but the theatrical myth that all leading men sleep with all their leading ladies, though perhaps flattering, is just an invention of the gutter press. I can assure you I have never been to bed with Flora Le Bonnier. She may be one of the most beautiful women of her generation, but she's too much like a piece of Dresden china for my taste. I have always gone for something rather earthier in my women. Dirty knickers, I'm afraid, are my thing. So Flora Le Bonnier has never ticked any boxes for me.'

'So you never even went out together?'

'Oh, we did a bit of that. For the benefit of the press.'

'What do you mean?'

'Flora and I first met at the Rank Charm School. Being trained up to become film stars. The publicity department there was always dreaming up romances for their stars. So Flora and I might be photographed leaving a restaurant together, but it was only to increase our public profiles, not because either of us had any genuine interest in the other.

'They were notorious, that publicity lot. They'd invent

anything to get a few column inches about their embryonic stars. I mean, that's where the nonsense started about Flora having a connection with the Le Bonnier family.'

'You mean there never was any truth in it?'

'No, complete fabrication from beginning to end. But she looked the part—and sounded it. Her very boring solicitor father had sent her to the right schools, so the cut-glass accent was there. She looked like an aristocrat, sounded like an aristocrat, so the Rank publicity boys thought: "Why not make her into an aristocrat?" '

'But people believed it?'

'The general public did, yes. In "the business" nobody had any illusions but, equally, nobody cared that much either. We'd all had our past lives reshaped in the cause of publicity. If Flora Le Bonnier wanted to claim an aristocratic lineage, good luck to her.'

'I'm surprised the press didn't expose her.'

'The press was different in those days, Carole. They were genuinely in love with the British film industry. Nothing they liked better than printing out word for word whatever press releases the publicity departments sent them. They knew it was mostly hokum, but they played along. They actually became part of the conspiracy.'

'But you'd have thought, in more recent times, when the nature of reporting has changed so much, somebody would have exposed Flora Le Bonnier's real background.'

'Maybe.' Rupert Sonning shrugged. 'But by then she had become a national treasure. And the public don't like having their national treasures shot down in flames. Anyway, for the tabloid-reading public, Flora's now way too old to be interesting. All they want to hear about is the doings of drugged-up girl singers or love-rat footballers.'

'So there never was a newspaper exposé of Flora?'

'There was one, actually, now I remember. Early seventies, as I recall. Done by a music journalist called Biff Carpenter. I think it was a hatchet job on Ricky Le Bonnier, actually, but it did bring in the fact that his mother's background was completely fabricated. There was a bit of a fuss at the time, but it soon blew over. The British public liked to think of their national treasure Flora Le Bonnier as an aristocrat, and they weren't going to let a little thing like the truth get in the way.'

Carole made a mental note to google the name of Biff Carpenter as soon as she got back to High Tor. Then she turned the conversation back to the fire at Gallimaufry. 'Suppose you'd got it wrong, Rupert? Suppose it wasn't about your residency at the beach hut that the police wanted to talk to you?'

'Ricky told me it was about my being in the beach hut.'

'But he might have been lying. Your being out of the way here might not be in order to protect you, but to protect Ricky himself.'

'But why?'

'Because, Rupert, you did see Ricky from your beach hut the night Gallimaufry burnt down, didn't you?'

'Yes, all right, I did, but there was no way I would have told the police that.'

'Why not?'

'Because I don't like authority.'

Carole took a risk and asked, 'Is that all?'

'What do you mean?'

'I got the impression, when we last met, that you might have a particular reason for wanting to steer clear of the police.'

His pale blue eyes looked sharply into hers. 'How much do you know?'

Carole wasn't about to answer this truthfully and say, 'Nothing.' She shrugged, hoping that her silence would prompt further revelations.

It did. Rupert Sonning's gaze moved rather shamefacedly down to his battered trainers. 'Last summer I had a bit of a set-to with the cops. I hadn't done anything, but if you live my lifestyle, you open yourself up to certain accusations.'

'How do you mean?'

'As you know, I spend most of my time wandering along the beach and inevitably, during the summer, I walk past lots of families with young kids. Well, some of them don't like that.'

'You mean they think you have designs on their children?'

'Not to put too fine a point on it, that's exactly what I mean, Carole. The press is so full of hysteria about kids being abducted and paedophiles and . . . any man who goes for a walk on his own puts himself at risk of that kind of accusation.'

'So somebody did make that accusation against you?'

'Yes, some uptight Yummy Mummy whose daughters had been changing into their bathing costumes as I walked past. She called the police and made a complaint against me. So I was hauled in and . . . well, let's say, they didn't give me a very nice time.'

'Were you charged?'

'No. There was nothing they could charge me with. And that made them even more furious. Anyway, the result of that rather unpleasant experience is that I vowed never to go out of my way to co-operate with the police again.'

'Even if you were a witness to a murder?'

'Even then.' He looked up at her again, an expression of defiance now on his face. 'I don't know whether you want to believe me or not—that's up to you—but I can assure you that I have no interest in small children. The sight of a mature adult female in a bikini can still sometimes get the old juices flowing, but children—no. That has never turned me on. As I say, you don't have to believe me.'

After a silence, Carole said, 'Actually I do.' And she did.

'Anyway, it was an unpleasant experience—and one that's characteristic of the way things are going these days. I think there are too many people around in this country trying to tell the rest of us how to live our lives. What happened to the great British principle of minding your own bloody business? That seems to have gone from contemporary life. We've become a nation of busybodies, whistleblowers, informers, sneaks. Like all these officials who're trying to get me out of Pequod. We've lost far too many basic freedoms during my lifetime—particularly since we joined the European Union. I think people should have the right to use their own property as they think fit.'

'Even to the point of burning it down?'

'In Ricky's case, yes. His wasn't the first and it certainly won't be the last insurance fire in the history of the world. Gallimaufry was doing badly—hardly surprising, it was a stupid thing to set up in the first place—money was getting tight, so Ricky burnt it down.'

'Did you see him do that?'

'I saw him go in the back way carrying a can of something. Then I saw him drive away. A few minutes later I could see the flames licking upwards from the downstairs window.'

'What time would that be?'

'Soon after midnight, I think.'

'From what you say, Rupert, you don't seem to regard lighting an insurance fire as a crime?'

'Not really. Well, if it is, it's a victimless crime. The only people who suffer from it are some faceless bureaucrats in an insurance company.'

'You say they're the only people who suffer. You're forgetting that Ricky's stepdaughter was inside the shop when it burnt down.'

'Yes, but she must have been already dead. Ricky would never have lit the fire if he'd known she was alive in there.'

'Are you sure?'

'Positive.'

'So who do you think killed Polly?'

'As to that, Carole,' said Rupert Sonning, 'I have no idea.'

CHAPTER THIRTY-THREE

While she continued to play the Hiding Things game with Mabel, Jude took only Woolly Monkey out of the secret hiding place. She left the mobile phone sock where it was and slid the hidden drawer back into the skirting board. It moved with great ease, as if it had been recently oiled, but she reckoned the mechanism was probably quite old. Fedingham Court House had borne witness to many generations who had no doubt used the secret space to hide valuables, jewellery, private papers perhaps even the vessels and vestments for a Catholic Mass.

Mabel's parents didn't arrive back at seven, but if they had, they would have found all calm at Fedingham Court House. Their daughter had given Jude very detailed instructions about how to serve supper for herself and her brother, told her about the bit of CBeebies television they were allowed to watch, and talked her through the required rituals of bathtime. Henry, a model of docility, had a bottle of milk before retiring and allowed himself to be put back in his cot with no fuss at all. Mabel indicated to Jude the three stories she required to have read to her—all of which she seemed to know by heart—and then she, too, had her light turned off and settled down for the night. Neither child seemed at all fazed by having their bedtime routine conducted by a relative stranger.

As soon as Mabel's light was off Jude went back downstairs. She had no moral qualms about reopening the secret drawer and removing the fluorescent pink sock, which, as she had hoped, did still contain a mobile phone. She hadn't decided yet what she would do with this vital piece of evidence, but was glad her neighbour wasn't with her. Carole would undoubtedly say that they should hand it straight over to the police. Jude was quite prepared to do that . . . eventually . . . but certainly not until she had checked out the phone for any information it could provide. The odds are always so heavily stacked in favour of the police over the amateur investigator that she was not about to look this particular gift horse in the mouth.

She tried switching it on, but the battery had run down. So, having put the phone and its sock safely into her handbag, Jude did as Lola had suggested and poured herself a glass of white wine from the well-stocked fridge. Then she sat in front of the open fire in the sitting room, very near to the hidden drawer, and tried to control the excesses of her speculation until the Le Bonniers returned home.

At about eight she had a phone call from Lola, apologizing that they were only just then leaving St John's Wood. Flora had been 'at her most demanding. I had to unpack for her. She claims she can't do that with her hands in the state they are. And then she found plenty of small jobs for Ricky, which, of course, he did for her without complaint.'

Lola sounded pretty fed up. Then she asked after the kids, and was relieved to hear that bath and bedtime had gone without a hitch. She said she and Ricky would get back as quickly as they could, but it was unlikely to be before ten. The fridge, though, was full of food left over from the party and Jude was encouraged to help herself to anything she wanted.

In fact, the babysitting vigil didn't last as long as it might have done. At about twenty to nine, just when Jude was thinking of making a foraging raid on the fridge, the au pair Varya arrived back at Fedingham Court House. She looked pretty wan— the vodka in Southampton had evidently flowed with Russian generosity—but she was quite capable of taking over the babysitting duties. So Jude rang for a cab to take her home.

When she got back to High Tor after her encounter with Rupert Sonning, Carole had started googling. She still hadn't got far with the thousands of references to Flora Le Bonnier, and going through all of them in search of one particular article would be a deterrently laborious process. So, instead, she typed in the name Biff Carpenter.

For him, too, there was a surprisingly large number of entries. Clearly, though few of the names he wrote about meant anything to Carole, he had been quite a significant commentator on popular music in the sixties and seventies. 'Had been' were the operative words, according to his very brief Wikipedia entry. Born in 1941, Biff Carpenter had died in 1977.

There was very little other information. Carole wondered whether life was actually long enough for her to trawl through endless articles about Jethro Tull and Procul Harum and King Crimson.

Then she had the thought of googling Biff Carpenter and Flora Le Bonnier together. No relevant references. (Well, she didn't think a nineteenth-century family tree from Ontario featuring a 'Biff' and a 'Flora' was relevant.)

Carole then tried Biff Carpenter and Ricky Le Bonnier together, and that did produce a result. She was directed to the blog of someone who'd clearly been a drummer with various bands in the early seventies. The rambling style suggested that most of his writing was done under the influence of some powerful narcotic.

She was about to give up on the blogger's turgid and misspelt prose when she spotted Ricky Le Bonnier's name. She read the pertinent paragraph:

. . . Like back then we was getting the *Cameleon Haze*

album together and we was working with Rickie Le Bonier as producer and having some great all-niters kind of open party scene in the studio while we was recording and doing a lot of, like, wacky backy and a lot of real heavy stuff too. And Biff Carpenter who was, like, the journo for our kind of music used to hang out at the studio which was good cos if he wrote about a band well you knew that like ment youd made it. Biff was writing for *NME* and all over including a new magasine called *Prog Printz* and he said he was going to do somthing about us for that which would have been like great. And Biff was good mates with all of us especially Rickie and they were smoking some seriously good shit together and injecting too but then, like, they had some bust-up which was bad karma for us because, like, suddenly Biff's off writing a peace for *Prog Printz* that is not about the band but is, like, rubbishing Rickie Le Bonier, not only Ricky but his mother whose, like, some actress or somthing. And Biff really has a go and when the magasine comes out Rickie really loses his cool and suddenly he's not producing our album any more and we're halfway thro and the bread's running out and we're totally buggerred. And then later we hear *Prog Printz* has folded and Biff Carpenter's snuffed it o/ded on the old horse and I'm not talking geegees here and were well up shit creak with no sign of any like padels . . .

Thereafter, the blog seemed to maunder off into incoherent self-pity. Carole thought it reasonable to assume that Biff Carpenter's exposé of Flora Le Bonnier's past was included in the article he wrote attacking Ricky, but she wasn't optimistic about tracking it down. She googled up a couple of references to *Prog Printz*, but they weren't very helpful. The magazine had only run for three editions, and copies were now valuable collector's items. There was no means of accessing their content online.

Carole was thoughtful as she closed down her laptop. Suddenly there were two drug-related deaths in Ricky Le Bonnier's life—Polly's mother and now Biff Carpenter. Of course, it could just be coincidence, a reflection of the lifestyle that Ricky indulged in at that time.

But Carole, being Carole, as she went next door to share her findings with Jude, wondered whether there was more to it than that.

Of course there was still no display on the screen of the mobile. Assuming it was Polly's—and every indication supported that idea—the phone hadn't been used for nearly a fortnight. Its battery was extremely dead. And, frustratingly, neither Jude nor Carole had a charger that fitted it.

They would have to wait till the morning. Fethering didn't boast a mobile phone shop. It was even doubtful whether there was one in Fedborough. Unlocking the secrets held in Polly's mobile might require a trip to Worthing or Chichester. It was profoundly annoying, but there was nothing else they could do but wait.

And what Carole had found out about Ricky Le Bonnier and Biff Carpenter was also frustratingly incomplete. Neither woman slept well that night. Worthing was marginally closer than Chichester, so on Friday morning they made it their destination. Even though Carole had pinpointed the phone shop they wanted to go to from researches on the Internet, their purchase took them a long time. Worthing was extremely full of people who, released from the chore of being nice to relatives over Christmas, were desperate for retail therapy. And most of the residents of Worthing seemed to be in that one phone shop. Those who didn't want to change the mobile they'd been given as a Christmas present were bent on upgrading their handset to the latest model which offered even more technological bells and whistles than their previous one. Transactions like that with the sharp-suited teenage salesmen took an inordinately long time and, though all Carole and Jude wanted to buy was a charger, they had to wait in a queue which threatened to redefine the concept of eternity.

They hadn't risked just memorizing the details of the phone's make and model; they actually took the handset with them to ensure that there should be no mistake in the charger they bought.

When they finally reached the front of the queue, their purchase was quickly completed, though the sharp-suited teenage salesman who served them seemed very disappointed they didn't want to upgrade anything.

Back at Woodside Cottage Jude intended to plug in the phone charger straightaway, but was diverted when she noticed that the indicator light on her answering machine was flickering.

The message was from Ricky Le Bonnier. His voice sounded taut with stress. He asked Jude to ring him as soon as possible.

'I think you've got something of mine,' he said when she got through.

'Oh?'

'You know what I mean. Mabel told me you played the Hiding Things game.'

'Ah.'

'I'm going to come round to your place and, when I do, Jude, I think you'd better give me back my property.'

'Are you sure we aren't talking about your stepdaughter's property?'

'Don't split hairs. I've got to see someone in Fethering this afternoon, then I'll come to your place. Half past four, five, I should think it would be. Don't try and do anything clever with the phone. You're involved in something much bigger than you realize, Jude.'

She must have looked shaken when she finished the call, because Carole asked if she was all right. Jude repeated what Ricky had said.

'Then I'm going to be here when he comes,' announced Carole.

'I'm sure it'll be all right.'

'Jude, a person who has killed once to keep something quiet may not be troubled by the thought of killing again for the same reason.'

'I find it hard to think of Ricky as a killer.'

'It's hard to think of anyone as a killer, but there are still a lot of people who have been sent to prison for murder.'

'Yes, I know. I'll get us some lunch.'

'Not before you've checked that mobile, you won't.'

The charger was so secure in its packaging that Jude had to take a pair of scissors to the obdurate plastic. When she'd finally freed it, she pushed the three-pin plug into a wall socket and pressed the small connector into the bottom of Polly's phone. She switched the handset on and navigated through to the voice-mail.

Only a couple of messages had been saved. One was from Piers, another from one of Polly's actress friends. Both dated from before Ricky's daughter had come down to Fethering, and concerned arrangements for social meetings. It was hard to imagine that either could have any relevance to the girl's death.

'That's very disappointing,' said Carole glumly. 'I really thought we were going to get a breakthrough there.'

'Don't give up hope. We haven't checked her text messages yet.'

These were stored in the in-box with the most recently received message first. That had been sent at 7.29 P.M. on the

Sunday before Christmas, the date of Jude's open house. The message read:

SOMETHING REALLY IMPORTANT HAS COME UP ABOUT THE BOOK. DON'T GO TO LONDON. MEET ME IN GALLI-MAUFRY AT NINE THIS EVENING. DON'T TELL ANYONE ABOUT YOUR CHANGE OF PLANS UNTIL WE'VE SPOKEN.

Jude checked the number from which the text had been sent against the mobile number on the card Ricky Le Bonnier had given her. They were identical.

CHAPTER THIRTY-FOUR

Four-thirty passed, so did five and five-thirty, and there was still no sign of Ricky. After six Jude tried ringing his mobile number, but was only asked to leave a message. She didn't.

They discussed having a drink. Carole was of the opinion that a drink might weaken their defences for the confrontation that lay ahead. Jude reckoned that a drink would strengthen them for the confrontation that lay ahead. Her counsel prevailed. She poured out two large glasses of Chilean Chardonnay. (The booze for the open house still showed no signs of running out.)

Soon after a quarter past eight, Jude's landline rang. She snatched at the handset, expecting to hear Ricky, but the voice at the other end was a woman's.

'Jude, I have some news for you, strange news.' The voice sounded so weird and ethereal that Jude took a moment to recognize it as Kath's. 'Do you wish to know where Ricky Le Bonnier is?'

'Yes, I do.'

'I felt his aura. I knew he was coming to Fethering today.'

'He was coming to see me, but he hasn't arrived.'

'I will tell you where you will find him. He is in his car near the Fethering Yacht Club. He has parked it in the same place as where I saw him the Sunday before Christmas.'

Immediately, Jude had a vision of Ricky once again taking risks to see Anna. 'Is he alone?' she asked.

'Oh yes,' replied Kath with considerable satisfaction. 'He is alone. The Devil Women have no power over him anymore. Their power is broken. I am the only one who now has power over Ricky.'

The woman was beginning to sound as nutty as an entire fruit cake factory, but there was something in her words that disturbed Jude. She felt a sudden urgency to find Ricky Le Bonnier, to check that he wasn't in danger. She ended the phone call.

Walking to the Yacht Club would not have taken long, but they went in the car. Jude's sense of emergency had communicated itself to Carole and neither of them spoke as the Renault hurtled through Fethering.

The Mercedes 4 × 4 was exactly where Kath had said it would be. Parked facing the sea between the end of the shopping parade and the entrance to Fethering Yacht Club. Its lights were on, sending strips of brightness out across the shingle of the beach until their glare faded into darkness.

Carole parked the Renault, and Jude was first to the Mercedes. She could see Ricky Le Bonnier slumped in the driver's seat.

The door was unlocked and when Jude opened it the interior light went on. There was no sign of any injury on Ricky's body, no blood, no evidence of a weapon.

And yet neither Jude nor Carole had any doubt that he was dead.

CHAPTER THIRTY-FIVE

'I just don't know what to tell Mabel. She adored Ricky. He was her Daddy and nobody could replace him. I haven't told her about Polly yet, but she didn't see Polly that often, so I can break that to her gently. But Ricky . . .'

Lola was very near to tears. Jude had rung through to Fedingham Court House on Saturday morning. Her motive had little to do with criminal investigation. She just knew from previous encounters how fragile Lola was beneath her glamorous carapace.

'Mabel will survive,' she said. 'Children are very resilient. But what about you, Lola? How are you feeling?'

'Numb at the moment. Every now and then I almost forget what's happened, my imagination can't cope with the idea of it being true. But then the reality crashes back in with a hideous thump and I'm left winded and weepy and . . . Ricky was the love of my life, Jude. There'll never be anyone else. I daren't think what the future's going to be like.'

'Like Mabel, you will survive. It'll be grim, but you will come through this.'

'It's hard to believe that at the moment.'

'I'm sure it is, but what I say is true. And, in the meantime, you'll have a lot of practical things to do . . .'

'Yes. Arranging the funeral.' A sob caught Lola unawares. 'I suppose I always knew that I'd outlive Ricky, that at some point

I would have to face life without him. But not so soon. Not so soon.'

'Presumably, you'll have to wait a bit before fixing a date for the funeral, won't you?' asked Jude, with all the delicacy of which she was capable.

'Why?'

'Well, until the police allow you to have Ricky's body.'

'What have the police got to do with it?' Lola sounded appalled at the idea of their being involved.

'When there's a suspicious death . . .'

'There's nothing suspicious about Ricky's death. There'll have to be a post mortem, yes . . .' The image of her husband's body being carved up shook her for a moment. 'But all that the post mortem will find is that he died of a heart attack.'

'Oh?'

'There'd always been a risk of that happening. Before we got married, Ricky told me that he'd had a couple of minor heart attacks, that his heart was weak. He was very honest with me, he didn't want me to go into the marriage not knowing everything about him.'

'So he had congenital heart disease, did he?'

'No, not congenital. Again, he was very honest. There was one stage in his life when Ricky did a lot of drugs. Heroin, mostly. And I think there's medical evidence—there's certainly anecdotal evidence—that heroin buggers up the system, particularly the heart. There are plenty of examples of rock stars dying of heart attacks in their late fifties, early sixties. So Ricky's heart was fatally damaged by his early excesses. It was a time-bomb ticking away. Then with all the stress he's been under since Polly's death—and his bloody mother being as demanding as ever, putting pressure on him every way she knew how— which is quite a lot of ways . . .' The last sentence was spoken with deep bitterness.

'Anyway . . .' At the end of the line Jude could hear Lola take a deep breath as she struggled for control. 'What's heartbreaking about it is that Ricky had really changed. He hasn't touched any kind of drug for eleven years, he's clean. Even the drinking, even though he talks it up a lot, he's cut back hugely on that. And then marrying me, and having Mabel and Henry. It was a new start . . . it was . . .' Emotion robbed her of speech.

'Well, look, Lola, if there's anything I can do . . . Are you on your own there? Because I could come up and—'

'I'm fine, thank you, Jude. Varya's looking after the kids. And Piers is here again . . . though that is something of a mixed blessing.'

'Oh?'

'Piers has always had a tendency to self-dramatize. And he's overreacting like mad to Ricky's death. In a way, that's almost helping me. Seeing how ridiculous Piers looks being all weepy and hysterical is stopping me from going down the same route.'

'OK, well, you've got my number, Lola. If there's anything I can do . . .'

'I'll let you know.'

'And when you've got details of the funeral sorted . . .'

'I'll see to it you're informed. Everything should be pretty straightforward once the post mortem's been done. It's tragic and it's heartbreaking, but it was a natural death.'

Jude wasn't quite as convinced as Lola about that.

On the spur of the moment—which was rare, Carole Seddon was very wary of anything that happened on the spur of the moment—she invited Jude round for lunch. She was keen to use up the remains of the Christmas Day turkey which she'd frozen. The old year had passed and Carole wanted to tidy things up by removing all traces of it.

She did the turkey in a white sauce, served up with mashed

potatoes and peas. Though she said it herself, it did taste rather good. And there was still a bottle of the Christmas Chilean Chardonnay left to accompany the meal.

Inevitably the women's conversation soon moved to the murder—or what both of them felt convinced now was a double murder.

'The main question,' said Carole, 'is who Ricky was coming to see in Fethering before he came to see us.'

Jude nodded. 'Well, the two obvious contenders are his ex-wife and his lover. Kath and Anna.'

'And don't forget Rupert Sonning. He clearly had had some dealings with Ricky . . . well, Rupert jumped when Ricky told him to.'

'Yes. I take it we're assuming a connection between the two deaths?'

'We have to, Jude. Otherwise the coincidence is just too great. And I think we can also assume that Ricky was killed to stop him from divulging what he knew about Polly's death to us, or to the police, or indeed to anyone else.'

'That's certainly the most likely scenario. Pity, I was absolutely convinced he was our murderer—particularly after we found that text from him on Polly's mobile.'

'You say "text from him", Carole. But, in fact, we should be saying "text from his mobile". We don't know who pressed the buttons.'

'No. Say he'd left it at Fedingham Court House when he went to take Polly to Fedborough Station, then it could have been used by Lola . . . or Flora . . . or Varya, come to that.'

'What about Piers, though, Carole?'

'Piers sending the text? How on earth would he have got hold of Ricky's mobile? He claims to have been in his London flat that evening, waiting for Polly to join him.'

'He also says he spent the night with his new girlfriend.'

'Yes, I'm not certain that we can accept everything said by Piers Duncton as gospel truth.'

Jude took a pensive mouthful of turkey, then said, 'If Ricky isn't guilty of killing Polly, he's still in the frame for torching Gallimaufry.'

'More than in the frame. He did it. Rupert Sonning witnessed him doing it.'

'Assuming Rupert Sonning's telling the truth.'

'Yes, he's an odd man, spending the declining years of his life masquerading as a beachcomber. And he has a very strange sense of morality. He apparently doesn't see anything wrong with burning down a business to claim on the insurance. He called it "a victimless crime".'

'All right, Carole. So, moving on from the hypothesis that Ricky didn't kill his stepdaughter, but did start the fire . . . he did that because he found Polly in the shop dead, and he set the shop alight in the hope of protecting the person who he knew had killed her.'

This gave Carole a new idea. Her eyes sparkled with excitement as she announced, 'And that person must be his mother. Flora's such a powerful personality that Ricky would do anything to appease her. Yes, that makes sense. She had some animus against Polly . . . I don't know what, but we can work that out later. Ricky left his mobile at home and Flora used it to send the text which lured Polly back to Gallimaufry. Flora met her there and shot her!'

Carole sat back, glowing with the satisfaction of having solved the case. She raised her glass to toast the success, but lowered it when she saw the expression on Jude's face.

'What's wrong? I've just provided the perfect theory of what happened.'

'It's a good theory,' said Jude, 'but it does suffer from one major flaw.'

252

'I don't think it does.' Carole's confidence began to drain away. 'What major flaw?'

'Flora's hands. You've seen how arthritic they are. They're as useless as flippers. She can't grip anything. She has to use both hands to hold a wineglass. There's no way she could send a text message with those hands. And, by the same token, there was no way she could have held a gun to shoot Polly.'

'Oh, damn.' It was very rare for Carole to utter even the mildest swear word, but she had been severely provoked. Her splendid edifice of a solution had been undermined by one tiny detail. What made her even more annoyed was the knowledge that Jude was right.

Her mouth set in an expression of petulance as her friend mused, 'I wonder if there's more than one person involved? Someone sent the text from Ricky's mobile, someone else met Polly at Gallimaufry and shot her.'

'What makes you think that?'

'Well, it widens our range of suspects, for one thing. Also, if we're assuming the text was sent by someone at Fedingham Court House . . . though it needn't have been, because somebody might have stolen Ricky's mobile or he might have given it to someone or—'

'Just for the moment, Jude,' said Carole tartly, 'let's assume that the text was sent from Fedingham Court House.'

'All right. Well, if that is the case, it wasn't sent by anyone in Fethering—in other words, it wasn't sent by any of the three people Ricky might have come here to see yesterday afternoon . . .'

'Kath, Anna or Rupert Sonning.'

'Exactly.' Jude sipped at her Chardonnay. 'The fact that Ricky had Polly's mobile phone suggests to me that he definitely did find her dead in the shop. He took it to avoid anyone who was investigating the crime finding the message we found on it.'

'If he knew that message was there.'

'Yes. I wonder if, when he found her body, he also found the gun that had been used to kill her . . .'

'Well, if he did, he would have left it there.'

'Why?'

'Oh, come on, Jude, keep up. He'd have left it there, so that the police would find it—or at least the charred remains of it—thus supporting the suicide theory that he was so keen to persuade us to accept.'

'I'd forgotten about that. It seems such a long time ago.' Jude finished up the last of her turkey and aligned her knife and fork on the plate.

'If you'd like a sweet, there's a bit of Christmas pudding left . . . or some mince pies.'

Jude's brown eyes gleamed. 'Mince pies with brandy butter?' Carole nodded. 'Yes, please!'

As they settled down to their final Christmas indulgence, Jude began, 'Of the three people Ricky might have been coming to see yesterday . . .'

'Kath, Anna or Rupert Sonning.'

'Yes. We don't have an address for Anna . . .'

'We know her surname. Carter. Maybe she's in the phone book?' Carole checked and she wasn't. 'Probably moved into the area too recently.'

'Well, you can try another of your dog-walking missions tomorrow morning.'

'Yes.'

'I wonder if she's heard about Ricky's death yet. And what effect it'll have on her when she does. In the long term, I think she'll probably feel relief. The relationship was never going to go anywhere.'

'From what she said to me, she was quite deeply entangled with him. He meant a lot to her, as part of her reinvention of herself.' But Carole didn't want to spend long on psychological speculation. 'Anyway, we can't find Anna today, so that leaves Kath and Rupert Sonning.'

'Who may still be living at her place. I suppose we'll have to try Ayland's again, though whether Kath'll be there, who knows? She must take a day off sometime.'

A call to the boatyard produced nothing but an answering machine message. Jude sighed despondently. 'If only we had a home number or a mobile for her . . .'

Her neighbour beamed. 'But we do. I made a point of getting both from Rupert when I visited him on Thursday.'

'Oh, well done, Carole. I think a call might be in order, don't you?'

'A call saying what?'

'A call asking whether Kath Le Bonnier would care to join us in the Crown and Anchor for an early evening pint of Guinness.'

CHAPTER THIRTY-SIX

Kath did not seem fazed by the request for a meeting, nor, when she arrived at the Crown and Anchor, was she fazed by the fact that Jude had brought Carole along. And, remarkably for someone who had just lost the love of her life, she did not show any signs of grief.

After her introduction, Carole went to the bar to get the drinks and Jude expressed her condolences about Ricky's death.

'Yes, but he hasn't really gone,' said Kath. 'He's just in a different dimension.'

'Ah. And where is that dimension?'

'It's around us.' The woman smiled beatifically. 'It's all around us.'

'So is Ricky in a better place than he was when he was alive?'

'Oh yes.' Kath giggled. 'The Devil Women can't get at him where he is now. Only I can get at him now.'

The drinks arrived, and Jude felt quite relieved that her neighbour hadn't witnessed the recent exchange. Carole and New Age mysticism were a potentially combustible mix.

'Did you actually see Ricky yesterday afternoon?' asked Jude.

'Oh yes, I saw him.'

Carole came in with the next question. 'Did you talk to him?'

'I talked to him, yes.'

'And what did he say to you?'

Kath looked at Carole curiously. 'He didn't say anything. He was no longer in the dimension where he could speak.'

Seeing the exasperation building in her friend, Jude said quickly, 'You mean Ricky was already dead when you saw him yesterday?'

'Dead? What do you mean when you say "dead"?'

'She means,' said Carole severely, 'that he had stopped breathing and was showing no other vital signs.'

'Ah. In this dimension, yes.'

'What?' asked Carole.

'Kath,' Jude intervened hastily, 'did Ricky ring you to say he was coming to Fethering yesterday?'

'No. I just knew he was coming. I felt his aura.'

Avoiding Carole's eye, Jude asked whether there had been anyone else with Ricky.

'No. He was on his own in the car, leaving his body there while the real him moved into another dimension.'

Covering Carole's snort, Jude went on, 'You don't know whether Ricky contacted Rupert Sonning yesterday?'

'Rupert Sonning? I don't know anyone called Rupert Sonning.'

'Sorry. Old Garge. Who's staying at your place at the moment. You don't know whether Ricky contacted him?'

'I don't think so. Anyway, Old Garge isn't staying with me anymore.'

'Do you know where he's gone to?'

The response was a shrug which announced that she didn't know and she didn't much care.

'But Ricky did ask you to put him up, didn't he?'

'Oh yes. I don't like Old Garge. I don't like having anyone in my flat except for me and Ricky. But Ricky asked me to, so I let Old Garge stay.'

'Kath,' asked Jude, 'you haven't seen Ricky's latest Devil Woman recently, have you? The blonde one from the shop?'

'Not since I saw her in the car with him before Christmas, no.'

'But do you think Ricky came to Fethering yesterday to see her?'

Kath took a sip of Guinness before replying. 'I don't know. It doesn't matter now. None of the Devil Women can reach Ricky now. Only I can reach him. Everything is perfect now. Things have been arranged as they should be.'

Carole and Jude exchanged looks which contained not only exasperation, but also an element of suspicion. If Ricky's death brought Kath such a sense of peace and resolution, was it not possible that she might have helped him on his way?

'While Old Garge was staying with you,' asked Carole, 'did he say anything about—'

'I didn't listen to him when he talked.'

Carole continued evenly, 'Did he say anything about Polly's death?'

The eyes Kath turned on her questioner had a new shrewdness in them. She may have been loopy, but some bits of her brain worked extremely well. 'What sort of thing should he have said?'

'Old Garge has been described as "the eyes and ears of Fethering Beach". He told me he'd seen Ricky setting fire to Gallimaufry. I was wondering whether he'd said any more to you about what happened that night. I mean, he told me he had no idea who killed Polly. I thought he might have opened out a bit more to you.'

'Why should he? He was staying in my place under sufferance. I didn't encourage conversation while he was there.'

'Are you sure he didn't say anything about it?' asked Jude in a gentler tone than Carole's.

'All he said was that Polly's death was payback time for Ricky. He said there are some people you offend at your peril.'

'But he didn't mention any names?'

A resolute shake of the grey, sixties' hair. 'No names.'

Carole let out a frustrated sigh. 'Oh, it's so infuriating. If only we could talk to Old Garge . . .'

'I don't see why you can't,' said Kath. Both women looked at her. 'I'll lay any odds that what he did the minute he left my place was to go back to his beach hut.'

'When did he actually leave?'

'Yesterday. The minute I'd told him that Ricky had gone to another dimension.'

'How did he react to the news?'

'He said, "Good, if Ricky's dead, then that lets me off the hook." '

The winter air prickled against their faces. The damp, cold smell of the sea assailed their nostrils. They could see the tiny square of light from Pequod when they reached the Promenade, and as they drew closer they could hear the strains of Radio 3. Rupert Sonning's anxieties about being found overnighting in his beach hut had clearly been allayed.

Inside Carole and Jude's heads the same questions were churning. What had he meant by saying that Ricky's death had 'let him off the hook'? What precisely had been his movements, in his Old Garge persona, on the night of Polly's death? And still at the back of both their minds was the thought that he might have some closer tie than he claimed to the Le Bonnier family.

Carole, as the one who had visited Pequod before, knocked on the wooden door. It was a cautious moment or two before a slice of Rupert Sonning's face appeared at the crack. 'Ah, it's you.' There was the sound of him disconnecting a chain on the inside. 'Can't be too careful after dark. Sometimes get some louts in from Brighton whose idea of a good night out is beating up an old man in a beach hut.'

He ushered them into the warm. Back in his own environment, the Jack Russell Petrarch was totally relaxed, and showed no more than polite interest in the visitors. 'Thought I might be hearing from you again,' said Rupert.

'This is my friend Jude.'

'Oh, Jude and I know each other, don't we?' To Carole's annoyance, he winked. 'Talked on the beach many a time, haven't we? Always guaranteed to get more than a Fethering nod from the lovely Jude. Usually a nice cuddle, I'm glad to say. Would you find something to sit on? Coffee?'

They both declined the offer and he seemed to note the seriousness of their demeanour. As he resettled into his armchair, he asked, 'So what are you accusing me of now?'

'Nothing. We just want a bit of clarification,' replied Carole.

He grimaced. 'Sounds ominous. Are you still asking me to admit that I'm the late Ricky's father?'

Carole blushed. 'No.'

'What we do want you to tell us,' said Jude, 'is why you said that Ricky's death "let you off the hook"?'

'Oh, is that all?' He relaxed visibly. 'Very simple. Ricky's death will have wound up the investigation into the death of Polly Le Bonnier. There won't be any homicide police snuffling around Fethering Beach anymore. *Ergo,* I'm let off the hook and can return safely to my possibly illegal domicile—which is where you find me.'

Carole wasn't buying that, it sounded far too well prepared. 'Why do you think that Ricky's death will stop further investigation into Polly's?'

'It's obvious.' He explained as if he were talking to a child. 'The case is neatly rounded off. Ricky can't live with the guilt of having killed his stepdaughter, so he comes back to near the scene of her death and tops himself.'

'When we last spoke, you said you had no idea who had killed Polly.'

'Well, I didn't, did I? Ricky hadn't topped himself then, had he? But now he has—and I can't imagine a clearer admission of guilt than that.'

Strangely, in their responses to Ricky's death, neither Carole nor Jude had considered the possibility of suicide. Such a robust, positive figure would be the last person they could imagine taking his own life. But when Rupert hazarded that there might be a history of depression in Ricky's family, they were forced to admit that was true.

'And he'd taken a hell of a battering over the last couple of weeks, hadn't he?' the old actor went on. 'God knows how it feels to have killed someone, least of all your own stepdaughter. I've never had children—either my own or inherited—but if I had, I'd like to think I wouldn't raise a hand against them. The sense of guilt must be appalling. And then Ricky had the stress of the police sniffing around everything, and the strong likelihood that they might find evidence to charge him with the murder. All that, plus a relationship breaking up as well, I'm not surprised it was more than he could handle.'

'Relationship?' asked Jude. 'What relationship? He and Lola seemed fine.'

'Not his relationship with his wife,' said Rupert Sonning patiently. 'His bit on the side.'

'Anna?'

'Yes, the Marilyn-Monroe-lookalike-I-don't-think-so.'

'But had they split up?' asked Carole. 'When I last saw Anna, she spoke as if the relationship was still ongoing.'

'It didn't sound very ongoing when I heard them talking about it.'

'When was that?'

'That Sunday. The evening before the fire.'

Simon Brett

'Tell us exactly what happened,' said Carole.

'Well, I quite often walk along the beach after dark. Petrarch loves it then, somehow the smells seem sharper for him. That night we were on the dunes and I had a clear view of the back of Gallimaufry. I saw Ricky and his bit of stuff coming out—not the first time I'd seen them either.'

'Anna thought no one had ever seen them together.'

'Well, that just goes to show what a short time she's been living here, doesn't it? Nothing in Fethering happens unseen. There's always someone watching.' Ever the actor, Rupert Sonning deepened his voice to increase the drama of his narrative. 'Anyway, as I say, Petrarch and I were on the dunes and I could see Ricky and Anna through the tufts of grass, but they couldn't see me. And I could hear what they were saying too. Quite clear it was. He said, "We've got to stop this. It's not working anymore." '

He took on different voices for the two characters as he continued, 'And she says, "It is. It is working, Ricky. I need you. I can't live without you." He says, "You managed to live without me for a good few years before we met." She says, "But now I have met you, I can't go back to how I was before. If you end it, I won't be responsible for my actions." He says, "Oh, please don't try that line. I've met more than my share of women who say they're going to kill themselves. And they never do." And she says, "Be careful, Ricky. It might not be myself that I kill." '

There was a silence, then a rather cross Carole said, 'Why didn't you tell me this before?'

'Because you didn't ask,' said Rupert Sonning.

Jude looked across at Carole. 'I think we'd better find Anna as soon as possible.'

'We'll have to wait till tomorrow morning, on the off-chance that she's taking Blackie out for a walk.'

'Oh, surely there must be some way we can find out where she lives.'

'There is,' announced Rupert Sonning. 'It's not for nothing that I am called "the eyes and ears of Fethering Beach". Would you like me to give you Anna Carter's address?'

CHAPTER THIRTY-SEVEN

It might have been better if they'd had a phone number to warn Anna of their visit, but they hadn't. Anyway, such a call might have alerted her to danger and allowed her time to make good her escape.

Carole and Jude went back from the beach to High Tor and got in the Renault. The address they had been given was on the extreme edge of Fethering's gentility, bordering the less salubrious area of Downside. There would have been no problem walking there in the daylight, but after dark they felt more secure in the car.

The woman who answered the door was presumably the landlady, whom Anna had described as 'a nosy cow'. When they asked about her tenant, she certainly seemed to know a lot of detail. 'She's been in her room all day today. Hasn't come out even to get anything to eat. She's been crying a lot, and all. You can hear it from outside her door. And all over the house,' she added hastily, to cover up her surveillance activities, before continuing, 'I think it's because she heard about that man dying down by the Fethering Yacht Club. She worked for his wife at the shop that burnt down, the one with the silly name. I think there was something going on there.'

'Something going on?' asked Carole.

The landlady very nearly winked as she said, 'Something going on between my Miss Carter upstairs and that Mr Le Bonnier. That's why she's taking his death so hard.' Again, so much for Anna's blind faith that no one in Fethering knew of their liaison.

'I wonder if we could see Miss Carter,' said Jude.

'Well, I don't know that she'd want to see anyone, but I could ask. And then she could come down and talk in my sitting room through there. I'll leave you on your own, just be through in the kitchen.' A kitchen which no doubt commanded an excellent position for eavesdropping.

'It's all right. We'll talk to her in her room,' said Carole.

The landlady looked disgruntled at that. Crying might be audible all over the house, but the intricacies of conversation could not be heard by anyone who wasn't actually lurking on the landing. And even the most inveterate snoopers have their pride.

She led them upstairs and knocked on the door. They heard a sharp yap from the West Highland terrier. 'What is it?' asked a pained voice from inside.

'Two ladies come to see you, Miss Carter.'

The door was opened to reveal a very depleted Anna Carter. The peroxide blond hair was straggly and her face, deprived of make-up, looked sad and old. Her eyes were rimmed with red. She looked at Carole and Jude blankly.

'Thank you very much,' said Carole to the landlady and then, uncharacteristically assertive, she stepped into the room, quickly followed by Jude. Blackie, barking suspiciously, came towards them, but a sniff at their ankles seemed to reassure him and he moved back to his basket.

The room's furnishings were minimal—a single bed, a dressing table, an armchair and an upright chair, all probably salvaged from the second-hand stores of Worthing. Clearly Anna Carter's reinvention of herself had been minimally funded.

The glass of water and box of tissues on the table beside the armchair showed where she had been sitting and when she

265

gestured her visitors to sit down, Carole took the hard chair and Jude sat on the edge of the bed.

'What's all this about?' asked Anna feebly.

Carole didn't have anything prepared, but she improvised, saying she'd heard about Ricky's death and knew that Anna would be devastated, and had come along to see if there was anything she could do to help. She explained Jude's presence by saying she was 'a friend and a professional counsellor, used to dealing with bereavement'.

'Well, that's very kind of you, but I don't think anyone can do anything at the moment. I've just got to get through this on my own . . . though God knows how long that's going to take.' The thought brought on a new outburst of crying. She rubbed savagely at her eyes with a tissue, careless of the discomfort it might cause.

'When did you last see Ricky?' Jude spoke very gently.

'You mean when did I last see him to talk to?' Anna asked through receding sobs.

'If you like.'

'Well, the time I told you about, Carole. That Sunday just before Christmas.'

'You didn't see him yesterday?' Anna bowed her head, but didn't answer Carole's question. 'Did you have a call from him yesterday?' Still silence. 'Anna, Ricky was going to come and see Jude and me yesterday afternoon. He said he had to see someone else in Fethering first. Was that someone you?' Nothing. 'I ask you again, did you have a call from Ricky yesterday?'

The lack of response continued, so Jude tried another tack. 'Old Garge—you know, the one who lives in a beach hut, has a Jack Russell—he overheard a conversation between Ricky and you that Sunday before Christmas, the night of the fire. He said Ricky was threatening to end your relationship, and you threatened to kill him if he did.'

This did finally have an effect. Anna Carter looked up from the tissue in which she had been hiding her face and said, 'Oh, so that's it, is it? I'm now a suspect in some game of murder investigation you're playing?'

'You can't blame us for being intrigued,' said Jude.

'I suppose not,' Anna said bitterly. 'Nobody has any secrets anymore, do they? Everyone's common property. All right, I'll tell you what happened—if only to stop you from adding more lies and insinuations to the Fethering grapevine. I told you about when my affair with Ricky started, Carole, and I'm sure you passed it all on to Jude, didn't you? And yes, as Old Garge overheard, that Sunday before Christmas Ricky did talk about breaking it off. It was just as we were leaving Gallimaufry. Normally, we'd leave separately to avoid being seen together. That night, just as I'd gone out of the back door, Ricky came after me and we had the conversation Old Garge described to you. I was pretty furious, nearly hysterical, which was why Ricky suggested we talk in the car. I think he was worried about someone hearing the commotion. That was why I was in the Mercedes with him that evening. We never had been at any other time. Anyway, we sat in the car and talked and it seemed to be OK. We kind of realized how much we did mean to each other. Ricky said he'd ring me over the Christmas period, but he never . . .' Her lower lip wobbled.

'Had he talked about leaving you before?' Jude used the soft voice of a therapist.

'No. Well, only in the way lovers do. He'd say, "You know, we shouldn't be doing this," but that was more as a come-on than an expression of guilt. It added to the excitement of the times when we were together.'

'And was there anything different about him that Sunday evening? Was he particularly tense or nervous?'

'Yes, he was. He tried to hide it—Ricky never liked showing

any weakness—but I could tell he was strung up. And it seemed worse after he had the phone call.'

'Phone call?' Carole repeated, instantly alert. 'Did he have his mobile with him?'

'No, he'd forgotten it, left it at home. The call came through on the landline at Gallimaufry. There was a handset in the flat, not in the bedroom, in one of the other rooms. When it rang, I told him to leave it, that it would just be some customer checking our opening hours running up to Christmas or something like that, but he insisted on answering.'

'Did you hear what he said?'

'No. He was in the other room.'

'Did he say who it was on the phone?'

'No, but I would assume it was Lola. Who can't have been over the moon to find him answering the phone in the shop at that time, anyway. The call unsettled him, though, really put him off his stroke. Straight afterwards he said we should get dressed and get out. And I'm sure it was the phone call that made him suggest we should split up.'

'Why?'

'Well, if Lola had tracked him down to Gallimaufry on a Sunday evening, she must have been suspicious of something, mustn't she? Why else would she have rung the shop?'

'Maybe. And then yesterday . . .' Jude prompted. 'Tell us what happened yesterday.'

'All right. I hadn't heard from him since that Sunday, and I was feeling pretty low about it and thinking that he really had dumped me, but hadn't got the guts to tell me so. And I thought I could see him at their New Year's Eve party, but when the time came, I hadn't the nerve to go. Then I had a call from him early yesterday afternoon. He said he wanted to meet. I felt so happy that I . . .'

The realization of her changed circumstances threatened to

overwhelm her again, but she bit her lip and struggled on, her voice taut with the effort of will. 'He said we'd meet down by the Fethering Yacht Club, where he usually parked the car, where we'd been when I last saw him. I got there at the time he'd said. The car's engine was switched off, but the headlights were on. I looked inside. Ricky was dead.'

'And you didn't see anyone else around?' asked Carole, trying to work out the sequence of people discovering the body, whether Kath had been there before Anna.

'No.'

'So what did you do then?'

'I came straight back here. I started crying, which is more or less what I've been doing ever since.'

'You didn't think of reporting the death to the police?'

'No!' replied Anna with a sudden, blazing bitterness. 'His dead body's nothing to do with me. That's something for his bloody family to sort out!'

She seemed exhausted by her narrative. There was a long, long silence. The landlady, who couldn't have failed to hear Anna's recent outburst from anywhere in the house, must have wondered what was happening.

It was Jude who finally broke the silence. Her voice was softer and more soothing than ever. 'Anna, did Ricky say why he wanted to see you yesterday? Did he say that he wanted your affair to continue?'

'Not in so many words. But what he said implied that we would have a future together, that we would go on seeing each other. He said I was one of the few people he could trust, and he wanted me to look after something for him.'

'Did he tell you what it was?'

'He said it was a flash drive . . . you know, one of those memory sticks. He said it was very precious to him, and he didn't want to leave it lying around at home because he didn't feel his home was secure.'

Jude had the passing thought that her finding Polly's mobile might have something to do with his risk assessment.

'Did you get the flash drive?' asked Carole, trying without great success to hide her urgency.

'How could I have done?'

'It was probably on his key-ring, or in his pocket.'

'Look, I'd just come across the dead body of the man I loved, possibly the only man I really loved. I wasn't about to start riffling through his pockets.'

'No, of course not,' said Carole, properly abashed for her insensitivity.

Jude asked the important question. 'Do you know what was on the flash drive, Anna?'

'Ricky said it was a copy of a book that his stepdaughter Polly had written.'

CHAPTER THIRTY-EIGHT

'The agent,' said Jude, as soon as they got back into the Renault. 'We've got to get in touch with the agent who read Polly's book.'

'The one who'd been at Cambridge with Lola and Piers?'

'That's right. Serena Somebodyorother, if my memory serves me right.'

'I suppose we could try to contact Piers. If he's still at Fedingham Court House.'

'We don't need to do that.'

'What do you mean?'

'I'm pretty sure I'll have Serena's number at Woodside Cottage.'

'Oh?' said Carole.

'Because that's where Polly's mobile is.'

'Ah,' said Carole.

Sure enough, in the Contacts list on the dead girl's phone, there was an entry for 'Serena.' On the assumption that the name was unusual and this must be Serena Fincham, Jude rang the number straightaway. As soon as she said she was calling about Polly Le Bonnier, the rather Sloaney voice at the other end became very concerned.

'That was terrible. I only got the news from a chum a couple of days ago. I'd been away skiing over Christmas. What a disaster—poor Polly. Do you know anything about exactly what happened?'

'I know quite a bit, and I'm trying to work out the rest. I wonder, would it be possible for us to meet?'

'Sure. When?'

'Sooner the better. Is tomorrow possible for you?'

'No, I'm staying with my parents in Gloucestershire. Back to work on Monday, though. Could do after work, sixish. My office is in Earls Court.'

'Would it be possible to make it a bit earlier?'

'Not sure. There's bound to be a log-jam of manuscripts. Aspiring writers don't seem to observe public holidays.'

'It is rather urgent.'

'Oh. Well, I suppose I could nip out for a coffee sometime in the morning. Since it's about Polly. I mean, I really am devastated.'

They fixed to meet in a coffee shop near Serena's office at eleven o'clock on the Monday morning. Anticipating the reaction when she relayed this to Carole, Jude said, 'And you'll be there too.'

She was on her own in Woodside Cottage at about half past nine on the Sunday evening when the phone rang. It was a very weary-sounding Lola.

'How're you holding up?'

'Pretty grim. But it helps having to do stuff with the children. Though I'm still no nearer breaking the news to Mabel. I fobbed her off this evening with something about Daddy being away, which has been the case often enough so she didn't suspect anything. But there's only so long I can keep doing that.'

'You'll find a way to tell her.'

Lola sighed deeply. 'I'm sure I will, though I can't for the life of me imagine what it'll be.'

'Is Piers still with you?'

'Yes, and getting to be a bloody nuisance. Emoting all over

the place. It's quite honestly the last thing I need at the moment.'

'He's a sensitive soul.'

'Huh. Is that what you call it? A self-appointed "sensitive soul". His only real concern is his own emotions, he never considers anyone else's. Anyway, Jude, reason I rang . . .'

'Yes?'

'I just wanted to say thank you for being such a support over the last few days. I don't know how I'm going to get through what lies ahead, but at least I've got friends like you to help me through.'

'Of course you have,' said Jude. 'If there's anything I can do, just ask.'

And she felt very guilty that Lola Le Bonnier was still on her list of suspects.

CHAPTER THIRTY-NINE

They'd travelled up from Fethering to Victoria on the first cheap train, and were in Earls Court well before eleven. From the wide array offered by the coffee shop, Carole asked frostily for 'an ordinary black, please.' Jude opted for a cappuccino, and also had a sticky *pain aux raisins.* Serena Fincham was late. It was after twenty past eleven and they were beginning to think she might have ducked the encounter when a red-haired girl in her thirties came rushing in through the door, clutching a battered leather briefcase overflowing with papers. She identified the only two women sitting together and came bustling across to them.

'So sorry. All hell breaking loose at the office. Now which one of you is Jude?'

Introductions sorted and a 'tall skinny latte' ordered, Serena Fincham sat down at their table. She was glowing with health from her skiing. The sun had brought out the freckles on her nose, and her brown skin made the other customers in the coffee shop look pale and wintry. 'I'm still reeling from the news about Polly,' she said. 'Are you two relatives of hers?'

'No,' Jude replied. 'Just people who want to find out how she died.'

'Yes, well, it seems to get ghastlier the more details I find out. Shot dead before the shop was burnt down around her— horrible.'

'How did you find out about it?'

274

'Oh, the Cambridge Mafia. I deliberately refrained from checking any emails while I was in Davos, because I knew they'd just be from needy paranoid authors, so I didn't get the news till Saturday.'

'You haven't spoken to Lola, have you?'

'No, I thought she'd have enough on her plate with her stepdaughter having been killed. Her husband must be devastated.'

Ah, so it seemed Serena hadn't heard about Ricky's death. Probably nothing to be gained by telling her unless she asked after him.

'What about Piers? Have you spoken to him?'

'Texted him. Said how devastated I was. How ghastly it must be for him. I mean, whatever he may have thought about Polly, they had been together for, I don't know, twelve years, something like that.'

'You say "whatever he may have thought of Polly". What do you mean?' asked Carole.

'Well, I gather from mutual chums that things haven't been too good between them recently. And Piers always treated her a bit as though she was second best. I mean, when we were doing Footlights revues and things, Polly was always the hanger-on, the outsider, you know, not at Cambridge, not part of the group. But maybe Piers'd treat any woman he was going out with like that.'

'Oh?'

'Not lacking in self-esteem, our Piers. Biggest ego on the planet. The only thing he really cares about is his writing, his bloody career, and now with this sitcom of his apparently going into production, all his ambitions are going to be realized.'

'The real reason why we arranged to meet you, Serena,' said Carole, 'is that we wanted to find out more about this book Polly had written. She was talking to me about it when I met her the afternoon before she died.'

'Oh yes, the book.' The agent sighed as this was a subject that had already caused trouble.

'She did offer it to you to read, didn't she?'

'Yes. Happens quite a lot. This terrible myth that "everyone's got a book in them". And, in most cases, that is precisely where it should stay. But because people know I'm a literary agent, I get lots of manuscripts passed on from second cousins and friends of friends . . . you know how it is.'

'So Polly sent her manuscript to you through Piers?'

'No, she didn't. Apparently she'd suggested that, but he wasn't keen. Usual Piers thing—he didn't want any competition. He was the writer in that set-up, didn't like the idea of having a girlfriend with literary pretensions—in case she might turn out to be more talented than he was. From what Polly told me, he'd positively tried to stop her contacting me. But she was very determined, and she'd met me enough times back in Cambridge to make a direct approach herself. Which is what she did.'

'So you read it?'

'Yes, every word. Which, let me tell you, I don't do with every manuscript that comes thudding into my in-box. I have a fifty-page rule—which I think is bloody generous of me, actually. A lot of agents don't even go that far. But with me, I give the author a chance. If he or she has failed to engage my interest in fifty pages, then it's the standard rejection letter.'

'So what did you think of Polly's book?' asked Jude. 'We've heard mixed reports.'

'She told me you'd liked it,' said Carole, 'but Piers implied you'd only told Polly that out of kindness.'

'Huh. Bloody typical Piers again.'

'Oh?'

'As I said, he really hated the idea of Polly having talent in

276

her own right. OK, she was an actor, he didn't mind that. At least he didn't mind it, because she wasn't a very successful actor. If she'd suddenly become a star, I'm not sure the relationship would have survived. He doesn't like competition.'

'According to Piers, the relationship wasn't going to survive, anyway,' said Jude. 'He said he was going to wait till they got through Christmas and then give Polly the old heave-ho.'

Serena Fincham smiled sardonically. 'So typical of Piers. Ever the sensitive soul.' It was significant that she used exactly the same phrase as Lola to describe him.

'Anyway, please tell us,' Carole demanded impatiently, 'what did you think of Lola's book?'

'Bloody great,' said Serena. 'I'd have taken it on straight-away—I know a good few publishers who would snap up something like that—and pay a decent advance for it, even in these benighted times. But Polly wanted to do a bit more tinkering with it, so I told her to get back to me when she'd got a final draft she was happy with.'

'Which, of course, she never did.'

'No.'

'What kind of a book was it?' asked Jude.

'Well, it was a novel, but one of those novels which is clearly very thinly disguised autobiography. About a girl—who wasn't called Polly, but clearly was Polly. And about the difficulties of her upbringing—feckless father, parents both doing drugs, divorce, mother's remarriage to another unreliable male, break-up of that relationship, second divorce, mother's death from an overdose . . . you know, all the cheery ingredients of normal family life. Had it been nonfiction, I suppose you would have called it a "misery memoir", but it was better than most of those are. Better written, for a start. Polly really did write beautifully.'

'And do you think, if the book were published, it'd be successful?'

'Oh yes. Though I say it myself, I do have an instinct for these things—which is why I do the job I do. I've represented a few turkeys—haven't we all—but, generally speaking, I've got a good nose for a successful book. And Polly's fell straight into that category, no question.'

'Presumably, with a book like that,' Carole began, 'thinly disguised autobiography, there's a potential libel risk, isn't there? I mean, if people in the book recognize themselves, they could take the author to court?'

'Yes, but Polly had managed that very skilfully. The characters were changed just enough to get round the libel risk. But, of course, particularly because she comes from quite a famous family, everyone would suspect who the originals were. So, come the publicity circus, Polly would have been asked all those questions: "Is the irresponsible stepfather Ricky Le Bonnier? Is the dominant grandmother Flora Le Bonnier? Is the arsehole of a boyfriend Piers Duncton?" And then, of course, in all the interviews Polly would have hotly denied that was the case, which would only feed more curiosity in the listeners and viewers—and would sell more books.'

'You used the word "arsehole" for the way Piers came across in the book . . .'

Serena quickly picked up Jude's cue. 'Yes, and I was being kind. I think Polly must've been saving up her spleen for some years. The Edwin in the book is Piers all over, very funny, lots of surface charm and a cold-blooded eye to the main chance. But at bottom a self-centred bully. If the book ever had been published, I don't think Polly's relationship with Piers could possibly have survived.'

Carole and Jude exchanged looks. Both knew how close they seemed to be getting to an explanation of the tragedy at Galli-

maufry, but both knew how seriously they lacked evidence.
'Serena,' said Jude softly, hardly daring to put the question in
case their hopes were to be dashed, 'you don't by any chance
have a copy of the book, do you? I mean, the draft that Polly
sent you?'

'She actually emailed it to me.'

'So you never had a hard copy?'

'As a matter of fact, I did. When she sent it to me I had a
problem with my laptop—it was being repaired—so I did a
printout at the office and took it home to read over that
weekend.'

'Have you still got the printour?'

'Yes.'

Matching involuntary sighs of relief emanated from Carole
and Jude, as Serena reached into her capacious leather briefcase
and pulled out a dog-eared pile of typing paper held together by
a red rubber band.

'Would it be possible for us to have a look at it? Get a copy
made, if you like? We would look after it.'

'Yes,' said Serena ruefully, 'in fact, you can have it. Sadly, it's
of no use to me.'

Carole looked confused. 'But I thought you said it was
publishable.'

'Yes, it very definitely is. Even in this state. Polly wanted to
make more changes, but that was only because she had a
perfectionist streak in her. All this manuscript needs is a little
copy-editing and it could go straight to the printers tomorrow.'

'Then why do you say it's of no use to you?'

'Because,' the agent replied, 'amongst the many emails I came
back to on Saturday, was one from Piers. He said the Le Bonniers had had a family conference, and they'd decided they
didn't want Polly's book ever to be published.'

'He said that, did he?' Carole looked headily across at her neighbour. Unusually, there was a beadiness in Jude's eyes too.

CHAPTER FORTY

The moment Serena Fincham had gone back to her office, Jude rang through on her mobile to Fedingham Court House. It was some time before Lola answered the phone. She sounded weary to the marrow of her bones.

'I'm still alive,' she replied to Jude's solicitous enquiries. 'Mabel asked where Daddy was this morning, and when he was coming back. I only just stopped myself from bursting into tears in front of her. God knows how I'll break the news.'

'You'll find a way,' said Jude, not for the first time.

'Hope so.' Lola made an attempt to pull herself together. 'Anyway, what can I do for you?'

'I wonder . . . is Piers still there with you?'

'No, he isn't.'

There was a harshness in Lola's tone that made Jude ask, 'Has he been causing any trouble?'

'You could say that. If you call coming on to a woman who's been widowed little more than twenty-four hours causing trouble.'

'Piers?'

'Yes. He had the nerve to come into my bedroom last night. I didn't have much prospect of sleeping anyway, but he ensured my night was completely ruined.'

'What did he do?'

'Oh, he sat on my bed, and he started pawing at me, and he said our time in Edinburgh together was the best bit of his life, and he'd always really loved me, and now Polly and Ricky were out of the way there was no reason why we couldn't become an item and . . . It was horrible. I couldn't believe anyone could be so insensitive, least of all someone who I've always thought of as one of my closest friends. It took me hours to persuade him that I didn't love him, that Ricky was the only man I'd really loved and . . . and then Piers started hitting me. I actually had to call for Varya and physically push him out of my bedroom.' She sounded perilously close to tears.

'So where is Piers now?' asked Jude.

'At his flat in London, I assume. I sent him off this morning with a flea in his ear.'

'You wouldn't have his address to hand, would you?'

'Yes, I know it off by heart. Near Warren Street tube. He's been there a while. I used to spend a lot of time with them there before I met Ricky.' She gave the details.

'What time did Piers leave this morning?'

'Varya drove him to Fedborough Station to catch an early train, the seven-forty-two . . . leaving me to somehow get across to my children that their father's dead, let alone start organizing his funeral . . .'

'You're allowed to do that, are you? The police have released the body?'

'Yes, they said they've had a preliminary report from the surgeon who did Ricky's post mortem.' She hurried over the words, not wanting to dwell on them. 'And I can start making funeral arrangements. Ricky died a natural death.'

In the teeth of the evidence, Carole and Jude were still not convinced about that.

'There's something I've just remembered,' said Jude.

'What?'

'The morning after we heard that a woman's body had been

found in the ashes of Gallimaufry I spoke to Lola on the phone. I asked her if she had any idea who the victim might be. She said she'd checked that Anna and Bex were all right, and that Ricky had checked that Polly was safely in London with Piers . . .'

'Are you saying that Ricky was lying?'

'No. I'm saying that Piers was.'

The flat off Tottenham Court Road which Piers and Polly had shared showed little sign of a feminine touch. Its aggressive tidiness suggested more the hand of a masculine control freak. Framed on the walls were posters going back to Piers's Footlights days, and more recent stills for television shows he'd contributed to. Posters of plays that Polly Le Bonnier might have been in did not feature. A smell of Piers's cigarette smoke hung heavy in the air.

He had sounded unsurprised when Jude had rung to ask if he minded her and Carole coming to see him. They had stayed in the coffee shop flicking through the manuscript for half an hour or so, which had been long enough to form a pretty clear picture of the hatchet job Polly had done on her boyfriend. Then they'd rung Piers.

On arrival at the flat, they were greeted with the minimum of courtesy, no offer of a drink but instead the immediate question, 'What's all this about?'

'We were hoping you might be able to tell us that,' replied Carole.

'We're interested in the deaths of Polly and Ricky,' said Jude.

'You're not alone in that. Everyone seems to think it's their business to speculate on the subject.'

'We particularly wanted to talk to you, Piers, because we've just been reading the manuscript of Polly's book.'

He went pale as he demanded, 'Where the hell did you get that?'

'From Serena Fincham.'

'Damn! I should have rung her and told her not to talk to anyone about it.'

'What?' said Carole. 'And then you would have suppressed every copy of it, wouldn't you? Did you know, incidentally, that Ricky had Polly's flash drive with a copy of the book on it?'

'Ricky's dead. He's not going to pass it on to anyone now.'

'Perhaps not. But if it was in his possession when he died—and we have reason to believe it was—then it's probably now in the hands of the police. They're going to be very interested in its contents, I would imagine, given that they're still investigating Polly's death.'

If he'd looked pale before, a new adjective was required to describe the pallor with which he reacted to this news. He fumbled for a cigarette and lit up.

'Anyway,' said Jude easily, 'that character of Edwin in the book doesn't seem very pleasant, does he? Domestic violence is never very pretty, is it? You always wonder about the personality of someone who gets a thrill out of beating up a woman. If he's capable of that, what other crime might he be capable of? And of course, if every copy of Polly's manuscript had been destroyed, the story of your violent behaviour would have died with her, wouldn't it?'

Piers had by now recovered himself sufficiently to say, 'You can't prove anything. And if there were anything to prove, the one witness who might have testified is sadly dead.'

'Sadly . . . or conveniently . . . ?' suggested Carole.

'Are you accusing me of killing Polly?'

'Not necessarily. But we would like to know your arguments for why we shouldn't accuse you of killing Polly.'

'My arguments remain exactly the same as they have always

been. I wasn't in Fethering on the night that Polly died. I was with a woman.'

'Oh yes, the actress from the sitcom.'

'Exactly. And just so's you know, she has been approached by the police investigating Polly's death. They wanted to check my alibi. An intrusion into her privacy of which she took a pretty dim view, let me tell you. In fact, it may have ruined what promised to be a very good relationship.'

'Or a good relationship until you started hitting her?' suggested Carole.

'Listen, I don't care what you say. You're just two nosy old women who have no authority at all. If the police are satisfied my alibi is true, then I think you should accept it as well.'

'You mean you're not going to give us a contact for your new girlfriend, so that we can check for ourselves?'

'You are bloody right, Jude. I am not.'

The two women looked at each other. Of course, Piers could be lying—he was quite capable of it—but both had a depressing feeling that he was telling the truth.

'So did you have any contact with Fethering during that time?' asked Carole.

'I spoke to Lola probably about eight.'

'About what?'

'I just told her about the date I'd got set up for the evening. The restaurant we were going to, that kind of stuff.'

'This would be your sitcom actress?'

'Yes. Lola and I always used to confide in each other about our dates . . . well, we did until she met Ricky. Thereafter, there wasn't much to say on her side, but I'd still keep her up to date with whom I was seeing.'

'I thought you were cohabiting with Polly, I thought you'd been with her since before Cambridge. So what dates are you talking about?'

He looked only slightly discomfited by Jude's words; he was more interested in his self-image as the great lover. He lit a new cigarette from the stub of his previous one, and there was pride in his voice as he said, 'There were a few skirmishes with other women.'

'All of which conquests you described in detail to Lola?'

'I don't know about "in detail", but I'd keep her up to date.'

'Telling her every time that none of them were more than "second best", and that she was the one for whom you would always hold a candle?'

He looked so embarrassed that Jude knew she'd hit the bull's-eye.

'So, apart from having to listen to you crowing about your latest potential conquest, did Lola say anything of interest to you?'

'Not much. She was having a difficult evening. Mabel had got an ear infection, and the dog was having puppies, and Lola was trying to get everything ready for Christmas, and her mother-in-law would soon be back being as demanding as ever and—'

' "Soon be back"?' Carole repeated. 'Did Lola say that, that Flora Le Bonnier had gone out that evening?'

'Yes,' Piers Duncton replied.

CHAPTER FORTY-ONE

The lunch which the two women had in a pub in Grafton Way was not a relaxed occasion. Neither really noticed what they were eating—which was just as well because it wasn't very nice. Jude had one glass of wine, Carole stuck to black coffee. And, meanwhile, they both trawled through different sections of Polly Le Bonnier's manuscript.

They were about to enter the Warren Street tube station when Carole suddenly noticed a PC World on the other side of Tottenham Court Road. Since her much-delayed introduction to computers, she had, with the fervour of a convert, become something of a devotee of PC World.

'Had an idea,' she announced. 'Just going to buy something.'

Flora Le Bonnier's flat in St John's Wood was as punctiliously maintained as the old lady herself. She had made no demur when Jude had rung, suggesting they pay her a visit, and she looked the model of elegance when she opened the door to them. But neither had the feeling she had dressed up specially. She always looked like that. Flora Le Bonnier was one of those women who didn't possess any casual clothes. The idea that her wardrobe might contain jeans, T-shirts or jogging bottoms was as unthinkable as the idea that her upper-class accent might ever slip.

When she closed the front door, they noticed that there was an extension on the inside handle so that she could manipulate it with her crippled hands. No doubt there were other devices in the flat which had been tailored to her disability.

She ushered them into a sitting room whose dark green walls set off the numerous silver-framed photographs that they bore. All were movie stills or production photographs of Flora Le Bonnier in her greatest roles. Interestingly, none of the pictures featured anyone else. Though she had acted with many of the great theatrical names of her generation, apparently Flora had not wished for any of them to share the limelight in the gallery she had selected for display.

The only other ornaments in the room were a collection of glass walking sticks—multicoloured, twisted and intricately wrought. They, too, graced the walls between the photographs.

The room was very overheated, but neither Carole nor Jude removed her coat. Flora Le Bonnier, ever the magnanimous grand dame, gestured her two visitors to chairs and then took her place in a winged armchair not dissimilar to the one they had last seen her in at Fedingham Court House. She seemed to favour thrones. 'I would offer you some tea or something, but with my hands . . .' She waved the incurling fingers eloquently. 'There is a woman who comes every morning, helps me dress, does a few chores, prepares my lunch and a cold plate for my supper. Sadly, she is not here now, so unless you feel like making a drink for yourself in the kitchen . . .'

'No, thank you. We've just had lunch,' said Carole.

'Any more trouble from your back or neck?' asked Jude.

'No. Oh, the usual aches and pains attendant on my great age, but nothing worse, thank goodness. I'm so grateful to you for the way in which you eased the pain I had down in Sussex.'

'It was no problem.'

'And we, erm,' Carole began awkwardly, 'we should offer you our condolences for the loss of your son.'

'Yes.' But the old lady did not seem unduly afflicted by grief.

Her eyes were fixed in the middle distance as she said, 'He was a foolish boy, dabbling with drugs. Taking drugs, like drinking too much, is a sign of indiscipline. Discipline is important in all walks of life, but particularly in the arts. Mine is a hard profession and I would not have survived in it so long if I had not had rigid self-discipline.'

'So rigid that you can control all of your emotions?' asked Jude.

'Controlling emotion is inevitably something you have to learn in the acting profession. You have to build up, as it were, a repertoire of emotions within yourself, so that you can summon up the required one for the part that you happen to be playing at any given time.'

'But you lost control of your emotions over Christmas, didn't you?'

'I don't understand what you mean, Jude.'

'According to Ricky and Lola, after Polly's death you virtually cracked up. You were in a terrible state of nerves.'

'To lose a granddaughter is a powerfully traumatic experience.'

'Was it, though, for you?' asked Carole. 'You hadn't seen much of Polly since she was a child. She was no blood relation of yours. Did her death really leave that much of a hole in your life?'

'You could not possibly understand the sufferings of a grandmother if you have not been one.'

'I am one,' Carole asserted with some pride.

Jude sat forward in her chair. 'Flora, you know that Polly wrote a book . . .'

'I believe she mentioned that she had at some point. I didn't take much notice of it at the time.'

'I think you know rather more about her book that that.'

'What do you mean?'

Carole took over the prosecuting role. 'I think you had read at least some of Polly's manuscript. You read the bit about her grandmother, about her pretentious grandmother, who's an opera singer in the novel rather than an actress, and who prides herself on a family name supposed to date back to the Norman Conquest, whereas in fact the grandmother has no connection with the family whose name she stole. The name the character in the novel invented wasn't Le Bonnier, but the story's the same.'

There was a long silence, then Flora said in her even, beautifully modulated voice, 'I am a Le Bonnier. The world knows me as a Le Bonnier. My autobiography is about being a Le Bonnier. I cannot have that taken away from me.'

'Even if it's not true?'

The old actress turned on Carole a look of pure malevolence. 'True? What do you know about truth? Most people never find real truth. I have been blessed to find it through my professional work. I have been nearer to pure truth on stage than you ever have been in your entire miserable life. People with my talent don't have to obey the rules created by ordinary people. I am Flora Le Bonnier. That is my name. That is true.'

'But it's not your name.'

'I cannot expect someone like you to understand.' The line was spoken with enormous dignity, and Jude felt sure Flora was quoting from some play she had once been in. That was really the trouble. The old actress could no longer distinguish between reality and the parts she had played.

'I can understand this much,' said Carole. 'That you killed Polly down at Gallimaufry and then persuaded your son to torch the premises in the hope of covering up your crime.'

Flora Le Bonnier offered her clawlike hands. 'I shot someone? These hands were able to hold a gun and pull its trigger? I wish that were true. I wish I were capable of shooting someone.

Because then I would also be capable of doing a lot of other things which these hands will not allow me to do.'

Jude tried another tack. 'Do you deny that you have read any of Polly's book?'

'Yes, of course I do.'

'Do you know where there are copies of the book now?'

A sly smile crept across the old lady's patrician features. 'Polly was, I believe, carrying a copy of the manuscript in the haversack she brought down to Fedborough. It was destroyed in the fire at that ridiculous shop of Lola's.'

'And that was the only copy?'

'I believe so, yes.'

'But in these days of computers,' said Carole, 'copies of any text are ten-a-penny. The original stays on the writer's computer.'

'It is my belief that Polly also had her laptop computer in the same haversack. That, too, was burnt beyond recognition or repair.'

'How fortunate then that I have this,' said Carole, producing the flash drive that she had just bought at PC World.

'What on earth is that?'

'A miracle of miniaturization, Flora. This tiny object, called a flash drive or a memory stick, is a wonderful device for storing data. You can put an enormous amount of text on a little thing like this. A whole book, if you want to. And that's what Polly used this one for. The whole text of her book is retrievable from this tiny little rectangle of plastic.' As she spoke, Carole placed the flash drive casually on the table next to Flora Le Bonnier.

Then she looked glumly across to Jude. 'Sorry, it looks as if we've been barking up the wrong tree.'

'Oh?' Jude wasn't quite sure what her neighbour was up to, but was happy to play along until an explanation arrived.

'Our clever theory about Polly having been killed by her

grandmother looks a bit threadbare now, doesn't it, Jude? With her hands in that condition, Flora wouldn't have been capable of holding a gun, let alone pulling its trigger. And she certainly wouldn't have been capable of sending the text message from Ricky's phone that summoned Polly back to Gallimaufry. I'm sorry, Flora, I think we owe you an apology,' Carole concluded, standing up as she did so.

'Apology accepted,' said the old lady gracefully. 'I'm afraid the shock of tragic events has a tendency to stop people from thinking straight.'

'Well, goodbye,' said Jude, also rising from her seat. She still didn't know what Carole's plan was; she just hoped her friend had one.

'Excuse me if I don't see you out, but movement is getting increasingly difficult for me.'

'No, of course. That's fine,' said Jude, looking enquiringly at Carole in hope of some elucidation of what the hell was going on.

But she got nothing. Dutifully, she led the way into the hall and reached up to open the front door. Just at that moment, Carole said, 'Oh, good heavens, I forgot the memory stick!'

Both women turned back towards the sitting room. And both women saw Flora Le Bonnier's hand reach instinctively forward to grab the memory stick. Between her fingers. Which, though their knuckles were swollen, were otherwise straight and fully functional.

'. . . and none of us likes losing power,' said Flora, 'particularly when one has been powerful, when one has been the centre of attention. And for most of my life I had certainly been the centre of attention.' She sighed. 'Anyway, the acting work just wasn't there anymore. Enquiries to my agent were getting more and more infrequent.' Carole remembered Rupert Sonning describing the same experience—death by a thousand silent telephones.

'And I didn't want to announce my retirement, because something might still have come up, and one must never say never. And my hands, which had once been one of my great beauties . . .' she stretched them out to look at them—'were getting misshapen with arthritis, and so I thought why not exaggerate that a bit more? Why not pretend I can't use them at all? And it seemed to work.'

'You mean it got you attention?' asked Jude, not very sympathetically.

'Yes. It didn't quite get me back centre stage—nothing was going to do that—but it did mean that people took more notice of me, felt sympathetic towards me because of my disability, helped me out. And with the autobiography written—'

'Did you have a ghost-writer for that?'

'Yes, but it's mostly me. I talked into tape machines at great length, then this little chap typed it all out, and I went through it and cut out all the extra stuff he'd added.'

'Personal stuff?' Carole suggested.

'Most of it was. Stuff that I didn't want made public, anyway.'

'By the way, who was Ricky's father?' asked Jude.

'Do you know,' said Flora Le Bonnier with a winsome smile, 'I really can't remember.' And it might even have been true.

'And do you feel any guilt about having murdered Polly?'

Flora gave Carole's question a moment of thought before answering, 'No, I really don't. She was not a happy child. She never really recovered from her mother's death. And, anyway, that book she had written, it was a complete betrayal of her family.'

'One could argue that it was simply telling the truth about her family.'

'One could argue that, but for me it would always be a betrayal.'

'When did you decide to kill Polly?' asked Jude.

'A couple of weeks before Christmas. Well, I didn't decide to kill her. I decided to offer her the opportunity to destroy all copies of the book. Had she done as I requested, the girl would still be alive.' Flora Le Bonnier's tone made it sound as if Polly's intransigence was responsible for her own death.

'How did you come to know the book's contents?'

'The girl actually came round here to see me. She gave me a copy. She was proud of what she'd done, she wanted me to read all the cruel things she had written about me.'

'And did you read the whole manuscript?'

'I did. Then, of course, I had that copy destroyed. And I contacted Polly to find out how many more copies there were. But she refused to suppress the work. It was then that I thought more drastic action might be required.'

'Where did you get the gun from?' asked Carole.

'It was used in a film I made in the late fifties. Called, perhaps not surprisingly, *The Lady with the Gun.* One of my rare forays into the contemporary thriller. At the end of the filming I was given the gun as a souvenir. I showed it once to a close friend, who told me, to my surprise, that it was in full working order. There was rather more laxity about safety issues on film sets in those days. I kept the gun and tracked down some ammunition for it. Having it gave me a sense of security. I never knew when I might need it.'

'So you took the gun down to Fedingham Court House with you?'

'Of course.'

'And,' said Jude, 'you cold-bloodedly planned to kill your own granddaughter?'

'No. And I wish you would stop calling her my "granddaughter". She was my *step*granddaughter. Anyway, if she had destroyed the book as I requested, nothing would have happened to her.' Again she made the murder sound as though it had been caused by Polly's unreasonable behaviour.

'Did you tell her you might want to meet before you sent the text from Ricky's phone?'

'I had prepared her for the possibility.'

'And why did you fix to meet in Gallimaufry?' asked Carole.

'It had to be somewhere that could be burnt down. Then, when the girl's body was found, it would be assumed by the police that she had died in the fire.'

'But it wouldn't work like that. The police forensic examination would be bound to find the bullet in her body and the real cause of death.'

'It worked like that in *The Lady with the Gun*,' Flora Le Bonnier asserted.

So she had based her homicidal plan on the plot of a fifties' thriller movie.

'How did you get from Fedingham Court House to Fethering?' asked Carole.

'I got Ricky to take me there. I rang him when he was in the shop with his latest bit of skirt.'

Which explained the call he had taken while he was with Anna. 'How did you know about that?' asked Jude.

The old actress smiled complacently. 'Ricky always tells me everything.' And only then did Carole and Jude realize the strength of the hold Flora Le Bonnier had exercised over her son.

'Was he with you when you confronted Polly?'

'No, I told him to wait outside.'

'Did he even know it was she that you were meeting in the shop?'

'No.'

'So when you told him to torch the place, he didn't know his stepdaughter's body was inside?'

'No.'

'Why did you do it, Flora?' asked Jude.

'Because I had to defend the Le Bonnier name. I couldn't have lies told about my family. It would have upset my public.'

The full extent of Flora Le Bonnier's selfishness, and the delusions which fed that selfishness, became clear. According to her priorities, even a murder was justified in the cause of maintaining the old lies about her family history. Lies which had been long discredited. Lies which, if she'd read the newspapers, she would have known scarcely anyone believed in. Flora Le Bonnier and reality had parted company a long time ago.

There was a silence in the little, overheated flat. Then Carole said, quite gently, 'You realize we'll have to tell all this to the police.'

'Yes, I suppose you will. And I will have to submit myself to the due processes of the law.' But she spoke calmly, there was even a hint of pleasure in her voice. She was, after all, being offered another role to play. And Flora Le Bonnier had always been good in courtroom dramas.

CHAPTER FORTY-TWO

In the event, Flora didn't get her day in court. A few days after Carole and Jude's visit, her home help came in one morning to find the old lady dead in her bed. The newspaper obituaries were effusive, on television and radio elderly thespians vied with each other to say how 'wonderful' she had been, 'what heaven to work with'. In some of the papers there were hints about her true origins. One was blatant enough to assert that she 'supposedly came from an aristocratic family, but that was a stunt dreamed up by some publicist at the Rank Charm School'. So, as Carole and Jude had deduced, the secret she had gone to such vicious lengths to keep had been one that was common knowledge anyway.

Some of the press played along, still under the influence of her charm. Flora Le Bonnier was described by *The Times* as 'an aristocrat of the theatre, and one of the few who was actually also an aristocrat in real life.'

No one mentioned the fact that she was a murderer, but then, of course, no one knew. Except for Carole and Jude, and Lola and Rupert Sonning, whom they had told. Oh, and the police, who now had assembled enough information to secure a conviction—or, as it turned out, to close the file on the murder of Polly Le Bonnier.

Lola's recovery from her husband's death was a long, slow process. At times she was overwhelmed by hopelessness and depression, and remembering Jude's offer, turned to her for help and encouragement. Though healing could never reconstruct the past, it could over time do something to ease the pains of bereavement.

In fact, Lola's rehabilitation came ultimately from adversity. When investigated, Ricky Le Bonnier's affairs turned out to be in a terrible state. His flamboyance had been achieved at the cost of living way beyond his income for years. Fedingham Court House had to be sold and, when all the outstanding mortgages and other debts had been settled, Lola was left with very little. She had no alternative but to start up her own retail business to provide for her family, and it was through the success of that enterprise that she found her salvation.

Her children grew up healthy, and Henry, taking after Ricky, showed a considerable talent for music. Mabel, who had been deeply affected by the loss of her father, developed into a quiet, serious, lonely little girl.

Lola deliberately lost touch with Piers Duncton, not initiating any contact with him herself and not replying to his messages or texts. His television sitcom ran for a couple of series, but was then pulled because it wasn't getting good enough viewing figures. He continued to work as a jobbing comedy writer, providing gags and links for a variety of shows and growing increasingly bitter as he saw younger and, to his mind, less talented writers become more successful than he was. What made things worse in his view was that quite a lot of them hadn't even come up through the Cambridge Footlights.

As for his love-life, the affair with the sitcom actress turned out to be very brief and it was followed by a great many equally brief affairs with other women on the periphery of show business. In his cups, Piers would frequently tell the decreasing number of people who would listen to him about how he'd tragically lost the great love of his life to a murderer's bullet.

Saira Sherjan continued to enjoy her life as a vet. She

completed the London Marathon, raising a great deal of money for animal charities.

And Rupert Sonning, entirely happy in his chosen role as Old Garge, continued to read poetry and listen to Radio 3 in Pequod, only returning to his rented room when warned of a local council inspection. He still spent long hours walking his Jack Russell Petrarch along the shoreline, and in maintaining his role as 'the eyes and ears of Fethering Beach'.

Occasionally he ran into Ruby Tallis, who would never fail to bring him the latest opinions of her husband Derek.

Anna Carter left the village early in the New Year. Perhaps she went off to reinvent herself somewhere else, but if so, nobody knew where.

In the Crown and Anchor Ted and Zosia ran a tight ship and, as spring approached and the fame of Ed Pollack's cuisine spread, business started to pick up.

Kath Le Bonnier continued to do the books for Ayland's boatyard for the rest of her life. And she was very happy that, having been rescued from the Devil Women, Ricky was hers for ever. Though not, of course, in this dimension.

Jude had a couple more meetings with the man with whom she'd spent New Year's Eve, but she didn't find him that interesting and the affair soon petered out. Her appointments book for healing was healthily full and, though occasionally afflicted by feverish wanderlust, she was content most of the time with her life at Woodside Cottage.

Next door at High Tor, with the zeal of a convert, Carole found she was spending more and more time exploring the Internet. Always upstairs in the same room, though. It still didn't seem quite right to her that a laptop should be moved about the house.

And her son Stephen, with Gaby's prompting, did stick his Glow-in-the-dark Computer Angel on his office laptop. It didn't do much in the way of staving off viruses, but it did make some of his colleagues think that perhaps old Stephen Seddon wasn't such a humourless nerd, after all.

Gaby put off going back to work at the agency, and Carole waited hopefully for the news of another Seddon pregnancy.

And Lily, in the eyes of her grandmother, just grew gorgeouser and gorgeouser.

ABOUT THE AUTHOR

Simon Brett worked as a producer in radio and television before taking up writing full time. As well as the much-loved Fethering series, the Mrs Pargeter novels and the Charles Paris detective series, he is the author of the radio and television series *After Henry,* the radio series *No Commitments* and *Smelling of Roses* and the bestselling *How to Be a Little Sod.* His novel *A Shock to the System* was filmed, starring Michael Caine.

Married with three grown-up children, he lives in an Agatha Christie–style village on the South Downs.